In the back of his mind, in a place he didn't like to visit very often, he wondered if a woman like Lauren could love someone like him.

A regular guy. A cop.

All at once Seth felt guilty. Here she was spilling her guts to him with no idea who he really was, or why he was here with her now.

"What about you?" she said. "Altex. Your job. I can see you're good at it. Do you like it?"

He felt uncomfortable lying to her—which was ridiculous. On an undercover job like this, it came with the territory. He had to lie.

Dear Reader,

Things are cooling down outside—at least here in the Northeast—but inside this month's six Silhouette Intimate Moments titles the heat is still on high. After too long an absence, bestselling author Dallas Schulze is back to complete her beloved miniseries A FAMILY CIRCLE with *Lovers and Other Strangers*. Shannon Deveraux has come home to Serenity and lost her heart to travelin' man Reece Morgan.

Our ROMANCING THE CROWN continuity is almost over, so join award winner Ingrid Weaver in *Under the King's Command*. I think you'll find Navy SEAL hero Sam Coburn irresistible. Ever-exciting Lindsay McKenna concludes her cross-line miniseries, MORGAN'S MERCENARIES: ULTIMATE RESCUE, with *Protecting His Own*. You'll be breathless from the first page to the last. Linda Castillo's *A Cry in the Night* features another of her "High Country Heroes," while relative newcomer Catherine Mann presents the second of her WINGMEN WARRIORS, in *Taking Cover*. Finally, welcome historical author Debra Lee Brown to the line with *On Thin Ice*, a romantic adventure set against an Alaskan background.

Enjoy them all, and come back again next month, when the roller-coaster ride of love and excitement continues right here in Silhouette Intimate Moments, home of the best romance reading around.

Yours,

Leslie J. Wainger
Executive Senior Editor

Please address questions and book requests to:
Silhouette Reader Service
U.S.: 3010 Walden Ave., P.O. Box 1325, Buffalo, NY 14269
Canadian: P.O. Box 609, Fort Erie, Ont. L2A 5X3

On Thin Ice
DEBRA LEE BROWN

![Silhouette]

INTIMATE MOMENTS™

Published by Silhouette Books

America's Publisher of Contemporary Romance

SILHOUETTE BOOKS

ISBN 0-373-27258-8

ON THIN ICE

Visit Silhouette at www.eHarlequin.com

Printed in U.S.A.

Books by Debra Lee Brown

Silhouette Intimate Moments

On Thin Ice #1188

Harlequin Historicals

The Virgin Spring #506
Ice Maiden #549
The Mackintosh Bride #576
Gold Rush Bride #594
A Rogue's Heart #625

DEBRA LEE BROWN

Award-winning author Debra Lee Brown's ongoing romance with wild and remote locales sparks frequent adventures in the Alps, the Arctic—where she has worked as a geologist—and the Sierra Nevada range of her native California. An avid outdoorswoman, Debra loves nothing better than to strand her heroes and heroines in rugged, often dangerous settings, then let nature take its course. Debra invites readers to visit her Web site at www.debraleebrown.com or to write to her care of Harlequin Reader Service, P.O. Box 1325, Buffalo, NY 14269.

For Michelle

Chapter 1

Thirty-six below. Forty-knot winds out of the east. It was gonna be a big one.

Lauren Parker Fothcringay zipped her down survival jacket to her chin, cinched the fur-trimmed hood tight and peered out the chopper's frosted window across an endless expanse of ice. In the dim winter light she could barely make out where land ended and the Alaskan coastline met the frozen Beaufort Sea.

"Whiteout comin'," the pilot shouted over the roar of the chopper's engine. He squinted into the blowing snow threatening to reduce visibility to zero. "Three hours, four tops. You sure you want me to drop you?"

Lauren shot him a wry look. "No, I changed my mind. Let's turn this thing around and head for Hawaii."

The pilot laughed, though she couldn't hear him over the engine noise. She settled back in her seat for the last few minutes of the trip out to Caribou Island, the site of Tiger Petroleum's latest oil exploration well.

It was simple, or should have been. Drill a ten-thousand-foot hole in the ground, collect rock samples over the target depth, document traces of oil, clean up the mess and come home. Your basic exploration well. Oil companies drilled them all the time on land leased from the government.

Caribou Island was nothing special, really, though it did sit just outside the boundary of a wildlife refuge, an area currently off-limits to oil exploration.

Tiger had leased the island's drilling rights on an exclusive basis. The rock samples and data collected would be proprietary, giving Tiger an edge in finishing its geologic maps of the area, and when bidding on future land leases. In the oil industry, figuring out where the oil was, was only half the battle. The other half was managing to lease the land overlying it before anyone else did. Land was everything. The only thing. And competition among oil companies was fierce.

As Tiger's most senior geologist and project manager, Lauren hadn't done any real fieldwork for years. Her early successes had catapulted her to the top of the technical ladder, and this next promotion would take her even further. She couldn't let anything screw it up. Especially a last-minute, routine assignment she had no time for, and that should have gone to one of her subordinates.

Both of the geologists originally assigned to Caribou Island had caught a nasty winter flu. Just her luck. Regardless, she was determined to get in, get her rock samples, and get out as quickly as possible. The well was nearly at target depth. A week should do it. Two, at most. She had three other projects to manage besides this one.

And she wanted that promotion. Bad.

Everyone expected her to get it, and she was never one to disappoint.

Lauren gazed out the window just as the chopper's high beams caught an arctic fox scampering across the tundra on the prowl for lunch. She caught herself smiling. The assignment wasn't really such a hardship. She was glad to be out of her hose and heels and into some comfortable clothes for a change. And she could breathe again. She'd forgotten how much she loved the Arctic. Untamed, fresh, real. So different from the life she'd been living these past few years.

On the corporate jet from Anchorage to Deadhorse, she'd slipped out of the expensive business suit Crocker had bought her on his last trip to San Francisco. He was always buying her gifts like that. No man had ever treated her with kid gloves before, not like Crocker did.

On board the chopper she'd coiled her carefully styled hair into a knot and stuffed it under her beat-up old hard hat. She felt good. Relaxed, almost. A break from the rat race was exactly what she needed. She grinned, wondering what Crocker would think if he were here with her now.

He'd never seen her in her field clothes: holey jeans, a turtleneck and the moth-eaten cardigan that had been her father's favorite when he was alive. She twisted her two-carat diamond engagement ring inside her glove, imagining Crocker's shock and her mother's disapproval.

There was a whole side of her, come to think of it, that Crocker knew nothing about. They were to be married in New York in the summer. A big, traditional affair. Mother had it all planned, down to the last white rose and swath of expensive silk. Lauren supposed she should be grateful. Her commitment to her career left no time for such details.

Besides, Mother was wild about Crocker. Who wouldn't be? As VP of finance for Tiger Petroleum, he was quite a catch, and one of the most respected oil company executives in the industry. Everyone liked him.

She was sorry, now, that they'd argued that morning. Crocker hadn't wanted her to take on the Caribou Island assignment herself. He said he didn't like the idea of her spending two weeks in close quarters with eighty guys—the type of men her mother called "oil field trash."

Lauren had dismissed his concerns. The way she saw it, she had no choice. Caribou Island was one of her projects.

Besides, the operation had been plagued with nothing but setbacks from the start. All the more reason for her to be on site herself.

"Roger that," the pilot yelled into his communications headset.

She looked at him, her brows raised in question.

"It's for you. Here." He ripped the headset off and handed it to her.

"Me?" Who on earth was calling her out here? If it was Mother, Lauren would have a fit. She didn't have time to discuss things like who was taking whom to Crocker's birthday bash at the Fairmont next month, or what she was expected to wear to the latest charity ball.

Lauren's life had changed radically after her father died and her mother remarried into the wealthy Fotheringay family. Mother had insisted her new husband legally adopt Lauren, so she might enjoy all the privileges associated with carrying the Fotheringay name. Sometimes Lauren wondered if her life had changed too radically.

Exhaling in exasperation, she pushed her hood back and slipped one of the earphones under the flannel lining of her hard hat. "Hello?"

"Hey, babe," the choppy voice came back.

"Crocker!"

"Just checking on—" Static ripped the end off his sentence.

"Crocker, you're cutting out."

"—that everything's okay." His voice sounded a million miles away. Still, she'd know it anywhere.

"Everything's fine, Crocker. Well, except for the weather." She glanced out the window at the dry snow blowing across the ice. What little light there had been was now obliterated by the onslaught. She could barely see a dozen yards ahead of the chopper.

"Be careful out there, babe."

"I will. And I'm sorry about this morning."

"Me, too. It was my fault. Don't give it another thought. Oh, and have Salvio call me on the satellite uplink as soon as you get there. Phones must be out. I want to—"

Another blast of static cut short his explanation. A deafening gust of wind blew the chopper sideways, and the connection was lost.

She handed the headset back to the pilot. "Guess we're out of range."

"Nope. It's the weather. Damned dangerous to be flying. I'm droppin' you and I'm outta here."

"Okay." She grabbed her duffel bag from the bench seat behind them, fighting a smile.

Crocker was likely going to ask Jack Salvio, Tiger's "company man" overseeing the Caribou Island operation, to keep an eye on her. Make sure she didn't run into any snags. Sweet of him, really. Crocker knew she was burned out and growing more and more disillusioned with the whole corporate scene.

Sometimes she wondered why she wanted the promotion at all. She'd even gone so far as to suggest that after they were married they stay in Anchorage instead of moving back to San Francisco like he wanted them to.

Crocker had not been very receptive to the idea, so she hadn't even broached the subject of her leaving Tiger and the oil business altogether to do something more meaningful with her life. Like teaching, maybe. She could teach earth science to elementary school kids, just like her father had always wanted to do, but never did because of her mother's objection.

She supposed it was a silly dream. And not at all in keeping with the ambitious edge that was her trademark. Oh, well. Maybe in the next lifetime.

She should make a point to spend more time with Crocker once this assignment was over. Between their two careers and his philanthropic commitments, they hardly had time to see each other. Crocker said all that would change once they were married, but she wasn't so sure it was even possible given their manic schedules.

When it came right down to it, she wasn't sure if they even had that much in common outside their jobs. Crocker had convinced her to push their wedding date up nearly a year. Lauren had wanted more time to get to know him, to make sure they were really meant for each other, but Crocker was insistent. He loved her, needed her, he'd said.

And she loved him, too. Didn't she?

"There she is." The pilot pointed a gloved finger to the north. Well, she guessed it was north, but couldn't tell any-more with the blowing snow. "Altex rig 13-E. What a hunk a junk."

Harsh sodium lights lit the site, bathing the island in a ghostly glow. Lauren's lips thinned into a hard line as the rusted orange paint of the steel walls housing the tired-looking drilling rig came into view just ahead.

Nothing had changed in the three years since she'd seen it. The last field operation she'd worked had been on that very rig. Against her will, her eyes glassed. She swiped at the tears with a gloved hand.

"Still gets to you, don't it?" The pilot shot her a com-passionate look as he slowed the chopper into a wide arc skirting the site.

She focused on the line of beat-up Suburbans, their en-gines running to keep from freezing, in front of the prefab buildings that made up the camp. Ninety-foot stands of drill-ing pipe hung in the oil rig's derrick, swaying in the near gale force wind. "Yes," she said. "A little."

Her father had been killed on 13-E when she was only eleven. He was a geologist just like her, working for a big oil company just like she did. But their reasons were dif-ferent. He'd done it for the money. Her mother had nagged him incessantly about it. She remembered Mother's tirades each time her father had talked about giving it up to teach.

Though the work was dangerous and the conditions harsh,

there had been only a handful of serious drilling accidents in the few decades since Alaska's North Slope oil fields were developed. It was a small, tightly knit community. Everyone knew about Hatch Parker and what had happened on 13-E. And everyone knew Lauren was his daughter.

"You're sure, now?" The pilot set the chopper down smooth as glass on an ice pad built fifty yards from the camp. "Last time we had weather this bad there was no gettin' in or out for weeks."

"I'm sure." Through the blowing snow she caught a glimpse of the brand-new geologist's trailer out behind the rig, by the big open pit—the "reserve pit"—that acted as an overflow for the oil well's drilling fluids. She checked her watch. Fourteen hundred. Two o'clock in the afternoon and it was pitch-black out. There was nothing quite like an arctic winter.

"Suit yourself, then. Take care, kid."

A roustabout, the oil field equivalent of a ranch hand, dressed in a down jumpsuit and white bunny boots, yanked the chopper's door wide. Lauren sucked in a blast of frigid air. Big mistake. Lung freeze. She'd forgotten you weren't supposed to do that.

The roustabout grabbed her duffel as she hopped out of the chopper with her overstuffed briefcase. They made a mad dash toward a waiting vehicle. Fifty yards to camp was too far to walk in this weather. Climbing into the Suburban, she waved to the pilot who gave her the thumbs-up before he took off.

For the barest second Lauren wished she was taking off with him. Too late now. She was here and, given the weather, here she would stay for at least a week. In a whiteout nothing could fly, and Caribou Island was over a hundred miles from Deadhorse, Tiger's outermost base camp. Too far to drive in these conditions, even if Tiger had maintained the ice road, which it hadn't. Budget constraints, her foot. She'd remember to talk to her boss about that. Not that it really mattered. She had a job to do, and she'd do it. She always did.

Two minutes later the wind blasted her through the main door to the camp and into the break room. A dozen pairs of eyes focused on her as she pushed her hood back, snatched the hard hat from her head, and shook out her shoulder-length hair.

No, nothing had changed at all. There was still that momentary shock in the crew's eyes that she was a woman. Probably the only one out here.

Nodding at no one in particular, Lauren snaked around the cafeteria-style tables littered with empty cigarette packets, disposable coffee cups and half-eaten glazed doughnuts, then pushed the door open into the mudroom.

A few seconds later, her steel-toed Sorels, hard hat and jacket tucked into an empty corner, she padded in heavy wool socks toward Jack Salvio's office. It was just like riding a bike. She bet she could traverse every inch of this place blindfolded.

The air was stale, as it always was in these oil field camps. She wrinkled her nose at twenty-odd years of cigarette smoke that clung to prefab walls like the inside of someone's diseased lung. This was *not* the Alaska she loved.

She turned into Salvio's office and did a double take.

"Hiya, Scout." Paddy O'Connor's weathered face cracked in a wide smile.

"Paddy!" The old toolpusher rose from the stained Naugahyde sofa that had been there since 13-E was new. "What are you doing here? I thought you'd retired from fieldwork years ago."

"Oh, no. Still at it, Scout." He pulled her into a bear hug, and she fought a painful surge of emotion that threatened her composure for the second time that day.

No one called her Scout anymore. No one except Paddy O'Connor, owner of Altex Drilling, a company that had been on its last legs for as long as Lauren could remember.

Most oil companies, Tiger included, didn't own their own drilling rigs and equipment. Nor did they employ the roughnecks and roustabouts needed to run an operation like Caribou Island. The job was contracted out to outfits like Altex. Only the geologist, an engineer or two, and company men like Jack Salvio who oversaw the whole operation, were Tiger employees.

Lauren's father had coined the nickname Scout when she was just a kid, tagging along with him on field surveys in the Brooks Range. Paddy had been one of his closest friends. She looked warmly into the toolpusher's bloodshot eyes and nodded.

His smile faded. "Lauren, we need to talk."

"Yeah, just as soon as you get that sorry-assed crew a yours back to work." Jack Salvio brushed past them, dropped into his creaky overstuffed chair and tossed his hard hat onto a desk covered in paperwork.

"How are you, Jack?" Lauren said and extended her hand.

Salvio waved it away. "I been better. We're behind schedule. And I could do without this frickin' weather."

Lauren nodded, glancing at the computer monitors on Salvio's desk, flashing stats on the weather, drilling depth, and a host of other specifics critical to the oil well's operation.

Hmm, that's strange…

Some of the measurements seemed to be off. Then again, these computer systems were always on the fritz. She watched as Salvio narrowed his eyes at the flashing readout on one of the monitors. Swearing under his breath, he abruptly switched it off.

Lauren had never liked Jack Salvio's nasty disposition and bulldog tactics, but she did respect him. He was the best company man in Tiger's history. He knew what he was doing, and she'd need his cooperation and his clout in order to get her work done on time.

"Where's your bag, Scout?" Paddy moved past her into the hallway. "I'll help you get settled."

"No." Salvio shot to his feet. "We got a well to drill. Get one'a your guys to help her." He grabbed Lauren's arm and steered her back into the hallway. No use protesting. On Caribou Island Jack Salvio was the boss. When he gave an order, everyone jumped.

The first shift break was over, and a few stragglers sauntered back down the hallway from their sleeping quarters toward the mudroom. Salvio whistled at one of them. "Hey, you there! Nanook."

Lauren winced. Apparently Jack Salvio had not been paying attention during the series of workshops on ethnic diversity Tiger Petroleum required all its employees to attend.

At the end of the hall an athletic-looking crew hand with *roughneck* written all over him stopped dead in his tracks, his back to them. He was tall—too tall for a native—and sported a dark, unkempt ponytail.

Lauren's gaze slid across the muscles barely hidden by his rumpled flannel shirt to the mud-spattered jeans hugging his backside like something off a Calvin Klein billboard. She suppressed the *wow* forming on her lips. His big, dirty hands fisted at his sides as he turned in response to Salvio's inappropriate comment.

He *was* a native.

Lauren knew the shock registered on her face.

"Get your butt over here and take the lady's bag." Salvio nodded at her duffel and briefcase sitting in the corridor outside the mudroom.

But then again, maybe he wasn't. It was hard to tell from this far away.

She guessed him to be in his early thirties, a year or two older than herself. His eyes were dark, his skin bronze, but the rest of his features didn't fit. He had what her mother would have called an English nose. Narrow and arrow-straight. Mother loved the English. But neither she nor

Crocker would love the way Lauren was looking at the roughneck.

Or the way he looked back.

She read a dangerous sort of instability in his eyes as he approached them. His gaze flicked from her to Salvio and back again. He passed her duffel, ignoring it. She fought the strangest urge to step back as he strode right up to Salvio and leveled his gaze at him.

"You talking to me?"

"Yeah." Salvio had to look up to meet that murderous glare of his. He *was* tall. But since she was only five-three, everyone seemed tall to her.

"The name's Adams."

Adams. Not your everyday Inuit or Yupik name. He was half-native, she suspected. And apparently he'd done something to anger Jack Salvio. Jack wasn't usually this nasty. Well, he was, but that was part of his nature. No, something else was causing the tension between them.

"I can take her bag out," Paddy said. As he stooped to retrieve it from the floor, he shot Lauren a loaded look. "Come on, Scout."

Paddy clearly wanted to talk to her alone. The way he fidgeted around Salvio, the tension in his expression, his bloodshot eyes... Something was wrong.

"No," Salvio said, not breaking the roughneck's gaze.

"But, Jack, I—"

"Nanook here will see her to her trailer. Won'tcha, boy?"

This was getting out of hand. Lauren pushed past them and grabbed her duffel and briefcase. "I can carry my own bag, thanks." Before they could react, she ducked into the mudroom and made a beeline for her jacket and Sorels.

Paddy followed her, Salvio and Adams in his wake. She laced her boots, shaking her head at their ridiculous behavior. This wasn't exactly the Ritz, and she didn't need a porter.

Adams plucked her bag from where she'd dropped it. "I'll take you out there. I've got a few minutes left before the shift starts up again."

"It's not necessary." She reached for the bag and, to her surprise, he let her take it. Their hands brushed in the transfer, their gazes locked, and for the barest second she imagined what those big hands would feel like on her body.

What was *that* about?

She shrugged it off and stepped around him, which wasn't easy in the close quarters, given Adams's size and the fact that she was dressed like the Michelin man in full survival gear.

"Suit yourself." Adams watched her as she snaked her way around the break room tables toward the exit. Her back was to him, but she felt his eyes on her all the same. Black eyes. Black as a winter's night in the Chugach.

"Scout, about that talk—" The door slammed behind her, cutting off the rest of Paddy's words. She'd catch up with him later. Right now all she wanted to do was get settled and get to work.

Heading straight for the geologist's trailer, she sucked in a blast of frigid air. On purpose. The lung freeze felt good this time. Hell, yes. She was back in the field.

She had a job to do. Failure was not an option. Not for the woman who was about to become Tiger Petroleum's next exploration manager. Not for Hatch Parker's little Scout.

Chapter 2

Seth Adams wasn't a betting man, but if he had to guess who the corporate thief was that the Feds had hired him to finger, he'd put all his stakes on Lauren Fothcringay.

Last year, a small, foreign oil company that had never set foot in Alaska before snagged a land deal netting what turned out to be a fortune in oil drilling rights. No way was it just dumb luck. They'd had an inside track. Access to geological data the FBI knew, because of the position of the leases, could have only come from one source—Tiger Petroleum.

The Bureau had already ruled out the possibility that the foreign company simply stole the data. Tiger's security was renowned in the industry. No, the data had likely been sold to them—and selling proprietary corporate data without that corporation's knowledge or consent was a crime. A big one.

There was a criminal at work somewhere in the Tiger organization, and the Feds, along with Tiger's CEO and some high-ranking Wall Street types, wanted that person caught. The Caribou Island operation was as good a place as any to start. Perhaps the thief would strike again. No one at Tiger knew, of course, that they were under surveillance, and the FBI wanted it kept that way.

Oh, yeah, Seth thought, as he watched Lauren Fotheringay out the icy window of the break room, lugging her duffel and briefcase across the site in near whiteout conditions.

The woman was tough as nails. And a hell of a lot more attractive in the flesh than she appeared in that society news clipping he'd seen showing her dressed to the nines with Tiger's money man, Crocker Holt. Seth had read all about the two of them in the dossier Bledsoe had provided.

Those big brown eyes of hers had given him the once-over, too. More than once. In an irritating way, she reminded him of Kitty, his ex. They both had that same finishing-school, expensive-women's-college, "hey, look at me, I'm a big lady executive" sort of arrogance about them.

Behind the scenes, women like that got their kicks from messing with the heads of men they considered a couple of rungs below them on the evolutionary ladder. Construction workers, auto mechanics, even a roughneck now and then. Yeah, he knew the type. Boy, did he ever.

What Little Miss Society In Geologist's Clothing didn't know was that he wasn't a roughneck. Well, not anymore he wasn't. Fresh out of high school he'd pulled pipe from Barter Island to Barrow, scraping together enough money to pay his way through college.

He'd graduated with honors with a B.A. in criminology from the University of Alaska, surprising the hell out of his old man. Seth would never forget the day he called him in his New York office with the news. Not that an important oil man like Jeremy Adams had time to attend his kid's commencement.

Remembering, Seth made a derisive sound in the back of his throat.

The FBI had recruited him right out of school. Some affirmative action thing, though he could have easily made the cut on his own. He ended up second in his class at the Academy. Even so, Bledsoe, his section chief in D.C., had never liked him. The feeling was mutual.

Three years later Bledsoe had him dismissed for reasons Seth didn't like to remember. He'd blown their cover on a major counterfeiting sting the FBI and Secret Service had spent six months and a bundle of cash setting up. The way Seth saw it, it was either that or watch his partner take one in the back. He'd had no choice. Bledsoe thought otherwise.

In the end, his partner nearly bought it. Bledsoe somehow managed to blame that on him, too. After Seth got the ax, he went home to his native village of Kachelik, and had worked as a borough cop there ever since.

It was a great job, and he loved the village. He had friends there, and family. His wife left him when the Bureau canned him and, in hindsight, he considered himself damned lucky. They were from different worlds, and Seth never intended to make that mistake again.

The past few years had been pretty uneventful. No real challenges, no serious girlfriends. Everything was rocking along just fine until a few weeks ago when two suits showed up at the village in the dead of night in an unmarked FBI chopper.

Bledsoe wanted him back. Needed him, was more like it. The Feds wanted someone undercover on Caribou Island, and couldn't find one among the ranks of bright and shiny new agents who'd fit in on an offshore oil rig in the Arctic. Seth was elected.

Altex's grim financial situation made it easy for the FBI to get him out on the island. Posing as a native Alaskan affirmative action group, Bledsoe's men had paid Paddy O'Connor a subsidy to hire Seth as a roughneck for the Caribou Island job. In a roundabout way, it was the second time he'd been hired by the Bureau because of his ethnicity.

It would be the last time.

He hadn't wanted the job at first, but a tribal elder had counseled him to take it. Seth wasn't sure why. He'd finally agreed, but it wasn't because of the elder's gentle prodding, or because Bledsoe offered him his old job back in D.C. if he fingered the perp. But this was no time to reminisce about his motives. He needed to focus on the facts.

He'd been on the job six days now, and so far everything about the operation seemed above board. He'd gotten the usual cold reception from the crew. If he hadn't, he'd have been suspicious. Jack Salvio was a nasty piece of work, too, but nothing Seth couldn't handle. Everything seemed normal, in fact, until fifteen short minutes ago when Lauren Parker Fotheringay landed on Caribou island.

Already he smelled blood.

Seth zipped his survival jacket all the way up, slammed his hard hat on his head and yanked the camp's front door wide. A blast of arctic air hit him full in the face.

Some routine maintenance had delayed the start of his shift, but he'd check in on the drilling floor anyway, just to make sure he wasn't needed. After that, he'd have plenty of time to pay a surprise visit to his number one suspect out there in her shiny new trailer.

That was probably Money Man's doing. The protective fiancé. Every geologist's trailer he'd ever seen on the North Slope had been beat-up and barely livable. This new one, which was bigger and nicer than half the houses in Kachelik, had been brought in special a couple of days ago for Her Majesty.

Seth dashed across the yard, took the slick outer stairs up to the drilling floor two at time, then skidded to a stop on the landing. Squinting back toward camp through the blowing snow, he saw Paddy O'Connor—that red hard hat of his was unmistakable—fighting the wind as he made his way toward Lauren Fotheringay's trailer.

Damn! He'd hoped to overhear their conversation. Paddy was also on his list of suspects, but only as an accomplice.

The Feds knew the thief was someone on the inside at Tiger, someone with a technical background who could interpret the data. But to pull it off, that person would need help in the field. And a drilling company toolpusher one short season away from bankruptcy was the most likely candidate.

Bledsoe had told Seth little else about the case. Just enough to get him started. He was supposed to finger the perps, then call in the cavalry. He wasn't authorized to take action on his own. That figured. His job was to stay undercover and report back to the almighty Doyle Bledsoe.

He jerked the door open to the "doghouse," the small break room just off the drilling floor, and ducked inside. The crew was standing around, drinking coffee. Big surprise. None of these yokels lifted a finger unless Paddy O'Connor was right there, making sure they were working.

That was fine with him. He shot back down the stairs and started for Fotheringay's trailer. Perhaps he'd get an earful of Paddy's conversation with her, after all.

"Yo, Adams!"

He turned in the direction the shout had come from, but couldn't see more than ten feet ahead of him. If the storm got much worse, they'd have to set up a rope between the rig and the camp, so no one would get disoriented walking back and forth.

A couple of roustabouts—Paddy O'Connor's men—fought the wind as they made their way to Seth's side.

"What's up, guys?"

"How 'bout giving us a hand?" One of them pointed back toward camp, where Seth knew a pallet of equipment sat waiting to be carried inside. "Forklift's down for the count."

Seth glanced in the direction of the geologist's trailer, but couldn't see it anymore through the storm. He bit off a silent curse. He wanted to get out there and see what was going on between Paddy and Lauren, but he also didn't want to arouse any suspicion, or give any of the crew any more reason to hate him than they already did.

Some of these good old boys didn't take kindly to natives taking up good roughnecking jobs they considered theirs by right. In winter the Arctic was a deadly environment. There was an unwritten rule out here that everyone pitched in and helped each other.

"Sure," he said, casting an annoyed glance in the direction of the equipment. It would probably only take a minute.

Twenty minutes later, when the pallet was empty and the roustabouts were on their way inside, Seth crept around the side of Lauren Fotheringay's custom-built trailer and peeked in the only uncurtained window.

There was nobody there.

At least not in the lab portion of the trailer. He scanned the clean white linoleum and sparkling steel countertops. A crate full of plastic bags filled with muddy rock samples sat by the door. Lauren's briefcase lay open on the desk next to a top-of-the-line laptop computer.

There was only one other room in the trailer. A small bedroom and bath in the back. He didn't think Paddy would be in there with her. But maybe so. He seemed to know her pretty well. What had he called her back in the mudroom?

Scout. Kind of an odd nickname for a society cupcake who wore the biggest diamond engagement ring Seth had ever seen up close, and who drove a seventy-five thousand dollar Porsche. Yet another little gift from her fiancé. Seth had done some last-minute homework on both of them using the Internet.

Skirting around the back of the trailer, he took care to avoid slipping into the murky-looking reserve pit. Due to the warm temperature of the mud and drilling fluids circulating in and out of it, it was the only thing liquid for miles. Everything else in the Arctic was frozen solid this time of year.

The wind was blowing so hard now, swirling dry snow

up around him like an icy white shroud, he could barely see his hand in front of his face. The bright, overhead yard lights reflected off all that white, making visibility almost worse.

Then he heard it. A woman's scream.

Seth froze in place, peering straight across the reserve pit from where the sound had come, ice and wind slicing at his eyes. It had to be Lauren. She was the only woman on the island.

It took him a full minute to traverse the narrow strip of ice sandwiched between the back of the trailer and the open pit. Where the yard opened up again, he took off at a run, then stopped dead in his tracks when he saw her.

She was kneeling at the edge of the reserve pit. In shirt-sleeves! No jacket. No hard hat. Was she nuts? Her auburn hair whipped at her face. Up to her forearms in mud, she was trying to pull something out of the pit—or push it in—he couldn't tell which.

As their gazes collided, he read panic in her eyes. "You!" she shouted at him over the roar of the wind. He took another step toward her, then caught a glimpse of something that made his heart seize up in his chest.

A red hard hat, lying next to her on the ice.

Only then did he notice what she was desperately clutching. Paddy O'Connor's limp, mud-covered body.

Seth narrowed his eyes, but not from the sleet blasting his face. "What the hell do you think you're doing?"

Chapter 3

For the first time in her life Lauren was knee-knocking, bone-shaking terrified.

Adams bore down on her like a predator. Once, years ago, she'd watched as a polar bear slaughtered a lone seal who'd drifted away from its herd. It all came back to her now as she felt a dazed sort of panic, the kind she'd seen reflected in the seal's eyes the second before the bear took it down.

Three strides, then two. Adams was almost on her, but she couldn't will herself to let go of Paddy's jumpsuit and run. She locked gazes with the roughneck, her teeth chattering from the cold. Adams reached out and—

To her astonishment, he grabbed the collar of Paddy's jumpsuit and in one smooth motion pulled him out of the pit onto the ice.

"Move away from him."

"Wh-what?"

"You heard me, move!"

She slid to the side, her arms dripping mud that would be frozen in— Oh, God, it was already frozen.

Adams shot her an icy look as he checked Paddy's body for a pulse. Lauren knew he wouldn't find one. That was the first thing she'd done when she'd discovered him face-down, floating in the reserve pit.

"Get the medic."

The world spun around her. Bright yard lights reflected off blowing snow. Bone-chilling wind sliced her skin like a razor. She sat back on the ice as visions of Paddy O'Connor and her father—collecting rock samples, inspecting a worn drill bit, sharing a beer after a job well done—screamed through her mind in an avalanche of pain and tenderness.

She was barely aware of Adams starting CPR.

"I said get the medic! Now!"

His command snapped her out of her daze. "Y-yes. Of course." She scrambled to her feet.

"Wait. Here." He stopped the chest compressions long enough to shrug off his survival jacket and toss it to her. Then he watched her as she struggled into it, teeth chattering, her gaze pinned on his. For the barest moment she read something in his eyes, something she wasn't prepared for.

Accusation.

"Have them bring the stretcher. Tell Salvio to order a medevac out of Kachelik. It's closer than Deadhorse. That chopper that dropped you here isn't set up for it."

She nodded, took a second to get her bearings, then took off at a run, Adams's unzipped jacket whipping her in the wind.

Two minutes later the camp was in an uproar. Twenty minutes after that, in the camp's tiny infirmary, the medic— a freckle-faced kid fresh from advanced life-support training—pronounced Paddy O'Connor dead.

Lauren felt sick to her stomach.

Salvio wrapped an arm around her and moved her toward the door. "Come on, I've got just the thing for you."

She tried to wave him off through a haze of tears, but he persisted, steering her back down the hallway toward his office. They passed Adams, gathered with the rest of the crew just inside the camp's kitchen. His face was hard, his eyes black and unreadable. Surely he didn't think it was her fault that Paddy'd been, that he—

"Did he make it?" one of the crew asked.

Salvio shook his head.

Some of these guys had worked for Paddy O'Connor since the beginning. Lauren had known the toolpusher all her life. What on earth had happened?

They turned into Salvio's office and he directed her to the beat-up sofa. "Sit down."

"No, I—"

He pushed her down onto the stained Naugahyde. She watched, in a daze, as he fished something out of his file cabinet.

"Here. Drink it." He handed her a small, silver flask.

It didn't surprise her at all that Jack Salvio ignored Tiger's strict rules prohibiting alcohol in the field. She stared blankly at the flask. Why not? It couldn't make her feel any worse, and it just might settle her nerves if not her stomach. He opened it for her, and she took a healthy swig. Whatever it was, it burned all the way down.

"Good. Now get some rest. You look like hell."

She'd shed Adams's jacket in the mudroom. Her clothes and her hair were caked with drilling mud, but that could wait.

"No, I've got to call in."

"Phones are out. The weather."

That's right. She'd forgotten. Crocker had mentioned it to her on her chopper flight in. "So there'll be no medevac to transport Paddy's body?"

"Nope."

"What about the satellite uplink? I've got to call my boss and tell him what's happened."

"Walters can wait. Along with the rest of the world. The uplink's down, too."

"But—" The satellite link was *never* down. "How can that be?"

"Dunno. All I know is it is."

"What are we going to do?"

Salvio shrugged. "Shut it all down, I guess. The whole operation."

"You're kidding, right?"

"I ain't kiddin' at all. The second we report what's happened we'll be crawling with Tiger execs, OSHA agents, borough cops—the whole frickin' state'll be out here. Might as well get a jump on the shutdown."

She looked at him incredulously. "But the exploration well... We're nearly at target depth. The rock samples... If we don't get them, if *I* don't get them—"

Tiger had spent a huge chunk of this year's exploration budget on the Caribou Island project. Her boss, Bill Walters, was counting on her. The accuracy of their geologic maps, Tiger's position in the next round of land leases, her promotion—everything depended on finishing the well.

"Uh, excuse me..." The roughneck, Adams, stood just outside the half-open door. Lauren wondered how much of their conversation he'd heard. "I thought someone might want this."

With a shock she realized he was offering her Paddy's hard hat. Her stomach tightened. A man was dead, and all she could think about was the damned job. Tears pooled hot at the corners of her eyes. By sheer will she beat them back.

"You were out there." She rose and stepped toward Adams's outstretched hand. "Why?"

"Who, me?" he said, far too casually.

Salvio got to him first, and snatched the hard hat from his hand.

"Yeah, you." She narrowed her eyes at him, wondering what he was hiding. It was that chiseled expression of his that made her suspicious. He was just too cool about the whole incident.

"Whaddya mean he was out there?" Salvio stepped between her and the roughneck. "When?"

Adams didn't answer. He just stood there looking at her, those black eyes burning an impression right into her—a heady fusion of danger and sexuality that hit her like a punch. A second later she looked away.

"Remember to tell that to the cops when they come," Salvio said.

"I—I will." She didn't trust Adams. There was something not right about him.

Funny that none of the other geologists in her department had ever mentioned him before. Over the years Tiger had drilled dozens of exploration wells in the Arctic. It was a small, tightly knit community up here. You got to know the drilling crews pretty well. But no one had ever mentioned a half-native roughneck named Adams to her.

"Get back to work, boy," Salvio said.

A healthy spark of rebellion ignited in Adams's eyes. He stood there, unmoving, just long enough to piss Salvio off. A split second before she was certain the company man was going to deck him, Adams did an about-face and was gone.

"I'd steer clear a that one, if I was you." Salvio shot her one of his rare paternal looks, then dropped into his overstuffed desk chair. "He's trouble."

She wondered for the dozenth time what Adams was doing out by the reserve pit when he was supposed to be on shift. And how Paddy O'Connor—a seasoned professional who'd worked every major oil field in the world, from West Texas to Saudi to the North Sea—had drowned in a reserve pit that was only five feet deep.

She nodded at Salvio, promising herself she'd stick close to him and do as he advised. "Yes," she said, and stepped into the hallway just as Adams turned the corner into the break room, flashing a cool look back at her. "Trouble is right."

* * *

They drilled a hundred more feet of hole before the shift was over at midnight. Geologist's orders. A man was dead, and they were still drilling. Seth couldn't believe Salvio had bowed to Lauren Fotheringay's demand.

In the claustrophobic bunk room he shared with three other guys, Seth stripped off his work clothes, grabbed a towel and headed for the showers down the hall.

The hot water felt good on his sore muscles. He'd been in pretty good shape when he arrived on 13-E last week, but roughnecking twelve-hour shifts, day in, day out, was enough to make any man bone-tired.

He threw on some jeans and a clean flannel shirt, then followed his nose to the kitchen. His stomach growled as his gaze zeroed in on New York strip steaks sizzling on the grill, stuffed baked potatoes and a half-dozen other side dishes ready and waiting for the crew to fill their plates.

A few guys pushed past him in line as he stood there contemplating his next move. He needed to check out that reserve pit now. Wind and blowing snow had probably already destroyed any evidence of what had really happened to Paddy O'Connor.

He swore under his breath as he palmed a couple of dinner rolls, then started back down the hall toward the mudroom, wolfing them down on the way. Salvio's office was dark. He'd be sleeping this time of night. Good. Seth hoped he was having nightmares.

There was a lot about Jack Salvio that Seth didn't like, but he had to keep his own personal opinions out of the investigation. The company man was a suspect like everyone else, but Salvio had been with Tiger nearly thirty years, and nothing like this incident last year—where someone had sold a foreign oil company stolen data—had ever happened before. Besides, Salvio hated foreigners.

No, it didn't add up. Salvio was a pain in the ass and a bigoted jerk, but Seth didn't think he had the smarts or the connections to put together a corporate piracy deal potentially worth hundreds of millions of dollars.

But Lauren Fotheringay did. Along with the technical knowledge required to know exactly which geologic data was valuable and which was useless. The question was, if Lauren was the thief, would she repeat last year's caper, this time with data from Caribou Island?

Suited up in full survival gear, Seth battled the wind as he trudged across the yard toward the reserve pit. Three quarters of the way there, he made out the outline of the geologist's trailer. The bedroom was dark, but an eerie light shone from the bare lab windows. Perhaps he'd pay the esteemed Ms. Fotheringay an unexpected visit.

First, he'd check out the reserve pit. Skirting around the trailer, he narrowed his eyes against the ice shards pummeling his half-exposed face. He was used to North Slope winters and the burning, biting wind. All the same, it was almost impossible to see anything.

As he'd suspected, the crime scene had been completely obliterated by the weather. No footprints, no outward signs of a struggle, nothing. "Damn." He should have stayed out here and surveyed the scene instead of helping to get Paddy's body inside.

Ten minutes after the toolpusher was pronounced dead, Salvio had rousted them all back to work, and had supervised the first part of the drilling shift himself. There'd been no way for Seth to slip out and investigate. Now, ten hours later, there was nothing left to see.

He kicked at the dry snow covering the spot where Lauren had been kneeling. The only evidence that she or Paddy had been there at all was a slick coating of muddy ice where she'd struggled with his body.

He glanced in the direction of the trailer, his mind made up. An open crate of rock samples, probably left outside by mistake, provided just the excuse Seth needed to intrude.

He grabbed an armful of the frozen plastic bags, jerked the door open to the lab and stepped inside. "Anybody home?"

Lauren jumped at his voice, nearly upending the lab stool on which she was perched. She'd been looking at samples under a microscope with a black light that bathed the room in a ghostly bluish glow. Soft music strained in the background—a raw Celtic ballad. It surprised him a little. Given what he'd read about her, he would have pegged her for classical or jazz.

"Don't you guys ever knock?" She swiveled toward him, then froze in place when she recognized him. "Oh, it's you."

"Yeah. I was just—"

"Put them on the counter." She hopped off the stool, strode past him and flipped on the overhead fluorescent lights. "Over there."

He set the samples down next to the scope, then turned to face her.

"What do you want?"

She'd been crying, and she hadn't slept. He could tell from the dark circles under her red-rimmed eyes. Brown eyes. Pretty, he thought, for the second time that day.

"I saw the samples outside and thought I'd give you a hand."

"Right. You saw them. All the way from camp, in this weather." She crossed her arms over her chest, and arched a neatly plucked brow at him.

She was smart as whip. Smart enough, he reminded himself, to commit murder and hide the evidence.

"No," he said. "I was out here already."

"For the second time today. Why?"

She was right to challenge him. Typically the crew didn't lurk around the geologist's trailer. It was off-limits to them unless they were acting under specific orders. Especially if the well they were drilling was important.

Data—especially rock samples with traces of oil—was

the whole reason they were out here. Good geologists protected their data, and right now Lauren Fotheringay was glaring at him with all the mistrust of a grizzly protecting her threatened cubs.

He needed to figure out how to reach her, how to get close to her, and fast. If he didn't, he'd never discover if she was the one the Feds were after. Or if she'd had a hand in Paddy O'Connor's murder. The medic had called it a drowning accident. Not a chance. No one drowned in a reserve pit.

Seth decided to gamble and go for the truth. Part of it, at least. He had to get Lauren to trust him. If the truth failed, he'd try seduction. That always worked with women like her—cool corporate princesses out of their element, thrilled by a chance to drag the bottom for some rough company.

"Okay," he said, flashing his eyes at her. "So the rock samples were just an excuse. I really wanted to talk to you."

The gamble paid off, though he wasn't sure if it was truth or the promise of seduction that roused her interest. All he knew was that her frosty stance softened, along with the hard look in her eyes. She nodded at the desk chair in the corner. "So talk."

He sloughed off his jacket, set his hard hat on the counter, but ignored her offer to sit. She watched him like a hawk. Every move. He recognized the music now. The Chieftains. He liked this particular cut, in fact. "Nice music," he said, and risked a smile.

Those warm brown eyes of hers instantly frosted over again. She snapped the CD player off and resumed her icy pose of a moment ago. "Paddy didn't fall in that pit. And he didn't drown. He was murdered."

Her plain statement of the facts caught him completely off guard. For a split second he read something in her eyes, in the way she unconsciously bit her lip, that unnerved him. A feminine sort of fragility he wasn't prepared for. A moment later it vanished, and her features hardened.

"You were out there," she said.

"So were you."

"You think *I* killed him?"

"Didn't you?"

Her mouth dropped open. "You're joking, right?"

"Am I?" Now he was getting somewhere. He'd push her right to edge and see exactly what she was made of.

"You're insane. Get out." She turned away and gripped the edge of the counter. He could tell by the way she wavered on her feet that she was exhausted.

Sheer instinct drove him closer. Perhaps she was more of a mystery than he'd first suspected. He'd thought he had her figured out, but he wasn't always good at reading people on first impressions.

"What did you and Paddy talk about?"

"Nothing. I left the camp to come out here and—" She spun toward him and shot him exactly the kind of condescending look his ex-wife had been famous for. "What business is it of yours?"

"I'm a witness. I saw Paddy come out here to your trailer, myself."

"He did no such thing. After I left the camp I didn't see him again until…" She looked away, her cheeks flushed.

"I saw you with his body. You were—"

"Trying to save him."

"That's not what it looked like."

She pursed her lips and glared at him, deadly silent, her small hands fisted at her sides. He could tell from the fire in her eye that she was mentally counting to ten. He used the time to consider the facts.

Paddy O'Connor had been in damned good shape for a man pushing up against the far side of sixty. Someone as petite as Lauren could never have muscled him into that reserve pit against his will.

Seth hadn't had the chance to check Paddy's body for marks. He'd been too busy trying to revive him. Now it would be nearly impossible to confirm his suspicions. Wrapped in plastic sheeting, the body was sequestered away in the big freezer in the camp's kitchen, which was open around the clock.

Lauren could have hit him with something, right here in the privacy of her trailer. Could have knocked him out cold, dragged him to the pit, shielded by the weather, then drowned him.

He glanced around the trailer at the neat stacks of papers, rock samples and supplies. Everything in order, neat as a pin. No blood. No signs of struggle, or obvious weapons in sight. Not even any mud on the floor, except for his own footprints. Lauren Fotheringay was either innocent, or very very good. Seth suspected the latter.

"I think you'd better leave." She turned her back on him and shut down the microscope she'd been using when he'd arrived.

He wasn't giving up that easily. He decided to try a different approach. "You knew Paddy pretty well, didn't you?"

"Yes, I did. He was…" She paused, and for a moment he thought she might not continue. "He was my father's best friend." She swept some glass slides into a drawer and slammed it shut, her back rigid.

Four feet away he could feel her anger, and something more. A carefully shielded vulnerability evidenced by the way her hand shook as she again gripped the counter for support.

Seth knew all about her father. Everyone here did. But he hadn't known Paddy O'Connor had been Hatch Parker's friend. The dossier Bledsoe had given him hadn't included that fact.

"I'm sorry," he said, and on impulse stepped toward her. "That's okay. I'm just…"

He looked down at her from behind as her knuckles turned white clutching the counter. Her shoulders shook almost imperceptibly, then her ragged breathing seemed to stop altogether. With a shock he realized she was crying.

"Hey, don't." Without thinking, he gripped her shoulders to steady her. By accident he grazed his lips across her hair, catching a whiff of herbal shampoo as he leaned down to whisper in her ear. "It's okay."

A fierce sort of compassion welled inside him. That wasn't good. He was a federal agent, for Christ's sake. Well, an ex-federal agent. Still, he was a cop, and he had a job to do. He was supposed to be questioning a suspect, not comforting a weeping woman.

She turned in his arms. As her feet twisted between his, she faltered and reached for him. He caught her up, and her arms snaked around his neck. A second later her face was buried in his chest. She worked to get a grip on herself, but gave up the fight as he gently massaged the tight muscles of her back.

"It's okay," he whispered, again, and stroked her soft auburn hair. "It's good to cry. Get it all out."

What the hell was he doing? He wasn't sure. All he knew was that she was warm and soft, and she needed him. Her father had been killed on this very rig, and now another man she'd been close to was dead, too.

He'd been too hasty, perhaps, in thinking her capable of murder. Selling proprietary corporate data was one thing. A nice, clean, white-collar crime. Lots of money involved, but no dirty work. And no one ended up dead. Lauren Fotheringay might be a criminal, but he sensed she wasn't a murderer. Her anguish over Paddy O'Connor's death was real.

Holding her close, feeling the soft weight of her breasts crushed against his chest, he thought about how long it had been since he'd really wanted a woman. Sure, he'd done his share of dating since he and his ex had split, but he hadn't let himself get close to anyone again. Had never let his guard down.

As he stroked Lauren's hair and soothed her with comforting words, he realized he was in danger of doing exactly that. His lips grazed her ear, her cheek. One more move and he'd be kissing her.

"Uh, sorry," she said, and pushed against his chest.

He instantly backed off.

"I—I don't know what came over me. I was just…" Her eyes darted away. She wouldn't look at him. Her face flushed with embarrassment.

"Don't worry about it." He was embarrassed, too. As he turned to leave, she touched his arm.

"I stepped out of the trailer to grab some rock samples from the crate outside. That's when I saw his hard hat."

"Paddy's?"

"Yes." She gripped his arm tighter, her eyes locked on his. "I looked around but didn't see him. That's when I heard it."

"Heard what?"

"I wasn't sure. I thought it was shouting, but the wind was so deafening, I couldn't tell."

"So you…" He nodded, urging her to continue.

"I picked up his hard hat and walked toward the sound. Over by the reserve pit."

"Without a jacket, in this weather."

She shrugged. "I know. Stupid. But that's what I did."

"And then?"

"As I got close, I saw something in the mud. When I realized it was Paddy…" She looked away again, struggling to keep her composure.

"You tried to save him."

She nodded. "But he was already dead."

He wanted to believe her. The thought of her killing someone bothered him more than he wanted to admit. On impulse he grasped her hand and squeezed it. "You'll be okay out here?"

"Yes. I just need some sleep."

He was halfway out the door, zipping his jacket, when she stopped him one last time.

"Thanks," she said, and shot him a tiny smile.

"Any time."

He stood there in the biting wind after she closed the door, wondering why he'd acted like a schoolboy in there instead of a cop. She was damned attractive, that was why. And not as tough as he'd first made her out to be.

Maybe she wasn't the one he was after. He'd like to believe that. Hell, ten minutes with her and he half believed it already.

A flash of white shot across his field of view. "What the—?" Arctic fox. Two of them, racing across the yard in the direction of the camp. Seth knew exactly where they were headed. To the Dumpster behind the kitchen.

He jogged after them, fighting the wind and trying to forget how good Lauren Fotheringay had felt in his arms. A few minutes later his suspicions were confirmed. One of the cooks had left the heavy, metal Dumpster lid open again.

A half-dozen arctic foxes huddled around a black plastic trash bag that had blown off the overflowing pile of garbage. One of them had a glazed doughnut in his mouth. No wonder the EPA was all over these drilling companies.

Seth let out a *whoop* and the foxes scattered. What a mess. He reached for the open bag, then froze. "Son of a—"

He forced his eyes wide against the wind and blowing snow, not wanting to believe what he saw. The overhead yard lights lent a harsh reality to the blood-covered tool stashed amidst the frozen remnants of that day's breakfast.

Its shaft was thick and sheathed in blue rubber, the head square. The claw end was like a pickax, long and curved to a single sharp point. Seth had seen plenty of them growing up to know exactly what he was looking at.

A geologist's rock hammer.

Chapter 4

Where had these rock samples come from, the moon?

Lauren pushed back from the microscope and focused her eyes out the trailer window. Not that it helped. She couldn't see a thing except blowing snow. The wind velocity had increased overnight to dangerous speeds. She'd woken with a start that morning when an empty fifty-five-gallon drum had blown up against the side of her trailer with a powerful *thunk*.

She grabbed her calculator and ran through the sequence one more time. "This can't be right." For the third time she checked the smudged label marking one of the small plastic sample bags littering her workstation.

Someone had clearly made a mistake.

As drilling progressed and the well got deeper, rock samples mixed with mud and fluids were sucked up from the bottom of the hole. At the surface they were collected and bagged by one of the Altex roustabouts. It was a dirty, thankless task, usually assigned to the lowest man on the totem pole. She wondered who among the Altex crew had been elected.

The Caribou Island well wasn't at its target depth yet, so at this point Lauren didn't expect to see anything out of the ordinary, like traces of oil, in the samples. And least of all rocks so unusual she was certain some mistake had been made.

She shut down the microscope and grabbed her jacket, then paused to consider her options. She wasn't that anxious to make another appearance in camp. Earlier that morning she'd been bombarded with crew members' questions—the same question, actually, over and over.

Are we going to keep drilling?

Didn't they understand? They were so close to finishing the well, it didn't make sense to shut it all down now. Tiger had invested a small fortune to get the data from Caribou Island. Her boss Bill Walters, the VPs—Crocker included— and Tiger's CEO would be counting on her. On all of them.

And she wasn't about to let them down.

Last night after she'd left the camp, Salvio had changed his mind about continuing the drilling. But only temporarily, he'd warned her this morning. Fine. She'd take whatever she could get. Once communications were up, they could let the bigwigs at corporate decide what to do. Until then, she wasn't changing her position.

She breezed out the door, then locked it with her key. No one was touching these rock samples until she figured out who had screwed up. The bags were clearly mismarked. It was impossible for that kind of rock to exist at the Caribou Island location. She should know. She'd interpreted all the subsurface maps of the site herself, just last year.

There would be hell to pay with her boss if she didn't get this mess sorted out. And fast. No way was she shipping mismarked samples back to Tiger's lab in town. But with Paddy gone and all communications down, she wasn't sure who exactly from Altex to talk to about it.

Adams, maybe.

Warmth washed over her as she recalled the feel of his arms around her last night in the lab. Strong, solid, comforting. When was the last time Crocker had held her that way? Stroked her back, soothed her? It dawned on her that she didn't even know Adams's first name.

The camp's forklift rumbled past, jerking her from her thoughts. Sheesh. Forty below, winds screaming across the tundra like a banshee, and she was lost in some fantasy about a roughneck. Great. Just what she needed. To act like an idiot out here on the job.

A man was dead. Tiger's operation was weeks behind schedule, and the biggest promotion of her career hung in the balance. She needed to focus, to do what was expected of someone in her position. Not break down like a crybaby and fall into the arms of one of the crew, for God's sake.

It had taken her years to win the respect of her male peers, of Tiger's senior personnel, not to mention the rough-and-tumble drilling crews, most of whom still believed women didn't belong in the field.

She wasn't about to throw it all away because the going got tough. Her father would have told her to buck up, meet the challenge. That's exactly what she intended to do. She'd see Salvio right away about those samples.

Hand over hand, Lauren pulled herself along the rope that had been set up as a guide between her trailer and the main camp. The weather was the worst she'd ever experienced, and showed no signs of breaking. Visibility was a joke. It took her nearly five minutes fighting the wind to make it to camp.

Salvio wasn't in his office.

"Damn." She plopped down into his beat-up desk chair and raked her fingers through her half-frozen hair. Fine. She'd talk to him later. Until then, she'd ask around among the crew.

The first shift was on break, and she heard laughter com-

ing from the kitchen. The greasy aroma of hamburgers sizzling on the grill and her growling stomach reminded her
she hadn't eaten yet that day. Lunch sounded good. Maybe
she'd grab a quick—

The thought vaporized as her eyes focused on the drilling
stats blinking at her from one of the computer monitors on
Salvio's cluttered desk. She leaned closer and scanned the
real-time drill depth readout.

"Fifteen two?" She blinked her eyes a couple of times
to make sure she wasn't reading it wrong. Fifteen thousand
two hundred and six feet. That couldn't be right. They were
at nine thousand last night, nine two this morning. The top
of the target zone for the Caribou Island well was nine thousand four hundred feet. Straight down. Easy as pie.

Altex had drilled dozens of oil exploration wells for Tiger, just like this one, over the past twenty-five years. Caribou Island should have been a routine operation, but Mur-
phy's Law seemed to be in full effect out here.

She hit the side of the monitor with the flat of her hand
and watched the screen. The green numbers jumped, then
blinked back at her. Fifteen two. "This is crazy."

"Fotheringay!" Jack Salvio's gravelly voice made her
jump. He shot through the door, a nasty expression screwed
into his face. "I'm having enough trouble with this frickin'
equipment as it is."

"I was just—"

"Damned thing is always screwed up." He leaned over
her, typed some two-fingered gibberish into the keyboard
and hit the Escape key. The monitor did a split-second reset,
then flashed back to life.

Lauren focused in on the depth measurement. "Nine
thousand three hundred feet."

"There. It's fixed."

Frowning, she studied the blinking stats again. Everything
seemed to be normal now. The drilling depth looked fine.

"Don't touch it again, ya hear?"

"Sorry." Lauren had never seen so much computer equipment in a company man's office before. Personally, she'd opt for a sheet of paper, a pencil and a plain old calculator any day over all the fancy analytical instruments Tiger had insisted they install at Caribou Island.

Bill Walters, her boss, had insisted, actually. She remembered a presentation he'd given months ago on the financial return of using some new computerized drilling system. It was supposed to have made the job easier, and to have saved them money. Funny that Bill even considered the financial end of things. That had been a first. Shaking her head, she gave the numbers on the monitor a final glance. The new system was clearly junk. As soon as communications were restored she'd give Bill a call to let him know.

Salvio grabbed his hard hat from a hook on the wall and turned to leave.

"Oh, Jack—wait." She'd almost forgotten why she'd come to see him in the first place. "Do you know which roustabout was assigned to collect rock samples here last Tuesday?" That was the date scribbled on the bags of samples left outside her lab, though the crate they'd been boxed in was missing its label.

"Beats me. Why do you want to know?"

"There were some really strange samples in front of my trailer when I arrived, and—"

Without a word, Salvio jammed his hard hat onto his head and stormed out the door.

What's with him?

Ignoring his trademark rudeness, Lauren scanned the messy bulletin board on the wall over his desk. A second later she found what she was looking for—the crew manifest detailing who was on shift last week. Maybe now she'd find out which roustabout had—

"That's odd." The routine paperwork indicated a whole new crew had come in last Wednesday. Roughnecks, roustabouts, two cooks, the medic, the housekeeper, *everybody*.

There was always a lot of overlap on an operation this big. Eighty guys staggered on four-week shifts, for as long as it took to drill the well. They never all changed out at once. It was hardly possible, just given the logistics of getting everyone on and off the island.

Lauren shook her head.

Strange-looking rock samples, computer stats that weren't possible given their operational plan, the worst weather in years, and a complete crew change just days before their toolpusher was killed in what Lauren knew in her gut was not an accident.

Something was going on here, and she intended to get to the bottom of it.

Pushing back from the desk, she made a mental note to query the one person who didn't seem to belong on Caribou Island at all. "Whatever-your-name-is Adams."

"It's Seth."

His low, smooth voice startled her. With a shock she glanced up to see the target of her thoughts standing in the doorway, his broad shoulders filling it.

"Seth Adams," he said, and shot her the most dangerous-looking smile she'd ever seen in her life.

That wide-eyed innocent look didn't fool Seth for a second. Lauren held his gaze just long enough for her cheeks to warm to pink, then she wet her lips and pretended to study the numbers on one of the monitors.

"You called?" he said, adding the narrowest edge of seduction to his voice.

A beautiful woman was the hardest kind of criminal to catch. And once caught, the hardest to put away. There was always some gullible sucker around willing to do anything to help her. Seth felt himself slipping easily into the role.

How predictable. Bledsoe had wanted him on the job because he thought playing the dumb roughneck suited him perfectly. Maybe it did. But for different reasons altogether.

"Um, yes. I uh…saw you in the hall."

He smiled again, thinking what a perfect touch that coy little flustered look was to her whole act. "And?"

"I wanted to ask you something."

"Go ahead, shoot." He pulled a chair up close—a lot closer than he would have if she was a man—and shot her another smile.

"How long have you been out here?"

"Came in last Wednesday. Why?"

"No reason. I just wondered." She gave up a smile.

"Matter of fact, a whole new crew came on that day. Was that your doing?"

"*My* doing? No, how could it be? Geologists don't make those kinds of decisions. Only the—"

"Toolpusher?"

"That's right."

His eyes fixed on the tiny mole near her mouth. Sexy as hell. He'd noticed it for the first time last night in the lab.

"Who's in charge of the crew now that Paddy's…" All the light went out of her eyes, and he found himself feeling sorry for her again. All part of her plan, he reminded himself.

"Don't know. Salvio, I guess." Jack had been riding roughshod on them since the second Paddy O'Connor was pronounced dead. It made sense, since Salvio was Tiger's senior man and in charge of the whole field operation.

"Jack wants to shut it all down," she said absently.

"Makes sense, given what's happened." Seth cast a look out the window in the direction of the drilling rig, barely making out the outline of the derrick.

"I'm going out there to talk to him."

"Hey, wait."

She ignored him, and a minute later was suited up and out the door to the yard. Seth was right behind her. He was late as it was. Lunch was over and everyone was back on shift.

Lauren slipped on the ice as she grabbed the guideline connecting the camp to the rig. He caught her just in time.

"Thanks."

He barely heard her over the wind. She smiled up at him, her auburn hair whipping around her face. He grabbed the fur ruff of her hood and pulled it snug, holding her close longer than he should have.

Again he had to remind himself he was acting. So was she. All in a day's work. He was a cop, and she was a murderer. He hadn't wanted to believe it when he was with her last night, but what he'd found in the Dumpster convinced him. He'd wrapped the evidence in a paper bag and stashed it in his duffel. It wasn't enough. He'd bet his life there'd be no usable fingerprints on that rock hammer. All the same, he had to get a look at Paddy's body.

As they pulled their way along the guideline to the rig, he mentally checked off what he knew about Lauren Fotheringay. Not nearly enough. Not yet. The homicide alone might be tough to hang on her. But proof that she was the corporate thief would likely buy her the murder rap, too.

His goal was clear to him now. Forget the murder. Finger her for the illegal sale of Tiger's proprietary data. Rock samples and maps—that was likely what she was selling. The rest would follow if he could establish motive. This much he did know about her:

Oil industry papers had rumored Tiger's CEO was thinking of promoting Lauren over her boss, Bill Walters, to VP of exploration. No small leap. She couldn't be that good. There must be another reason. Maybe she was sleeping with him.

Maybe she was sleeping with all of them—Tiger's CEO, her boss, not to mention that pretty-boy fiancé of hers. Seth watched her shuck her jacket off inside the first-floor stairwell of the drilling rig, his gaze pinned on the curve of her hip, the swell of her breasts against that ratty old cardigan she seemed to live in.

He reminded himself that even if she wasn't a perp, she was still off-limits to him: a rich sorority princess with a fancy career and ice water in her veins. He'd gotten burned on that type once already, and wouldn't make that mistake again. Women like Lauren Fotheringay didn't love men, they used them. That fact made it easier to focus on his goal.

Bledsoe had ordered him to hold his cover even after he'd fingered the ringleader and his or her accomplices. They wanted to take everyone involved in this corporate piracy case down at once. No one was sure how high up in Tiger the fraud went, but Seth suspected pretty high.

Based on what he knew so far, if he had to guess, he'd make Lauren as the kingpin here in the field, and Paddy O'Connor her accomplice. Paddy must have gotten scared or screwed up, done something to make it dangerous for Lauren to let him live. Maybe he was getting ready to blow the whistle on the whole operation.

Seth didn't know, but he was going to find out.

Amazingly enough, his own father—a shrewd business-man who watched the movements of oil companies oper-ating in the Arctic like a hawk—had been the one who'd tipped off the Feds to what he'd first thought was some kind of illegal collusion between Tiger and that foreign company. How ironic that Seth should catch the case. He wondered if his father knew. And if he did know, if he'd care.

Oh, he'd care all right. The great and powerful Jeremy Adams would expect Seth to screw it up somehow. Just like he thought Seth had screwed up his career with the Bureau and his marriage. Not to mention a hundred other things growing up.

Lauren started up the metal stairs, and Seth followed, his gaze fixed on her jeans-clad behind. Mmm, nice. The view drove all thoughts of his father from his mind.

The higher they climbed and the closer they got to the drilling floor, the more deafening the noise became. The screeching sounds of machinery one floor above them told Scth they'd already started the rest of the shift without him. He'd catch hell from Salvio for sure now.

He swore silently under his breath. One of these days he and Jack Salvio were going to have a serious disagreement.

They topped a landing, and Lauren stopped short. Seth crashed into her from behind. "Whoa, sorry." He grabbed the greasy metal handrail to keep from falling backward down the stairs.

Over the noise, he heard her rattle off a litany of cuss words the average society cupcake shouldn't even know. But her tirade wasn't on his account. She pointed across one of the catwalks circling the central drilling pipe that stretched from ground level up five stories to the drilling floor just above them.

Seth looked past her and saw two roustabouts—the same guys who'd corralled him yesterday into helping them move that equipment. He'd found out soon afterward that they'd lied to him about the camp's forklift being down. The question was why?

His hunch was that they'd deliberately wanted to divert his attention. Away from a murder being committed not fifty yards away as he humped crates off a pallet? Maybe. Maybe not.

Seth filed that question away for the time being, and watched them scoop samples out of the big metal vat of drilling mud and rock being circulated out of the well. "Want me to—"

Lauren didn't wait for him to finish. In three seconds she was across the catwalk, shouting something at the two roustabouts that Seth couldn't make out over the noise. A second later he bumped up behind her again.

"What's going on?" Seth looked to Pinkie for an explanation. The roustabout had gotten his nickname when he lost one of his little fingers in a drilling accident years ago, so Paddy O'Connor had told him.

"Nothin'," Pinkie said.

"Yeah, nothin'." Seth looked hard at Pinkie's greasy-looking friend. The name *Bulldog* was painted in crude letters across his hard hat. "We was just takin' samples like—"

"Like we're supposed to." Pinkie shot Bulldog a cautionary look.

Something was off about these two. Seth had thought so since his first day on the job. They were thick as thieves and strangely aloof from the rest of the crew. Come to think of it, neither of them had seemed overly concerned, as had the rest of the men, when Paddy O'Connor turned up dead in the reserve pit.

Lauren grabbed a half-full plastic sample bag out of Bulldog's hand, yanked off her glove and ran a finger over the crudely marked depth measurement on the plastic. "Ninety-three ten."

"Yeah," Pinkie said. "What of it?"

Lauren shook her head. "Nothing. I just wanted to have a look, is all." She dipped a finger into the muddy, crushed up rock and sniffed it.

Seth leaned down and smelled the open bag. "What's wrong?"

"Nothing. I just—"

"We gotta get back to the floor." Pinkie tried to squeeze past them, but Seth blocked his way.

"Salvio ask you two to take samples?" Seth remembered that another roustabout, a young kid, new to the oil field, had been doing the sampling up until now.

"Yeah. Why?"

"No reason." He let Pinkie pass.

"I'm going with you." Lauren handed the sample bag back to Bulldog.

Pinkie turned on her. "Salvio says no one who ain't needed is supposed to come up there—geologists included."

"What?" Lauren's mouth gaped.

That figured, Seth thought. And it made sense. You didn't want too many people around distracting the drilling crew. He'd been more than distracted himself the past twenty minutes.

"Salvio put me in charge a-makin' sure." Pinkie flashed a hardened look at her. "Know what I mean?"

Seth had had enough of these two. "Get going." Oil field hierarchy, punctuated by the fact that Seth was bigger than both of them, insured their compliance.

Pinkie smirked, then nodded at his partner. Bulldog zipped the sample bag closed and tossed it into an open box beside the mud vat. Seth followed them both out onto the catwalk.

"Damn split-tails," Pinkie said, to no one in particular. "Women shouldn't be out here, if ya ask me."

Lauren stood there, face flushed, her whisky-brown eyes flashing anger, as she watched the two of them jog up the metal staircase toward the drilling floor.

"Ignore him," Seth said. "He's an idiot."

"If he's assigned to sample collection I've got to work with him, now don't I?"

"Yeah, I guess you do." The thought bothered him more than it should have. Seth nodded at the samples in the box. "What's up with those rocks anyway?"

She shook off her foul temperament and turned her attention on the box. "You wouldn't understand."

She'd be right, if Seth was who he was supposed to be— just another roughneck working another job. If he was smart, he'd stick to that role. But years ago, in college, he'd taken an introductory geology course along with a handful of other science classes needed to fulfill his degree requirement. In the end, his pride got the better of him. "Try me."

She looked at him for a cool moment that seemed longer than a winter in Kachelik. Hell, what was she doing, sizing up his intellect? His ex used to do that all the time.

"Forget it," he said, and started for the catwalk.

"No, wait." She grabbed his arm. "I—I'm sorry. It's just that so few people are ever interested in my work. It surprised me, is all."

He shrugged, annoyed at himself for letting her get to him.

"Come on." She pulled him toward the open box of samples.

The machinery noise was so loud, he had to invade her personal space so he could hear her. At least that's what he told himself as he edged close enough to her to catch the lingering scent of shampoo in her hair. He knew being this close to her was dangerous. He couldn't think straight, couldn't focus. Come on, Adams, get a grip.

"These are totally normal," she said, snapping him back to the topic. "Exactly what I'd expect to see at this location and this depth." She snatched one of the sample bags from the box and handed it to him.

He pulled off his glove and squished the heavy plastic between his fingers, squinting in the bad overhead light, studying the grayish-brown rock chips floating in mud. "Shale, right?"

"That's right." She smiled at him. "That's exactly what we should be seeing at this point."

"So, what's the problem?"

"That's not what's in the samples that were waiting in the crate outside the lab when I arrived."

"You mean the ones I saw you looking at last night?"

Their gazes locked, and for the barest second he knew she was remembering what had happened between them in the trailer. Their embrace, the delicate kisses he'd brushed across her temple and her hair. The recognition in her eyes told him she knew he was thinking about it, too.

She snatched the bag from his hand and broke the spell. "Um, yes." Her cheeks flushed with color. Clearly, she was uncomfortable with the bit of spontaneous intimacy they'd shared last night.

He was uncomfortable with it, too. Damned uncomfortable. But he was determined to get close to her. Close enough to learn her secrets—exactly what information she was selling, and how. She'd responded to him last night, and whether it was all an act or not didn't matter.

For whatever reason, Lauren Fotheringay wanted him on her side, as an ally. Maybe more than that, given the way she stole a glance at him when she thought he wasn't looking. That's exactly what he'd become, then. Another dumb, unsuspecting primate she could use for her own purpose.

It couldn't be more perfect. Once he proved to her she could trust him, he'd be able to glean the facts he'd need to collar her and her cronies here in the field, and anyone else in on the scheme back at Tiger Petroleum.

Time to move in for the kill.

"If there's anything I can help you with," he said, drawing her gaze back to his, "let me know."

"Thanks." She smiled again, and this time he marveled at how genuine it seemed.

Looking at her standing there in her field clothes, her expression open, eyes wide and trusting, he could almost believe she was innocent. That she knew nothing about Paddy's murder or the illegal peddling of information worth millions to the right buyer. He wanted to believe it. More than anything.

Watch your step, Adams.

She tossed the sample bag back into the box and slid past him, pausing at the catwalk. "See you later?" It was more than a question. Her eyes held a subtle plea.

"Yeah," he said, and forced a smile. "Later."

As he turned toward the metal staircase leading up to the drilling floor, he saw Jack Salvio leaning casually against the railing at the top, watching them. Lauren saw him, too. Salvio flashed her a hard look, then waved Seth up to the floor.

Time to go to work.

Chapter 5

The rhythmic *whomp* of chopper blades ripped her from an uneasy sleep. Lauren sat up in the hard, single bed and blinked her eyes open to pitch-black. "Oh, right."

Before she'd gone to sleep last night, she'd drawn the blackout shades in the trailer's tiny bedroom. Not that it was necessary in the dead of an arctic winter when darkness prevailed twenty-plus hours a day.

She checked the glow-in-the-dark hands of her watch. 2:40 a.m. Great. She'd never get back to sleep now. Why had she dreamt of a helicopter? In this weather, it was the last thing—

Wait! There it was again. She scrambled out of bed and ripped the Velcro-lashed drape away from the window. The harsh yard lights made her squint. She blinked a few times, to make sure she was seeing what she thought she was seeing.

Absolutely nothing.

No blowing snow. Not a breath of wind, in fact. The yard between her trailer and the drilling rig and the rest of the camp was perfectly still. Then she heard it again. She hadn't been dreaming. From this vantage point she couldn't see the chopper pad lying out beyond the camp, but her ears told her everything she needed to know.

Someone was here. Thank God!

She flipped on the overhead light and snatched a pair of jeans and a T-shirt from the pile of clothes she'd unpacked last night. If the weather had cleared long enough for a chopper to get in, maybe she could get word to her boss. Let Bill know what had happened to Paddy O'Connor, about the faulty computer system and those strange rock samples she'd found outside her trailer when she'd arrived.

Not bothering to wash her face or run a comb through her tangled hair, she jerked the connecting door open to the lab, just as the fluorescent lights snapped on overhead.

Jack Salvio stood across the room, framed by the lab's open doorway, a master key in his hand. "Good. You're up."

"What's going on? There's a chopper outside."

"Grab your gear. You're outta here."

"What?" She padded across the linoleum to where she'd left her boots, and slipped them on.

Ignoring her question, Salvio brushed past her and made a quick survey of the lab, his gaze darting across the stainless steel countertops, pausing on the open notebook at her workstation. She knew what he was looking for.

"Those samples you took from my locked trailer yesterday—where are they, Jack?" She was still steamed about the whole incident. She'd come back here yesterday afternoon to find them gone. Salvio was the only other person with a key.

"I told you. They were from last week. Shoulda been shipped days ago back to the lab at Tiger. It's taken care of now."

"That's not the point."

He started to read her handwritten notes about the unusual

samples. Lauren closed the distance between them and snapped the notebook shut.

What Salvio didn't know was that he'd missed one of the samples when he'd confiscated the crate. Lauren's eyes darted to the open plastic bag sitting next to her microscope. Salvio's gaze followed. She snatched it off the counter and stuffed it into the pocket of her cardigan.

"What's that?"

"Nothing. Just something I was working on yesterday." She tossed him a blank look.

"Don't screw around, Lauren. There's no time." He continued to eye the bulge in her pocket, the lines in his face deepening into a scowl.

"I'm not screwing around." She tried to ignore the fact that for some silly reason he was making her nervous. "What exactly is going on here, Jack?"

"Like I said, you're outta here."

"That's ridiculous. I'm not leaving, I just got here."

"Yeah, you are. I'm sending O'Connor's body back to Deadhorse. You're going with it."

"What? I can't leave now. We're nearly at target depth."

No one else knew what to look for—where and how much to sample, or what the samples meant, whether they had to drill deeper, or if they could stop. No one could make those decisions except the geologist.

Besides, she wasn't going anywhere until she found out where those peculiar rock samples had come from, and what Salvio had done with the crate.

"You're the one who found the body. And someone from Tiger's got to make the report. It's you or me." Salvio nodded at the rig. "Unless you want me to shut the whole frickin' thing down like I wanted to in the first place. Then we can go in together."

"No. That's out of the question, and you know it."

"Well, then?"

Lauren swore. Salvio was in charge and couldn't leave

the island while they were drilling, especially now that they had no toolpusher to manage the crew. And if they didn't keep drilling, they'd never finish on time.

"Start packing." Salvio shot her a nasty look just begging her to challenge him. "The break in the weather's temporary. We got a half hour at best." He started for the door.

Lauren's hand closed over the rock sample in her cardigan pocket. Instinct told her it was the key to this whole nightmare. On impulse, she dashed into the bedroom and stuffed it into a half-full box of tampons. Safest place on the planet. No guy in his right mind would ever touch that box.

Grabbing her jacket, she followed Salvio out the door. The cold hit her like a brick wall. The wind had died, but the ambient air temperature had dropped. She jogged after him, teeth chattering.

The whole place was in an uproar. Salvio hadn't been kidding. Four men in bunny boots and survival gear exited the prefab camp, bearing Paddy O'Connor's stiff, plastic-wrapped body across the yard toward the chopper pad out back.

"Why didn't you wake me sooner? You can't make a decision like this on your own. What if the weather gets worse? I might never get back to the island. We need to call in, tell someone what's hap—" Lauren stopped dead in her tracks. "Wait a minute!"

Salvio turned.

"The chopper. How'd you get it?" She spun toward the tiny communications shack nestled between the camp and the rig. "The satellite link! It's up!"

"Not anymore. It was working just long enough for me to make the call to Deadhorse for the bird."

"But Bill Walters… Didn't you—"

"Never got the chance to call him. Besides—"

Lauren didn't wait for him to finish. Pushing through a line of men making for the rig, she stormed toward camp.

"Get your stuff together, Fotheringay!" Salvio shouted after her. "You're gonna be on that bird."

She blasted through the door into the break room and collided with one of the crew. "Dammit! Watch where you're going."

Seth caught her by the shoulders. "Whoa! What's the hurry?"

She gritted her teeth and mentally counted to ten, trying to calm her anger. He pulled her off to the side, so more men could file past.

"It's Jack," she said. "He has no right to do this without permission."

"Do what?"

"He's sending me back to Deadhorse with Paddy's body."

"Makes sense. Someone has to go."

"But why me, and why now?"

Paddy didn't have any family; his crew was his family. Altex was his whole life. There was no one else to notify except the borough police and Tiger's senior management, and that could all be done by phone.

"The weather's supposed to get worse. Another hour, maybe less, and it's coming back." His voice was calm, smooth as glass. Exactly the opposite of the way she felt. "With a vengeance, so the chopper pilot says."

"So I've heard." She brushed past him and started for Salvio's office.

"Where's your gear? Don't you need to—"

"I'm not going." Her declaration didn't seem to surprise him one bit.

She plopped into Salvio's desk chair and snatched the red phone receiver from its hook. Dead. "Damn!"

"Communications are down." Seth looked at her hard, as if he expected her to react in some way to his comment.

"Well, they were up at some point, now weren't they? Long enough for Jack to call in that helicopter."

"Yeah, I guess they were."

She glanced briefly at the computer monitors on Salvio's desk. They were blank. Figured. The whole system must be down.

She had to call in. Had to tell someone what was happening. Her boss would be furious if he knew Salvio was trying to send her back to Deadhorse without consulting anyone else.

"I'm going over there." She pushed back from the desk.

"Where?"

"Sat-comm shack."

"I'll go with you."

She looked up at Seth, and their gazes locked. She realized he expected her to protest. To tell him no, that she didn't need his help. Common sense told her to steer clear of this guy, but instinct told her different.

"Okay," she said. "Thanks."

By the time they slipped out the camp's rear emergency exit, the wind had started up again. Visibility dwindled as the gale whipped swirling, needle-sharp blasts of dry snow into her face. Lauren pulled her fur-ruffed hood tight as they jogged along the back side of the metal building.

Where the snowdrifts deepened, Seth grabbed her gloved hand and guided her on, sheltering her from the wind with his body. He was so…what was the word? Chivalrous came to mind.

She recalled the last time she and Crocker had been caught in a snowstorm. It was during that awful ski vacation in the Alps. She had wanted to ski down the mountain, leaving space on the cable car for children and seniors who hadn't the stamina to brave the weather. But Crocker wouldn't hear of it. He'd pushed his way onto the car. Lauren was so angry at him, she'd skied down alone.

As Seth's grip on her tightened, she felt a warm sort of satisfaction blossom inside her. No man had ever gone out of his way to protect her before. Well, not since she was a kid and her father was alive.

"Wait here!" Seth shouted over the wind. He ducked inside the back door to the machine shop and emerged thirty seconds later with a pair of bolt cutters. Of course! The sat-comm shack was always locked for security reasons. Jack Salvio had the only key.

Together they rounded the corner and peeked between the buildings. No one was around. He pulled her into the tight space between the two steel structures. "Come on."

A dozen paces later they stopped dead. The door to the sat-comm shack was cracked, light spilling from inside. The heavy padlock lay open on the ground.

The door crashed wide, and Lauren's heart leaped to her throat. Seth pushed her hard against the wall of the shack and flattened his body over hers. It was dark, and if they were lucky—

Pinkie, the roustabout who'd given her trouble yesterday afternoon on the catwalk, stepped from the shack and stopped, not six feet from them. He ripped a cigarette from his pocket and tried, unsuccessfully, to light it.

Lauren felt Seth's body tense as Pinkie kicked the door shut, plucked the padlock from the ground and clicked it into place. She didn't breathe until he'd rounded the corner into the yard.

"That was close." Seth stepped away and pulled her with him. "You okay?"

She nodded.

"Good. Here we go."

As Seth sheared the lock with the bolt cutters, it struck her that he'd never even asked her why she wanted to access the operation's communications equipment. He'd just come with her. No questions.

And now, as if they were doing nothing out of the ordinary, he was assisting her in breaking into the one place on the island she had no business being. If they were caught, he'd lose his job in an instant.

"Okay, it's open." He pocketed the broken lock, flipped on the overhead light, and followed her inside. "Now what?"

Lauren studied the complex array of telecommunications equipment. The only familiar-looking hardware was a keyboard, monitor, and what looked like a high-tech scrambled-signal phone. "Now we try to call out."

Her knowledge was exhausted in the first thirty seconds. This was a system unlike any other she'd seen. Strange that Tiger would splurge on something this state-of-the-art for a routine operation like Caribou Island.

Seth took over, and seemed to know a whole lot more about the equipment than she ever would have suspected.

"How do you know about stuff like this?" she asked as he yanked a screwdriver out of his pocket and took the back off of the biggest of the CPUs. "Computers and telecommunications, I mean?"

He shot her a bitter smile. "What, you think I spend my days at the village hunting seals and carving totem poles?"

"No, it's just that—"

"That what?" He tossed the screwdriver aside and peered into the guts of the main system. "That it's amazing a guy like me, a native, would know anything about high-tech stuff?"

"That's not what I meant." Shame heated her face. She realized that was exactly what she'd meant.

As a child, tromping all over Alaska with her father, Lauren had spent time in many native villages. She'd never had preconceived notions about any group of people before.

But when her father died and her mother remarried, whisking her off to New York, Lauren's life had changed dramatically. Mother had made sure their world was populated only by the *right* kinds of people. And, when Lauren was old enough to date, only the right kinds of men. In her mother's mind, that didn't include native Alaskans, or any persons of color. Well, unless they happened to be rich. Then it was all right.

Lauren shook her head, remembering.

"What the—?" Seth grabbed a funny-looking connection coming from one of the inner components of the system. It wasn't your typical computer connector. "Son of bitch," he breathed.

"What is it? Can you fix it?"

He stared past her at the closed door, grinding his teeth, his mind working, as if he was remembering something.

"Tell me. What did you find?"

Men's shouts interrupted both their trains of thought. Seth snapped to attention. "N-nothing. It's just broken." He quickly screwed the plastic cover back onto the CPU, then took her arm. "Come on, we've gotta get out of here before—"

"Fotheringay!"

They both froze. The gravelly, disembodied voice belonged to Jack Salvio, and he didn't sound happy.

"He must be right outside," Lauren whispered.

Seth grabbed her, pulled her with him into a corner, and flipped off the overhead light.

"It's pitch—"

Seth's hand covered her mouth, as he pulled her tight against him. They stood motionless for what seemed an eternity, listening to Salvio swearing somewhere in the yard.

Lauren was aware, for the second time in as many days, of Seth's size and strength, the warmth radiating from his body as he held her. She found herself relaxing in his arms.

He brushed his thumb across her lips—her breath caught—then he slid his hand from her mouth. Awkwardly, she turned in his embrace.

"He's looking for me," she whispered up at him in the dark. "I'm supposed to be on that chopper."

They both heard the sound of the helicopter's rotor escalating to maximum rpm. The weather was coming in fast, and the pilot wasn't waiting.

"But you're not going, are you?" Seth's mouth was so close to hers she could feel his warm breath on her lips.

"No."

A flurry of emotions clouded her thinking as they listened to the eerie shrieks of the waxing wind and Salvio's shouts fading in the distance.

It was almost as if Salvio was deliberately trying to get rid of her. She'd read anger and something else, a strange sort of uneasiness in his eyes when he'd caught her looking at his computer monitor yesterday, and again when he'd found her and Seth examining rock samples from the mud vat on the rig.

Thank God she'd had the presence of mind to pocket that last remaining sample from the confiscated crate before Salvio realized what it was.

Something was going on at Caribou Island. Something fishy. And she was going to get to the bottom of it, if it was the last thing she did. They were a hundred feet from the target zone. A lousy hundred feet.

Her promotion hung in the balance. Tiger's senior execs would be counting on her to keep their interests in the forefront, even if their number-one company man, Jack Salvio, had temporarily lost his mind.

Crocker would be counting on her, too. To finish the job and get herself home in one piece. Though she found it difficult at the moment, in Seth Adams's warm embrace, to keep Crocker on her mind at all.

"It's probably your last chance," he said. "Once the chopper leaves, with the ice road ruined the only way in or out is by Rolligon."

She'd seen the enormous vehicle out back behind the drilling rig, with its tiny cab and low-pressure tires suited to rolling across the tundra without harming the fragile environment.

"I know. I don't care. It's just that—"

She gripped him tighter in the dark, remembering the horror of finding Paddy's body in the reserve pit, Salvio's odd behavior, Pinkie's warning, and now discovering the roustabout here in the sat-comm shack where he had no business being.

She closed her eyes and listened to the rapid-fire beating of her heart. "Seth, I don't know who to trust anymore."

He brushed a strand of hair from her face. His touch, his ragged breathing—even in the dark she knew what he intended, yet she made no move to stop him.

His lips trapped hers in the gentlest of kisses. Heat suffused her body from the inside out.

"Trust *me*," he said, and kissed her again.

Chapter 6

The job, his whole reason for being there, the fact that she was a suspect and he was a cop and that at any second someone might find them there together in the dark—all of it blazed away in a white heat as Seth felt the tip of Lauren's tongue, silky and hot, dance with his.

She was tentative at first. He felt her tremble in his arms, and both of them knew it wasn't from the cold. Unable to stop himself, he deepened the kiss. Lauren responded with a whimper that hinted more of need than seduction, clutching at his jacket as he backed her against the wall of telecommunications equipment lining the cramped space.

Somewhere at the edge of his awareness he heard the sound of the helicopter taking off, the thump of rotors barely audible over the shrieking wind. Salvio's shouts and men's footsteps died away.

And then there was only her. Soft lips and hot breath and hair that smelled of apples.

He knew he wasn't acting. Not anymore.

"Seth," she breathed. "Don't." She pushed against his chest, but not convincingly.

He kissed her again.

Their hands slid together, fingers twining. He couldn't think anymore, couldn't concentrate on anything except her and the moment. Then something hard scraped his palm, a reminder every bit as jarring as a cold shower or a slap in the face.

Her two-carat diamond engagement ring, emerald cut.

The world came abruptly into focus.

"We'd…better go," he said, breaking the kiss and backing away from her.

He couldn't see her face in the dark, but felt a sobering jolt of reality laced with confusion fill up the space between them.

"Okay," she said, her voice a whisper.

Ignoring the overhead light, he grabbed her hand and guided her in the dark toward the door. A moment later, the coast clear, they were outside. She wouldn't look at him. Maybe she thought not acknowledging what had just happened between them would make it go away.

He wished it was that simple.

Right now he had to focus on getting them both back to where they were supposed to be, without being seen. Then he'd allow himself to think about what the hell he'd just done in there, and what it meant.

While Lauren fumbled with her gloves, he pocketed the sheared padlock and clicked a new one into place across the door latch.

Her brows shot up when she saw it.

"There's a whole drawer full of these in the machine shop. I think they all have the same key."

She looked at him with an undisguised mixture of suspicion and disbelief.

"Come on. It's nearly four o'clock in the morning. Let's

get you back to your trailer. You'll have hell to pay when Salvio catches up with you.''

The weather was back—wind screaming like a banshee, dry snow blasting across the polished ice of the yard, pummeling them as he led Lauren quickly across the open space between the sat-comm shack and her trailer.

Lucky for them, everyone—Salvio included—had gone back inside. The second shift was in full swing now. Seth glanced briefly at the rig as they passed, noting the ninety-foot stands of drilling pipe swinging in the derrick in the wind. He didn't know how much longer they'd be able to keep drilling. They were just days away from target depth, but he hadn't seen weather this bad in…hell, maybe never.

Lauren let go of his hand long enough to fish her keys out of her jacket. A second later they were inside. Seth pulled the door shut and locked it, and for a moment neither of them moved. They stood there in the dark in their survival gear, breathing hard, their bodies drawing in heat from the trailer's propane furnace.

"If I turn the light on, Salvio will be out here in a second," she said.

"If he can see this far in the weather. And if he's still up."

Salvio didn't like to miss his beauty sleep.

"I hadn't thought of that." She moved across the linoleum to her workstation, then he heard her fumbling in a drawer. "Still, I don't want to risk it. Tomorrow is soon enough for me to face the firing squad."

He heard a striking sound and smelled burning graphite. An instant later the room was bathed in a soft glow. She'd lit a candle. And not one of those plain, white emergency candles. It was pink and heart-shaped, and looked as if it had been lit before. For some reason this surprised him. She hadn't seemed the candle type to him. In fact, he wasn't sure any more what type she was.

She shucked her jacket and boots, then turned to face him.

"About what happened…" She didn't look at him directly, and he could tell from the way she bit her lip she was searching for words. "Seth, I—"

"It was my fault." He moved toward her. Halfway there, she raised a hand to stop him. He nodded at her diamond ring, glittering in the candlelight. It reminded him of some of the jewels he'd seen in the Tiffany exhibit at the Smithsonian when he'd lived in D.C. "I forgot you were engaged." At last their gazes met. "That *is* an engagement ring, right?"

"Yes, it is."

He risked a smile. "Lucky guy."

"Look, Seth—"

A brash ringing startled them both. He spun toward her bedroom at the back of the trailer where the sound originated.

"Oh, it's my alarm clock. Just a sec." She dashed into the bedroom before he could stop her. For a split second he wondered if someone was back there waiting for her. Then he heard the slap of her hand on the ringer, and the room went quiet. He breathed.

"I'll be out in a minute," she called from the bedroom. He heard what he suspected was the bathroom door closing. Water started to run, and he used the time to shrug out of his jacket and get his head screwed back on straight.

Twelve short hours ago Seth would have bet the farm that Lauren was Paddy O'Connor's murderer and Tiger's corporate thief. Now he wasn't so sure. And his uncertainty had nothing to do with the fact that fifteen minutes ago he'd held her in arms and kissed her with a passion he hadn't felt in…well, he couldn't remember how long. Besides, that wasn't the point.

The point was that Pinkie the roustabout—one of Paddy's own men—had been in that telecommunications shack seconds before they had. He'd had a key, and from the casual way he'd clapped the padlock on the door and sauntered away, it was clear it wasn't the first time he'd been in there.

It was also clear that someone had sabotaged the equipment. But not permanently. One of the main CPU connectors had been altered. Disconnect it, and the whole system shut down. Connect it again, and everything worked.

The question was why?

Salvio's behavior was also cryptic. Lauren was right. It didn't make sense to fly the geologist off the site just days before the well reached target depth. What was Salvio's hurry? Seth didn't buy the obvious, that the company man wanted to go by the book, fly Paddy's body out ASAP, along with a Tiger rep to make the police report.

Jack Salvio, from what he could tell, didn't give a rip about Paddy O'Connor or the law. He did what he wanted, when he wanted, and few people crossed him.

The kicker in all this was that, now, Seth wouldn't get the chance to examine Paddy's body. To see if that bloody rock hammer he'd found in the Dumpster was the murder weapon. He hadn't seen traces of blood in Paddy's red hard hat. The funny thing was, the flannel liner had been missing. Nobody wore a hard hat without a liner in the Arctic in winter.

"Hi."

He glanced up to see Lauren's petite frame in the doorway of the bedroom. She'd combed her hair and washed her face. Her cheeks had a natural glow about them he found damned attractive. Her brown eyes were bright, alert, watching him.

It surprised him that she didn't wear any makeup. He recalled only a whisper of lipstick and mascara that first day she'd arrived fresh from Tiger's offices in Anchorage. No fancy clothes, no perfume, her auburn hair loose or swept into a casual ponytail skimming her shoulders.

She didn't look a thing like the pictures in her dossier.

She was beautiful standing there in the candlelight in that oversize, moth-eaten sweater and jeans.

"You'd better go now," she said, skirting the perimeter of the lab, careful, he noticed, to steer clear of him as she made her way back to her workstation.

"The second shift's working, the first shift's asleep. There's nobody around, nobody to see me here, if that's what you're worried about."

"I'm not worried about it. I'm just..." She absently twisted her engagement ring on her finger. That told him everything he needed to know. "I just think you should go."

He told himself it was all part of the job to question her. He wasn't ready to face the idea that maybe he was falling for her. It was an act. A cover. He needed to get close to her in order to collar her, or rule her out as a suspect. That was all. That's why he needed to know everything about her, and everything about her relationship with her fiancé Crocker Holt.

At least that's what he told himself as he ignored her request and slid onto a lab stool five feet from where she was standing, backed against her workstation.

"Tell me about him," he said, and nodded again at her ring.

"Crocker?"

"That's his name? Crocker what?"

"Holt. He's a—he's in the business. You might have heard of him."

She meant the oil business. And Seth already knew everything public there was to know about him, but she didn't know that. Besides, he wanted to know more. A lot more.

He shook his head. "Don't know him."

"No, I guess you wouldn't."

She didn't mean it in a disparaging way, though twelve hours ago he might have read it that way anyway. But now, at four in the morning after kissing her in the dark, recalling the feel of her hands on his chest, her hot mouth opening beneath his, he simply shrugged it off.

"Anyway…" She told him how her mother had introduced her to Crocker when he was still in banking. How he'd come to work at Tiger not long after he started dating Lauren.

"How convenient."

"What do you mean?" Those pretty brows of her arched.

He shrugged, and she went on, looking mostly at the floor or the steel countertops gleaming in the candlelight—anywhere but at him.

She told him all about Crocker Holt the financier turned oil company CFO, about Holt's accomplishments, his success in the business, his future plans. But at no point in her story did she say anything about how she felt about him, or about their upcoming marriage. He was her fiancé, for Christ's sake, yet her description of him was like something you'd read in a *Money* magazine article spotlighting the top fifty executives in the country. It was a glowing report, but with no underlying emotion to it.

For some reason that made Seth smile.

"What?"

"Nothing." He shook his head.

She went on, and after a minute absently opened a drawer and pulled out a cloth bag. She dumped the contents onto the counter beside her, and Seth did a double take.

"Walnuts?"

"Yes," she said. "I like them. I keep snacks out here so I don't have to go into camp every time I get hungry."

"Makes sense."

"Want some?"

"No." He shook his head. "Thanks."

She yanked open an industrial cupboard over the drawer, and her face twisted into a frown. "That's odd."

"What?" He slid off the stool and joined her at the counter.

"My hammer. It's missing."

"What hammer?" The second the words left his mouth, his gaze fixed on the blank spot on the Peg-Board inside the cabinet where a half-dozen common tools hung on metal hooks. Each tool had a carefully drawn red outline around it, so you'd know where to replace it after you'd used it.

"My rock hammer. I keep it right there."

He stared hard at the red outline on the Peg-Board. It was, of course, identical in shape to the bloody tool he now had stashed in his gear in his room at camp.

"I must have left it somewhere. Oh, well." She shrugged and shut the cabinet, then turned her gaze on his. "Seth, about what happened tonight…"

"Forget about it," he said, his mind racing. "You were scared, that's all. It was a dangerous situation."

"I don't want you to think that I—"

"I don't think anything. Like I said, forget it." She held his gaze a moment longer, and he knew she wouldn't forget it. Neither would he.

"Thanks for coming with me. For what you did."

"Any time." He shrugged, trying to project a casualness he didn't feel. His thoughts skimmed over the events of the past three days, recalling who was on shift when, if he'd seen anyone other than Lauren approach the trailer.

She could be playing him. Staging the little scene with the walnuts and missing hammer for his benefit. But if she was that smart, why would she have tossed a bloody murder weapon into the camp's Dumpster to begin with? That would be the first place the borough police would look once they saw the body and hightailed it out here.

"I'll see you, then," she said, and walked to the door.

He followed, sliding into his jacket on the way. "Lock your door after I leave."

She met his gaze and absently bit her bottom lip. He'd have given anything to know what she was thinking. "I always do."

The frigid air hit him like a Mack truck as he stepped out of the trailer. He sucked it in and felt the dry burn in his lungs. Grabbing the guideline leading back to camp, he turned into the wind.

Lauren managed a few hours' sleep despite the howling wind. With communications down, there was no way to transmit her morning geologist's report back to Tiger Petroleum. All the same, after Seth had left her trailer and before she'd collapsed, exhausted, onto her bed, she'd filled out the paperwork and tossed it onto the pile of unsent transmissions from yesterday and the day before.

Now, six hours later, restored by two cups of instant coffee she'd brewed on one of the lab's Bunsen burners, Lauren slid onto the stool in front of her workstation and opened her notebook.

A crate of rock samples collected from yesterday's drilling sat on the frozen ground just outside her trailer. She could see them out the window. Barely. Blowing snow skittered violently across the ice. The storm was getting worse.

She ought to haul the crate inside and take a look at those samples. This close to target depth, she should be paying attention. "Come on, Lauren, snap out of it."

The problem was, there was only one thing on her mind this morning, and it wasn't rock samples—strange or otherwise—or dead toolpushers, slightly off-balance company men, or anything to do with her work at Caribou Island.

"Seth."

She said his name out loud, feeling the sound of it on her tongue, remembering his hands on her body, the smell of him, the way he'd kissed her. The way she'd kissed back.

What am I doing?

She shot from the stool, ripped open the trailer door and went for the samples. Five minutes later, her workstation littered with open bags, rocks and mud, she flipped off her microscope and tapped her mechanical pencil against a blank page in her notebook.

Nothing unusual. Same as yesterday.

Absently, she traced the outline of her lips with a finger. *She* wasn't the same as yesterday, however. And that was the problem.

Thinking back on her two years with Crocker, she tried to remember a stolen kiss, a look, an afternoon of lovemaking—anything they'd shared that had been as explosive as the few minutes she'd spent in the dark with Seth Adams.

She couldn't.

Besides, there had been no afternoons of lovemaking, had there? And few stolen kisses. Crocker was always too busy. She'd been too busy, too. It simply wasn't a priority with them, and there was nothing wrong with that. She and Crocker had other things going for them besides passion.

So why was she having second thoughts?

How could one reckless moment in the arms of a stranger shake her confidence in a marriage that had been planned for months? Marriage to a man everyone said was perfect for her. She and Crocker were good together. A match.

A match with no spark.

A loud thump jarred Lauren from her thoughts. She slid off the lab stool, dropping her mechanical pencil onto the counter, and noticed her fingers had gone an angry red from gripping the metal so tightly.

The thumping sounded again. Someone was at the door.

"Yes?" She cracked it a few inches, feeling the cold air rush in, and peered out at the ski-masked face. Her heart flip-flopped. For a split second she was reminded of every bank robbery movie she'd ever seen.

"It's me, ma'am. Bulldog." The roustabout pushed his hood off and jerked up the ski mask so she could see his face.

"Oh. I didn't recognize you without your hard hat." His

name was painted across the front of it, she remembered from the incident on the catwalk yesterday.

"Yeah, I oughtta be wearin' it. Salvio'll skin me alive if he sees me without it." Everyone wore a hard hat on the job, even to walk across the yard. "Speakin' a-which, he wants to see you. Now."

She wondered when Jack would get around to sending out a posse for her. She'd put off going into camp this morning, and had gone to sleep earlier, half suspecting she'd be jolted awake by the man himself, and in no pretty mood.

She'd disobeyed his direct order. And while Tiger Petroleum wasn't the army, an operation like Caribou Island was run by rules every bit as stringent as those applied in the military. Still, she didn't regret her decision to stay on the island, and no way was she going to apologize.

"Tell him I'll be right in," she said, and waited for the roustabout to go. Bulldog didn't budge. "So you're my escort, huh?"

"Guess I am. Salvio says I'm to bring ya, personal like."

"Fine." She slipped into her survival jacket, snatched her hard hat off a hook on the wall and locked the trailer door behind her on the way out. "Let's go."

It took them forever to make the fifty yards to camp, sliding their gloved hands along the yellow guide rope. Lauren kept her head down and her feet moving. Bulldog glanced back at her every thirty seconds or so, to make sure she was still behind him.

A few minutes later, standing rigid in Salvio's office, she could see she'd been right. He wasn't in a pretty mood. Not by a long shot.

"You wanted to see me?"

His gaze burned right through her, and she could tell by the vein pulsing in his forehead and the way he ground his teeth that he was royally pissed off.

"Frickin' computers are down for good—" he flashed

steely eyes at the blank monitors on his desk ''—so we're drillin' blind now. The old-fashioned way.''

She nodded, familiar with the old manual method of calculating their depth.

''How far to target?''

''I'm not sure,'' she said, remembering the rock samples—nondescript shale and silt—she'd looked at a few minutes ago in the lab. ''Fifty feet. Eighty maybe. No way to tell at this point.''

''Well, whenever the hell we get there, I want you finished and outta here on the next chopper. Got it?''

She held his gaze and didn't flinch. If he was trying to intimidate her, he was doing a good job, but she'd be damned if she'd let him know that. ''Got it.''

He glanced out the undraped window into the yard where harsh sodium lights shimmered off blowing snow.

''Is that all?'' she said, stunned he didn't mention the events of last night and her overt insubordination. Jack Salvio lived for the smallest excuse to beat someone over the head.

''For now.'' He didn't look at her again, and inside she felt a small thrill of victory.

She turned on her heel and marched out of his office, relief surging through her like adrenaline. Delicious smells from the kitchen made her stomach growl. She checked her watch—11:00 a.m.—as she padded down the hallway in thick wool socks toward the sounds of men eating and talking and telling bawdy jokes.

The cafeteria tray was in her hand before she noticed him.

Seth sat alone at one of the big round tables, his black eyes fixed on hers. She gave a nod of acknowledgement, but no smile, and wondered if it was too late to return her tray to the stack and leave.

It was. Besides, it didn't matter what had happened last night between them. It was nothing. It meant nothing. She was getting married and that was that. At least that's what she told herself as she unconsciously loaded her plate with foods she didn't even like.

On purpose she chose an empty table across the room from where he sat, and set her key ring and tray on the Formica surface.

A couple of roughnecks at another table, packed with first-shift crewmen, made some disparaging comments about Seth, loud enough for everyone in the room to hear. Pinkie, the roustabout she'd met yesterday on the catwalk, snickered.

Seth didn't spare them a glance. It was almost as if he didn't hear them. He continued to stare at her as he ate, then out of the blue, Pinkie tossed a lewd comment in her direction. Lauren glanced up from her tray in time to see Seth's face harden to stone, his fork stall in midair.

She held her breath as he rose stiffly to his feet, a white-knuckled grip on the tray holding his half-eaten meal. Pinkie's face darkened, his small eyes riveted to Seth as he slowly walked to their table. The conversations and laughter of the other crewmen died as they turned their attention to Seth's imposing figure.

Lauren had learned a long time ago to simply ignore the kinds of comments men made about women when they got together in groups. Bars, construction sites, oil field camps—all were typical hotbeds of testosterone and bad judgment.

She tried to get Seth's attention, to make it clear he should just let the comment slide. It happened a lot out here, and she was used to it. It happened in town, too, where the ratio of men to women was nearly five to one.

Sometimes when she and Crocker went out in the evening, incidents like this would occur. Anchorage on a Saturday night was more like a frontier town than a twenty-first-century metropolis. Crocker would tell her to simply ignore the occasional catcall or lewd remark. He did the same, pretending the offender didn't exist. It was all very civilized.

But there was nothing civilized in the way Seth loomed over the table of crewmen, his eyes burning holes through a sober-looking Pinkie.

Lauren waited, her heart in her throat, a little thrill coiling inside her.

Seth didn't say a word. He simply stared at the roustabout.

Finally, when the tension was so thick she thought the whole table would spontaneously combust, Pinkie said, "Didn't mean nothin' by it." He shrugged. "Was just a joke."

"Yeah, a bad one," one of the crewmen said, and they all started laughing.

Everyone except Seth. He continued to stare at Pinkie, unmoving, silent. Pinkie wasn't laughing anymore.

Then, just as abruptly as it had started, the incident was over. Seth turned and walked to her table, set his tray down, and parked himself on one of the plastic chairs. She could see that his hands were shaking. His face was still hard, his eyes unreadable.

She was prepared to tell him that he needn't have bothered rushing to her defense like that—that it wasn't worth starting trouble over. That's what Crocker had said to her on such occasions. It wasn't worth the trouble. Perhaps what he'd really meant was that *she* wasn't worth it.

"Thank you," she said, surprising herself.

Seth's face softened, his black eyes warming to chestnut. "No problem."

They ate in silence. Well, he ate. She spent most of her time wondering what he was thinking, and pushing food around on her plate. Why on earth had she chosen broccoli? She hated broccoli.

"Not big on vegetables, huh?"

She put down her fork. "No. I never have been."

She only ate them because it was expected—both at home growing up after her father died, under the direction of the Fotheringay chef, and now at the endless parade of social functions she attended with Crocker and her mother.

"I'm more the meat-loaf-and-mashed-potatoes type," she said. "Simple stuff."

He made a funny sound in the back of his throat, and flashed his eyes at her engagement ring. "Yeah. Like the ring and the Porsche."

"How did you know about—"

He nodded at the distinctive logo medallion attached to the leather key ring resting on the table next to her tray.

"Oh, right." She shrugged. "It wasn't my choice. Someone bought it for me."

"Your fiancé." The way he said it irked her.

"That's right. My fiancé." She plucked her fork from the table and started stuffing broccoli florets into her mouth.

"I suppose you're going tell me you'd rather have an Explorer or Grand Cherokee, or something like that?"

She had, in fact, had an Explorer before she and Crocker started dating. One afternoon she'd come out of Tiger's offices to find it missing from the parking lot. A brand-new silver Porsche Boxter sat in its place, a big red bow tied over the hood. Crocker's idea of a surprise.

She put down her fork and stood. "I've got to go. So do you, by the look of things." She flashed her eyes at the other first-shift crewmen who were bussing their trays and starting to wander back down the hall toward the mudroom.

"Yeah," he said. "Shift starts at noon."

"Once the well's at target depth, I'll collect my samples and go."

He looked at her, his face hardening again. "Back home to the Porsche and the fiancé."

"That's right."

He smiled coldly. "Lucky you."

* * *

Late that night while the first shift was working and the second still asleep, Lauren defied Jack Salvio's direct orders and climbed the five flights of metal stairs to the drilling floor of the rig. She paused, her gloved hand on the steel door of the doghouse, and braced herself for what she knew would be an ugly encounter.

That morning when Salvio had summoned her to his office, she'd known better than to question him again about that crate of mysterious rock samples. But enough was enough. She needed to know where they'd come from, and what he'd done with them.

Her little escapade with Seth in the sat-comm shack and that incident in the kitchen had distracted her long enough from her responsibilities. It was time to get to work.

If Salvio thought he could just—

The door to the doghouse swung outward and Lauren lurched sideways, nearly tripping on the metal gridwork of the landing. Instinctively, she shot to the shadowed corner behind the door as it crashed wide, knocking her hard against a wall of greasy standpipes.

She steadied herself, twisting awkwardly in the tight space until she was turned around and could peek around the edge of the door. The sound of swearing carried over the constant roar of machinery, and a moment later the disembodied voices came into view.

Pinkie and Bulldog. They were carrying something heavy, a piece of equipment. It looked familiar, but she couldn't quite place it. Three years was a long time to be out of the field. Technologies changed, drilling equipment came and went. Still, there was something about it that bothered her.

Jack Salvio stepped out of the doghouse onto the landing, hands perched on his hips, shouting orders at the two roustabouts. Lauren didn't breathe. She'd come in search of him, but now she wasn't so sure she was ready for a confrontation.

He stopped Bulldog and Pinkie at the top of the stairs,

long enough to wrestle a dangling part back into place on the boxlike contraption weighing them down like pack mules.

She stared hard at the equipment. What was it? An odd notion came over her that, whatever it was, it didn't belong here. She pushed the door away from her body, leaning her head out to get a better look. Too late she realized her mistake.

Salvio turned on her. "What the hell are you doing here?"

Lauren's heart stopped beating. She felt her eyes widen of their own accord and every muscle freeze as Salvio ripped the door from her shielded body and slammed it shut, exposing her snooping.

"I—I was looking for you." Her gaze darted to the equipment as Pinkie and Bulldog humped it down the stairs and out of sight.

Salvio's steely eyes followed, then fixed on hers, his face cold as stone. "So you found me. Now what?"

Chapter 7

"I just wanted to ask you..."

What? What did she want to ask him?

Why two roustabouts were carting around strange equipment at midnight? Where that crate of mystery samples had gone? Why a state-of-the-art satellite communications system stopped working the second she arrived? Why their drilling computers were down, and their toolpusher was dead?

Salvio glared at her. "Out with it, Fotheringay. I ain't got all day."

Lauren had always considered herself a scientist first. She was logical, relied on facts, data, rarely on hunches or intuition. That's one of the reasons she'd done so well at Tiger, and was in line for the biggest promotion of her life.

But now, staring into Jack Salvio's cold eyes, all her left-brained training fled in the face of instinct. An overwhelming urge to shield her suspicions from him gripped her and wouldn't let go.

In the end, she gave him a shrug. "It's…nothing. I know you're busy. It can wait."

Salvio stared hard at her, as if he knew she was lying, and was trying to read her mind. "It's late," he said evenly. "And you shouldn't be up here. Go back to your trailer, Lauren."

He only called her Lauren when he meant business.

"I'm right behind you. I, uh, need some hand cleaner for my lab. There's some in the doghouse. I'll just get it and—"

Salvio didn't wait for her to finish the lie. He started down the stairs after Pinkie and Bulldog, and when he was out of sight Lauren breathed with relief.

She realized she was shaking. Why had she let Salvio get to her? She drew in a steadying breath and reached for the door. There was always coffee in the doghouse. It was always bad, but she didn't care. She needed something warm to hold on to, even if it was just a paper cup filled with tepid sludge brewed twelve hours earlier.

Pulling herself together, she stepped inside. A beat-up metal coffeepot sat on the counter next to the safety-glass window overlooking the rig's drilling floor. Drawn like a magnet, Lauren moved toward it.

Halfway there she froze.

Seth was out on the floor with the rest of the first shift crew, pulling pipe. He didn't see her. None of them did. For a long moment she just stood there in plain view, both wishing and fearing he'd look up.

If he saw her, would he experience that same, punchy, heart-in-the-throat thrill she did each time she ran into him? She realized she'd never felt that way with Crocker. Not even in the beginning, when they'd first started dating.

In the end, her nerve dissolved. Lauren retreated to the corner near the coffeepot, sloughed off a glove and grabbed a cup. Slouching, half-hidden by the metal pot, she watched Seth work.

He was good at what he did. He moved smoothly across

the drilling floor, working in concert with the others, his steady gaze alternating between the ninety-foot stands of pipe coming out of the hole, the crewman working the controls, and two other roughnecks she recognized as old Altex hands.

Insulated wind walls around the derrick and strategically placed heaters made the temperature on the drilling floor about eighty degrees warmer than it was outside. Like the others, Seth wore mud-spattered jeans, a thermal shirt that did nothing to hide the well-defined muscles working beneath it, hard hat and gloves. His dark hair was pushed haphazardly into a ponytail.

Lauren's gaze slid over his bronze, sweat-sheened skin, pausing at the vee in his shirt, before she allowed herself to fully appreciate the rest of his physique, and remember what he'd smelled like when he'd kissed her.

Hot and exotic and one-hundred-percent male.

Not the kind of man who showered three times a day, dousing himself in expensive cologne afterward. Not the kind of man whose muscles were hewn by machines in a gym, or whose idea of sports was a half hour of squash once a week at a private club or an afternoon of polo on a horse he owned but didn't care for.

Lauren tipped the cup, downing the bitter-tasting coffee like a shot of single malt. It shocked her to her senses— exactly the result she'd intended. Enough was enough. Salvio was right. She shouldn't be up here. She shouldn't be anywhere near Seth Adams. He was dangerous.

No. *She* was dangerous when she was around him.

She found herself wondering what would happen if she simply abandoned the painstakingly crafted plans in place for her marriage and her career. Plans her mother—and Crocker, too—had slaved over. Out of the blue, an odd thought struck her.

Maybe *she* was the slave.

Crushing the paper cup, she tossed it into the trash and

grabbed her gloves. Her biggest mistake of the day was looking up one more time.

Seth was staring straight at her. There it was again, that tingly feeling, as if her whole body had been asleep and was just now waking up.

He wiped the sweat and mud from his face with a gloved hand, not taking his eyes from her. Then he smiled. Not the dangerous, seductive smile he'd given her yesterday. Just a simple smile. Warm, just like she felt.

A second later she was out the door, struggling into her gloves, barreling down the metal staircase at the speed of light.

The weather raged on. Lauren had spent most of the day in her trailer, avoiding Seth. Salvio, too. Both of them made her jumpy, but for completely different reasons.

She'd been on Caribou Island four days now. Four days without any contact with the outside world. Four days that had all but turned her life upside down.

Paddy O'Connor's body would have reached Anchorage by now, along with whatever information Salvio had conveyed to the chopper pilot. Bill Walters, her boss, would be half-crazy wondering what had happened out here.

Crocker would be a wreck, too—worried sick about her. She'd never gone this long without talking to him before. He always made sure that, wherever each of them happened to be in the world, he could always reach her. He always checked in on her when they were apart. Always. At least once a day, sometimes more.

She'd thought a lot about Crocker these past couple of days, but they weren't the kinds of thoughts a soon-to-be bride should be having about her fiancé. Not that she wasn't having those kinds of thoughts. She was. Only she was having them about someone else.

Grabbing her jacket off the hook on the wall, she prepared to brave the storm and make the trek across the yard to camp. It was safe now, just after 7:00 p.m. Seth worked the first shift, noon to midnight. Their dinner break was over, and he'd be up on the rig now, working until the shift was over.

Lauren would be back in her trailer long before then. But if she had to sit out here one more hour, she'd go stir-crazy. Her work for the day was finished, reports she had no way of sending, complete. She needed a mental break from all that had happened since she'd arrived, some mindless entertainment to relax her.

Twenty minutes later, her jacket and boots stowed in the camp's mudroom, Lauren sank into the worn-out seat cushion of a dilapidated sofa in the camp's TV room, cradling a bowl of buttered popcorn in her lap.

On her way there, she'd noticed Salvio's office light was out, which meant he was either up on the rig or asleep. Thank God she didn't have to deal with him tonight.

With no satellite, there was no TV, but the camp did have a collection of videos. Most of the second-shift crew were still asleep, but a few early risers, guys she recognized but didn't really know, sat—with cups of what for them was morning coffee—across the room from her, facing the TV. Lauren nodded politely when one of them looked her way.

"This okay with you," he said, holding out the video *Death Wish II*.

"Fine," she said, relieved it wasn't an X-rated title. Oil field camps were notorious for their collections of bad porn films. Charles Bronson she could take.

A minute later the movie started, and one of the men flipped off the overhead lights. The room was warm and dark except for the television screen, and Lauren began to relax.

After nine dead bodies and God knows how many rounds of ammunition, she caught herself dozing. Good, she thought. She needed the rest. She'd tossed and turned all night last night, unable to get her mind off—

The door to the hallway opened and light spilled in. Lauren squinted at the tall figure silhouetted in the door frame. There was no mistaking who it was. She'd know those broad shoulders anywhere.

Seth.

He closed the door behind him, and Lauren held her breath as he moved slowly in the dark toward the sofa, easing down right beside her.

"Hi," he said.

She was so stunned that for a moment she couldn't speak.

"Are you sharing that, or keeping it all to yourself?" He nodded at her popcorn, which was cold now.

"What are you doing here?" She risked a longer look at him, and caught the light from the television dancing in his eyes.

"Looking for you."

She had that fluttery feeling again, and knew she had to put a stop to it before she did something stupid... A vision of them making love on the narrow bed in her trailer flashed across her mind. Heat rushed to her face, and she thanked God the room was dark so he couldn't see it.

"You're supposed to be on shift." The words came out a hiss under her breath.

"Not anymore. Salvio changed the roster. I'm on nights now—well, midnight to noon. It's *all* night this time of year."

One of the men sitting on the other sofa glanced in their direction, then whispered something to an older crewman slouched next to him. He looked over, too, then they both chuckled.

"Why did you sit here? Next to me, I mean?"

"I told you." He leaned down to whisper in her ear, and her heartbeat quickened when she felt his warm breath on her skin. "I wanted to see you."

"No. You can't see me. I mean we—" The crewmen were still looking at them, grinning now. The sounds of gunfire and a car chase screamed from the television, but her mind wasn't on the movie anymore. "We can't be seen together."

"Why not?" Seth turned toward her on the sofa.

"We just...can't. It wouldn't—it doesn't look right." She risked another look at him and in the light from the television screen she could tell that his eyes had cooled and that his teeth ground together behind his lips. Lips she'd kissed. Teeth, smooth as glass, that she'd felt with the tip of her tongue.

"Why not? Because I'm a roughneck and you're a—" He started to say something that she didn't think was *geologist,* then stopped himself.

Lauren bristled. Women professionals in the field never fraternized with the crew. It just wasn't done. If he was any kind of roughneck, he'd know that.

Still, she said, "No. That's not why."

"Because I'm half-Inuit, then, and these good old boys—" he nodded toward the sofa where they were sitting, engrossed again in the movie "—wouldn't take kindly to me messing with a white woman. Is that it?"

"No. That's not it."

"Maybe it's you, then. Maybe you don't think I'm good enough for you."

She grabbed his hand in the dark, and heard his breath catch in his throat. The hard muscles of his thigh tensed against hers.

"No. I just...can't." She met his gaze, and he waited for her to say more. His hand was so warm. His fingers closed around hers and she felt her heart beat faster. "I just don't want anyone to think we're involved."

He looked at her for a long moment, and what she read in his eyes scared her. "Are we? Involved?"

"I...don't know," she heard herself breathe.

Before he could react, she shoved the popcorn bowl into his hands and bolted.

By the time she heard his footfalls behind her in the mudroom, she was suited up and out the door of the camp. The wind caught her and she almost tripped down the metal stairs into the yard. It was bitter cold, and shards of dry snow and ice cut her face as she pulled herself back along the guideline toward her trailer.

Seth was right behind her.

Why wouldn't he leave her alone? She didn't ask for his attention. She didn't want it. Couldn't want it.

"Lauren!"

She ignored him and kept moving. Her hood blew off, but she didn't stop. By the time she reached the trailer, her face felt like a block of ice.

She fumbled with the keys, dropped a glove and didn't bother picking it up. Slamming the door behind her, she pushed in the button of the lock just as she heard Seth's fist beat against the door.

"Come on, Lauren. We need to talk."

Her heart pounded, and her breathing was short and choppy from fighting the elements as she'd practically jogged the fifty yards across the yard. Not easy to do in a blizzard in survival gear and heavy boots. She kicked them off and dropped her jacket where she stood.

And waited.

A few seconds later the pounding stopped. Still, she didn't move. A long minute after that, the trailer door flew open and, in a maelstrom of blowing snow, Seth stepped into the lab.

Chapter 8

This was either going to be the most brilliant move of his soon-to-be-resurrected FBI career, or the biggest mistake of his life.

Blindly, Seth closed the door behind him and punched the lock. Lauren stood rigid, her hands fisted at her sides, her brown eyes wide and riveted to his. He shucked his jacket and gloves, tossed his hard hat aside, and was ready for her.

Soft light spilled from the bedroom into the darkened lab where they stood. With purpose he moved toward her. Halfway there she read his intent and gave a little gasp. He didn't let it deter him.

A second later his hands closed over her narrow shoulders and he pulled her to him, not roughly, but with enough determination to let her know what was coming next. Her head angled back in response, and everything he read in her eyes—excitement, fear, desire—spurred him on.

He kissed her, and she let him.

Not only that, she was kissing him back. Her mouth

opened under his, and their tongues mated in a wild frenzy. He pulled her closer, feeling her breasts hot against his chest, her hips rolling into him as his hands slid down her back to cup her behind.

She moaned into his mouth—a needy little sound that drove him over the edge. Lifting her off her feet, he backed her to the steel countertop as her legs wrapped around his hips.

He was as hard as a teenage boy scoping his first girlie magazine, and had been from the second her thigh had connected with his on the sofa back at camp. He deepened their kiss and thrust against her, leaving no doubt in her mind as to what he was feeling.

What *was* he feeling?

Stirred up somewhere between lust and excitement there should have been victory. He'd conquered her at last. He'd won. After they had sex, she'd tell him everything he wanted to know about her. He'd make sure of it. And then he'd know one way or another if she was the one he was after.

The only problem was, he didn't feel anything close to victory. In fact, he knew in his gut that he was the one who was conquered, not her.

"Seth," she breathed, and pushed gently against his chest, her legs untwining themselves from his body.

He kept on kissing her, touching her, working to kill what he was feeling, trying to focus on the physical—but she was insistent. "Seth, stop."

Stop.

The four-letter word every man dreads hearing.

He obeyed, not just because she'd asked him, but because somewhere inside he knew he had to—for himself. He'd gotten carried away again, had lost his head for the second time in as many days. When he'd followed her to her trailer, he told himself he was doing this for the job, for his own gain, to cement her trust in him, to get her to talk.

Christ.

As for universal lies, this one was right up there with "the check is in the mail."

He was doing this because he wanted her. And for more than just sex. He liked her. He admired her courage and tenacity, even as he felt an almost visceral need to protect her when the slightest hint of fear or vulnerability shone in her eyes.

He was falling for her. Hard.

Harder than he'd ever fallen for anyone, even his ex. The signs had been there from the beginning, from the second he saw her standing in the hallway four days ago in that ridiculous sweater, her nose tipped in the air, her pretty mouth gaping in shock as his gaze met hers.

"We don't even know each other." She pushed him away from the counter far enough so she could snap her legs together.

She tried to hop down, but he stopped her, his hands on her shoulders, his eyes willing hers to look up. She did.

"I'd like to get to know you, Lauren."

"I don't think that's a very good idea."

He had to agree with her, but he didn't. Standing aside, he let her slide from the steel countertop, and watched as she padded across the linoleum floor of the lab and switched on the lamp at her workstation.

"Then..." He followed her, picking up his jacket and hers on the way, tossing them onto the hooks in the corner by the door. "We'll just talk business. How about that?"

"Business?" She turned on him and her soft brow wrinkled in a frown. "Why?"

"Because I don't want to leave yet."

Finally—the truth.

He didn't smile, and neither did she, but there it was. He waited, chastising himself for getting emotionally involved with her, at the same time praying she wasn't going to throw him out.

"I don't want you to leave yet, either."

He breathed.

"Good." He did smile then, moving slowly to one of the stools near to where she was standing, and eased himself onto it.

Instead of dropping into her desk chair or perching on another of the lab stools, she pulled herself onto the countertop facing him. He knew from her cool expression that it wasn't an invitation to repeat their groping of a minute ago on the other side of the lab. She was so much smaller than he was, it was her way of sitting above him, keeping her distance, maintaining control.

And that was fine with him, because right now he was very much out of control. Not physically, but mentally. He was out of his frickin' mind, as Salvio would say. He sucked in a breath, waited for his heartbeat to slow, then attempted to get his act together and salvage what was left of the opportunity.

You're a cop, Adams. Do your job.

She made it easy for him. "What do you want to talk about?"

He shrugged. "How about Tiger? Your job. What you're doing out here and where you're going next."

"That's a lot."

He checked his watch. 8:00 p.m. "I've got time." He smiled, and she smiled back.

They spent the next hour talking about Tiger and the oil business, about her boss, Bill Walters, Tiger's CEO and the other VPs. Well, all of them except one. She didn't mention Crocker Holt's name once, and Seth didn't, either.

"So this promotion means a lot to you, then?" he said, thinking about everything she'd told him, piecing together a new angle on the case. A new angle on her.

"It means everything." Her voice was strangely flat, her face blank, not animated like it had been when she'd told him why she'd become a geologist in the first place—about

her father and their trips together into the field when she
was a kid.

"You're not very convincing."

She didn't say anything for a moment. And then in a near
whisper, as if she was talking to herself, she said, "No, I'm
not, am I?"

"What about Walters? Seems to me he'd be hell-bent on
keeping you down, making sure he wasn't passed over."

"No, Bill's not like that. I think he's perfectly happy
being in charge of Tiger's Alaskan prospects. If he was exploration VP he'd have to uproot his family and move to
San Francisco, Tiger's headquarters. Bill's an Alaskan
through and through. I don't think he'd do it."

"What about you? You're an Alaskan. Are you so anxious to leave?"

He studied her face as she thought about it while absently
twisting the rock on her finger. She was considering more
than the job, he could tell.

"No, I'm not anxious to leave. In fact, I love it here.
Well—" she glanced at her surroundings "—not *here*, exactly, but you know what I mean. Alaska."

He knew exactly what she meant. He'd left the state when
the Bureau recruited him, and was gone for five years. He'd
hated D.C., and all the other big cities he'd worked cases
in. Urban life just wasn't for him. Neither were urban
women, he reminded himself.

"Yeah, I know what you mean."

She smiled at him, and he had to fight the urge to walk
over there and kiss her. Hold her. Not like he had an hour
ago, with the promise of hot sex oozing from every pore,
but gently, with warmth and an understanding of the things
he was beginning to suspect she loved.

In the back of his mind, in a place he didn't like to visit
very often, he wondered if a woman like her could love
someone like him. A regular guy. A native. A cop.

All at once he felt guilty. Here she was spilling her guts

to him with no idea who he really was, or why he was here with her now.

"What about you?" she said.

"Me?"

"Yes." She smiled again, and slipped from the counter, landing softly in stocking feet on the floor. "Altex. Your job. I can see you're good at it. Do you like it?"

He felt uncomfortable, now, lying to her—which was ridiculous. On an undercover job like this, it came with the territory. He had to lie if he was going to crack this case. And he was no closer to it than he had been ten days ago when he first arrived on the island.

"It's okay," he said with deliberate vagueness, and shrugged.

"Where do you live? I mean, when you're not working?"

"Kachelik. It's a village about—"

Her face lit up. "I've been there! Years ago with my dad. I remember it. It's small and…"

"Quaint?"

"No. That's not how I remember it at all. I was going to say…well…*warm,* but that sounds so stupid. I don't mean the weather. I mean—"

"I know what you mean. Yeah, it *is* warm. It's the people. They're open, friendly. Just the opposite of New Yorkers or District types."

"District types?" Her brows arched. "You've been to D.C.? New York, too?"

Once, he might have been irritated by her surprise that a guy like him—a half-native nobody from Kachelik—had been anywhere. But she hadn't meant it like that. Besides, the only one he was irritated at right now was himself.

He couldn't believe he'd made a slip like that. It wasn't like him to screw up. Bledsoe—and his father, too—would have argued that point, but Seth knew he was good at what he did. He was just too relaxed around her. That was the problem.

They'd been chatting together for over an hour now, and he felt himself connecting with her in a way that he never had with his ex, or with any woman, for that matter.

Keep your cool, Adams. Remember why you're out here.

"I've been a lot of places," he said with a noncommittal tone that bordered on cool. "Tell me more about Holt."

She went rigid, her gaze flying to his. "I thought we were going to talk strictly business?"

"Holt's a Tiger VP, right? That's business."

Her tight expression and body language told him he'd overstepped the bounds of their conversation. He expected at any second she was going to ask him to leave. But she didn't. To his surprise, she collected herself and shot him a matter-of-fact look. "All right. What do you want to know?"

"He's a pretty big fish, isn't he? In the oil business, I mean."

"Yes, he is. In banking, too. Or he was."

"VP of finance for Tiger Petroleum. A job like that's got to pay a lot."

She nodded.

"About ten times more than say a…roughneck, or a plumber, or even a borough cop."

"So?"

He shot her a bitter smile, knowing he was straying dangerously close to territory he shouldn't be anywhere near. "Guess a guy like that's pretty appealing to most women."

She looked at him for what seemed a long time before answering. "To a lot of women, yes. But—"

"Forget it," he said, and abruptly stood.

"Money isn't everything, you know." She moved toward him, slowly, gauging his reaction. "It doesn't really mean a lot to me."

"No?" As she inched closer, his mouth went dry.

"No. I mean…" She stopped and grabbed hold of the frayed ends of the baggy brown cardigan he'd seen her in from the second she'd arrived on the island. "Well...can't you tell?"

He laughed. "Yeah. I was meaning to ask you about that."

"It was my father's field sweater. The week after he was killed, my mother cleaned out his closets. She didn't even send his clothes to charity, she just dumped them in the trash. I rescued this." She smoothed the well-worn wool over her hips. "It was his favorite."

"It's beginning to be my favorite, too."

She blushed, and he had to physically stop himself from taking her in his arms again. He made himself check his watch and move his feet, until he was reaching distance to his jacket and the door.

"Shift starts soon. Gotta go."

She nodded, wrapping her arms around herself as if she was suddenly cold.

He slipped on his jacket and zipped it to the chin. His hand was on the doorknob when he remembered. "You came up to the floor last night. Why?"

"I was..." She paused, flustered. "Looking for Salvio."

"Oh." What had he expected her to say? That she was looking for him?

He was halfway out the door when she called his name. He turned, blowing snow flurrying around him.

"The door was locked and you came right in." She nodded to the doorknob and his gloved hand still around it. "How'd you get a key? There are only two. I have one. Salvio has the other."

He smiled. "I don't have a key."

"Then how?"

"I picked the lock." He stepped into the yard and cocked a brow in her direction.

"You can do that?"

"Yeah. I can do a lot of things. You'd be surprised."

She gave him a smile, her eyes dancing like snowflakes

in an unexpected storm. Nothing like the razor-sharp ice shards that were pummeling him now. But it didn't matter. He couldn't even feel them—just the warmth of her smile and the memory of her kiss.

"See you tomorrow, then?"

Why was he doing this? Innocent as a spring lamb or guilty as the last perp he'd put behind bars—it didn't matter which she was. He couldn't get involved with her. She was wrong for him. All wrong. And he was wrong for her.

"Tomorrow," she said, and pulled the door closed, clicking the lock into place as he stood there in the wind and silently swore.

That night Lauren slept better than she had in days. The next morning, after dropping a copy of her daily geologist's report in the overflowing in-box on Salvio's desk, she went to the kitchen in search of something to eat.

She'd forced herself to stay in her trailer during the hour she knew Seth and the rest of the crew on the midnight to noon shift would be in camp for breakfast.

"Steak and eggs?" the cook called out from behind the row of steam trays when she walked in.

"How about just one egg and some toast?" she said, and grabbed a tray. "I'll skip the steak."

"You got it."

She smiled at him, and poured herself some coffee. The kitchen was deserted except for the cook, which was why she'd planned her meal at this particular time.

The military-style clock on the wall read oh-nine-hundred. Salvio's office had been empty a minute ago when she'd dropped off her report. His hard hat was gone, too. That meant he was out on the rig somewhere, probably supervising the drilling.

They were close to target—less than fifty feet, now, judging by the rock samples she'd looked at that had been delivered to her lab earlier that day. The drilling was slow going, but given the weather—which still showed no signs of breaking—they had all the time in the world.

"Here ya go." The cook handed her a plate stacked with enough eggs, toast and hash browns to feed a family of four.

"Thanks," she said, and moved to a table.

The food was good, and she ate more than she intended, but afterward she felt better. Strong. Ready to do what she knew needed to be done.

There were two things, really. The first was the most important, and had to do with Seth. Their discussion would have to wait, of course, until he got off shift at noon. Besides, she wasn't quite sure how she was going to handle it.

She supposed she would simply tell him that they couldn't get involved. That she was engaged and had a whole life planned around Crocker and her work at Tiger. That what had happened between them shouldn't have happened. That the only reason it had, was the situation. Paddy's murder, the storm, Salvio's behavior, all of it.

She was alone here, isolated. What did he expect? It was totally natural for her to turn to someone strong and compassionate like him for comfort. And, well…she supposed she couldn't deny the animal attraction between them. But that's all it was. Attraction. Lust.

Healthy and to be expected, even, under the circumstances. She was merely sowing some last-minute wild oats before committing herself to the man she would spend the rest of her life with.

As for Seth…she didn't think for a minute his desire for her was anything more than the natural reaction of a man living in close quarters with eighty other men who didn't like him, and where she was the only woman for a hundred miles.

They were both alone on the island. Outsiders, each in their own way. That's all it was between her and Seth. That's all it could be.

If Crocker was here with her, she'd have never gotten involved with Seth, period. Crocker would have been the one she'd have turned to for comfort and for help. Though, she had to admit, Crocker wasn't very good at what he liked to call "the warm and fuzzy stuff." Lauren accepted that. Besides, she was used to standing on her own two feet.

Crocker had other attributes. He was a savvy businessman, a decision maker, and he knew how to handle tense situations. Like the one she found herself in now with Jack Salvio.

Which reminded her of the other issue she needed to deal with today. The cloak-and-dagger stuff going on with Salvio and those samples, not to mention that weird equipment she'd seen Pinkie and Bulldog moving off the rig two nights ago.

It was time to get her butt in gear and find out what was going on. Tiger wasn't paying her to sit around and moon about her personal life. They weren't paying her to question the actions of their best company man, either, but she had a feeling Bill Walters would back her up in this.

She downed the rest of her coffee, bussed her tray, and thanked the cook on her way out the door. Five minutes later she was suited up. Survival jacket, insulated boots, hard hat, gloves. Standard equipment for a walk in temperatures approaching fifty below zero.

Her destination was the warehouse at the edge of camp, not far from the chopper pad. If that crate of samples Salvio had confiscated was still here on the island, Lauren bet that's where it would be. Staged with other sample crates, used drill bits, and pallets of equipment waiting to be trucked back to Deadhorse when the weather cleared.

There was no guideline set up between the warehouse and the camp, and it took her ten minutes of fighting the wind to get there. The big roll-up door was closed, as expected, the camp's forklift idling outside.

She tried the small entrance door beside it. Locked. After

making her way around to the back, she pulled open the rear emergency exit and stepped inside.

It took her a moment to catch her breath, which frosted the air only a bit, since the warehouse was heated to a warm thirty-five degrees. Shirtsleeves weather in the Arctic. Some of the overhead lights were out, casting shadows over the haphazard rows of stacked sample crates, empty pallets and mounds of equipment packing the good-size metal building.

The aisles should have been wide enough to accommodate the forklift, but the storm had delayed their regular trucking schedule, and the warehouse was packed. Pallets rose in teetering stacks twelve feet high all around her. Sample crates were packed three deep in disorganized rows. It was downright claustrophobic.

Lauren retrieved a penlight from her pocket, then snaked her way through the labyrinth of crates, double-checking the name of the well, the date and the depth measurement scrawled on each label.

All of them were the same. Caribou Island 1. Depths ranging from five thousand to nine thousand feet. Nothing unusual. The mysterious sample crate she'd found in front of her trailer hadn't had a label, which *was* unusual. Roustabouts had gotten fired over less.

She heard voices as she made her way down the cramped aisle. No surprise there. The warehouse was a mess. It would take a dozen guys a week to get it sorted out. The voices grew louder, but not because she was moving closer. She'd stopped to listen.

They were arguing. No. Someone was chewing someone else out. And it wasn't too hard to figure out who the chewer was. Only one man on the island had a temperament that nasty.

Lauren switched off her penlight and inched around the corner into the next aisle. She was right. Jack Salvio stood beside a pallet of sample crates, his back to her, hammering a young roustabout she'd seen but didn't know, up one side and down the other. Poor kid. He looked all of about twenty. Jack was really tearing into him.

She noticed a few of the sample crates were open. Their wooden lids had been pried off and tossed into a pile on the floor, bent nails sticking into the air. Jack had the crowbar in his hand, gripping it as if he was trying to squeeze the life out of it.

He was yelling something about the samples. Lauren couldn't help herself. She inched closer, watching the Adam's apple in the kid's thin, white neck move up and down as he mutely weathered Salvio's abuse.

"I—I didn't know they were special," he sputtered. "There was no label, so I—"

Jack dropped the crowbar and, to Lauren's shock, grabbed the kid by the shirt collar. "What did you do with them?"

Lauren stopped breathing. Salvio wouldn't really hurt him, would he?

"I—I did what we're supposed to do. I opened 'em up. Looked at 'em. They were weird. Didn't look like all the other ones." He nodded at the open crates, eyes wide.

"Then what?" Salvio twisted the kid's collar, and Lauren watched in horror as his face turned red.

"I went to find—"

"Who?"

"That—that geologist. Like we're supposed to if something like this happens."

"Damn!" Salvio turned him loose.

"But—but I didn't find her, and when I asked Pinkie he said not to bother her. That the samples were mistakes. That they didn't need no label, and that I—I shouldn't put 'em in with the rest. He—he was gonna take care of 'em later, he said."

Salvio put a leathery hand to his face and exhaled in what Lauren could plainly see was relief. The roustabout's face relaxed, his normal color returning.

"So, where are they then?"

Salvio turned at the sound of her voice, as she stepped from the shadows. His face turned to stone before her eyes. She refused to let it faze her.

"The samples?" the kid croaked.

Salvio's face went beet red. Lauren breathed, willing herself to remain calm and cool as she watched the vein in his neck pulse.

"Yes," she said. "The unmarked samples. What did you do with them?"

"Lauren, get...your...ass...back...to...camp." Salvio's voice shook like she'd never heard it. He moved toward her, but she forced herself to hold her ground.

The roustabout moved with him. "I tossed 'em."

Salvio froze, his eyes nearly bulging out of his head. "What?" He whirled on the kid. "Where?"

The kid took two steps back. "Pinkie said they were mistakes. So I...th-thought I was doing him a favor."

"You didn't want to get anyone into trouble," Lauren said, trying to defuse the situation. "I can understand that."

He nodded vigorously. "Th-that's right. Pinkie said—"

"Where? Where did you toss 'em?" Salvio had forgotten about her, now, and focused all his attention on the terrified young roustabout.

"I—in the reserve pit."

Lauren closed her eyes and counted to ten. Salvio swore, every word in the book.

"When?" she said.

"Y-yesterday. No, the day before."

The unmarked samples were as good as gone. The reserve pit held over five-thousand gallons of overflow muck from the well, most of which would have already circulated through a recycling system that crushed any rocks or debris in preparation for trucking the mud out when they finished the job.

"Get outta my sight," Salvio said to the kid.

The roustabout didn't waste time. He was gone in a flash. Lauren jumped as the heavy metal door slammed shut behind him.

Now it was just the two of them.

Alone.

"As for you—" Salvio whirled on her, and the look in his eyes made her heart stop.

Lauren was usually assertive, and could hold her own in most situations. Well, situations that didn't involve her mother or Crocker, both of whom were experts at getting her to bow to their wishes. But this was different. Salvio was more than angry. He was enraged, unstable. Dangerous. She'd never seen him like this. She'd never seen anyone like this.

Instinctively, she backed up.

"Like I said—" Jack moved with her, and the hairs on the back of her neck prickled "—get your ass back to camp, and don't poke your nose into things that aren't your business."

"Uh…okay. Sure. I'm…out of here." Her feet were like weights, her boots glued to the floor.

But the ten minutes it had taken her to negotiate the distance out to the warehouse was quartered on her trip back. Speed records had been set with longer times.

Chapter 9

Just after midnight the well reached target depth.

Lauren worked straight through until noon the next day, analyzing samples. All through the target section the rock she saw was the same. Fractured limestone, littered with invertebrate fossils—exactly as expected. What she'd not expected was that she'd be writing these words on her final geologist's report for the Caribou Island well...

Hydrocarbons: none.

The well was a dry hole. Not even a hint of oil. Lauren tossed her mechanical pencil onto the counter and rubbed her tired eyes. For the first time since she'd arrived on the island, she was glad communications were down. The worst part of her job was delivering bad news.

Bill Walters, Tiger's VPs, their CEO...all of them would be disappointed. But it came with the territory. This was the business they were in. That's why it was called oil *exploration.* If it was a sure thing, everyone would be doing it. The odds of discovering a new, untapped oil field in the

Arctic were about a hundred to one. Good odds, really, in the scheme of things.

Lauren flipped off her microscope and worked to shake off her own disappointment. At least they had the samples, the data. Her team would be able to finish their geologic maps of the area, giving Tiger an edge when bidding on future land leases on which to continue their search for oil.

It was something. Not the best outcome, maybe, but one she and every other oil company geologist in the world was used to. That was the job.

Deal with it, and move on. That's what Crocker would say. He wouldn't waste a second brooding. An hour after Lauren's report hit the office, Crocker would have already calculated how much of the loss Tiger could write off in this year's taxes.

Money. That's what it was all about. Not the geology or Alaska or any of the reasons she, herself, was drawn to the Arctic. It was all about the money.

"Deal with it, Lauren. Move on."

She smiled bitterly, bagged the last of the samples from Caribou Island 1, tossed them into the open crate on the floor, and grabbed her hard hat on her way out the door.

"That's it then," Salvio said, when she dropped her report into his in-box fifteen minutes later. "Dry hole."

"As a bone." Lauren wanted to collapse on the Naugahyde sofa in Salvio's office—something she would have done under normal circumstances so they could commiserate about the outcome of the well. But she was convinced, especially after that scene in the warehouse yesterday, that the circumstances were *not* normal, and so she forced herself to stand.

"Plug and abandon," Salvio said matter-of-factly as he scribbled notes on his own report.

She watched him, remembering his warning of the day before—and her fear, which had been so palpable she could almost smell it, even now.

Seth had come to her trailer last night before his shift began, but Lauren switched the lights off and didn't answer when he knocked. She'd known it was him because she peeked out the window of the lab and saw him standing there in the wind and blowing snow.

She'd feared he would pick the lock again, and thanked God when he didn't and had headed back to camp. The incident with Salvio had been so unnerving, she knew if Seth were to see her in the state she was in, his first instinct would have been to take her in his arms.

And that would have been the end of all her good intentions. She'd never have been able to tell him that it was over between them. That it had never started. That she was getting married, and that her career came—

"Hey."

The warm timbre of his voice snapped her back to the moment. She and Salvio looked up at the same time. Her stomach did that little jittery thing it always did when she saw him.

"Adams," Salvio said. "What's the word?"

"Hole's cleaned out. We're done."

They'd finished drilling, and were ready to begin the operation's shutdown, which would take a few more weeks to complete. Longer, if the weather didn't cooperate. But Lauren wasn't thinking about that, as she watched Seth hand Salvio a ream of paperwork edged with greasy fingerprints.

As Salvio studied it, Seth's gaze found hers.

She thought about the other night when he'd eased her onto the countertop in the lab, pressing his hard body between her spread legs. She couldn't help herself.

He was remembering, too. She read it in the way he drank her in, the way he absently wiped a streak of drilling mud from his cheek, letting his forefinger trace a slow path across his lower lip, just as her tongue had.

"Did you hear me?"

"Wh-what?" Lauren snapped to attention.

Salvio stared hard at her, at them both, with steely eyes. "Sorry to break up the little moment you were having with Nanook, here, but—"

"The name's Adams." Seth took a step toward him, and for a frightening second Lauren thought Salvio would come off the chair. She would never forget the wild look in his eyes yesterday in the warehouse as he gripped that crowbar.

"Whatever." Salvio dismissed Seth with a look and turned his attention back to her. "As soon as this frickin' weather clears—"

"I know. I'm on the next chopper out." She nodded at her final geologist's report positioned facedown in his inbox. "When the uplink's back online—"

"Yeah, yeah. It'll get sent." Salvio waved her away.

His flippant attitude annoyed her. Geologist's reports were confidential. Even if Caribou Island was a dry hole, the data was still important. Salvio treated it, and her, far too casually.

"So…that's that, then." Seth trapped her gaze, but the moment, as Salvio had called it, was lost.

She remembered why she was here, what Tiger expected of her, what Crocker would expect.

"That's that," she said, and pushed past him into the hall.

Seth stood in the doorway of Salvio's office and watched Lauren march stiffly down the hall toward the mudroom. One minute she'd looked at him with enough heat to melt a polar ice cap, and in the next her brown eyes had frosted to a subzero glare.

She wanted him, but she didn't want to want him. He knew the feeling. Boy, did he ever.

"Snap out of it," Salvio said.

Seth turned his attention back to the company man. Salvio's face was hard, his eyes cool steel. "Stay away from her."

"That an order?"

"Yeah."

Seth bit down on his tongue so he wouldn't say something stupid.

Salvio grabbed at the keys dangling from his belt, secured by one of those retractable chains, and opened the locked drawer of his desk.

Seth just stood there.

"Something you want? Or are you just trying to piss me off by wasting my time?" Salvio snatched Lauren's report from his in-box and scanned it, one hand resting in the open drawer.

Seth's gaze was drawn to the pile of papers strewn in a careless pile inside. Staring back at him were the company man's daily drilling reports, along with copies of Lauren's daily geologist reports.

On an exploration well like this one, daily reports were sent via a secured, encrypted fax line over the satellite uplink. E-mail was used, too, but mostly for routine communications, not to transmit status reports or data. It was too risky, too easy for hackers hired by competing oil companies to intercept.

Salvio flipped to the second page of Lauren's report and kept reading, while Seth's gaze slid casually over the stack of older reports in the drawer. He did a double take, then frowned. Each report had an extra slip of paper stapled to it.

They were fax confirmations!

Those reports had been transmitted. He moved an inch closer, tilting his head to read better. He saw yesterday's date on one, the previous day's date printed on another, and the day before that on—

Salvio slammed the drawer shut. Seth was caught off guard by the hard-edged meld of suspicion and fury simmering in Salvio's eyes.

"Lookin' for something?"

Seth shrugged. "Just wanted to let you know we were

finished up there.'' He nodded out the window toward the rig.

"So you said.'' Salvio locked the drawer, then let his key chain snap back into place on his belt.

Seth eyed the dozen or so keys attached to the chain, remembering what Lauren had said about the company man being the only other person on site who had access to her trailer. Salvio's gaze followed his, and his trademark scowl deepened.

Seth turned to leave, but Salvio called him back.

"Where you from, Adams?''

Seth's mind raced over everything he'd seen and heard in the last week, and what those fax transmissions implied, given the fact that the satellite uplink had been rigged to go from fully functioning to nonoperational with the flip of a switch.

He forced himself to slump casually against the door frame, and said, "Kachelik.''

"Village boy, eh?''

"Yeah. What of it?''

Salvio snorted. "You don't seem the type, is all.''

"What type is that?''

"You know.''

Yeah, he knew all right. Salvio was eyeing him like he was the Alaskan equivalent of what some of these old boys from the South called "white trash.''

Seth didn't say a word. In his mind he was piecing together the puzzle, getting a picture that looked more and more like Jack Salvio. Seth liked him, or one of his cronies, for O'Connor's murder. But Salvio couldn't be in this corporate piracy scheme alone. There had to be someone else pulling the strings.

One short week ago he'd been sure it was Lauren—if not the key player, then at least involved in some way. But now he was just as sure it wasn't her. He swore silently, cursing himself. Either Lauren was innocent, or he was letting his personal feelings for her corrupt his objectivity to the point he couldn't see straight.

What he really suspected was that both of those statements were true.

A lot was riding on this case, on fingering the perps before they even knew they were under investigation. All of them, right up the tree to the top. He couldn't blow it now. If he wanted his Bureau job back—and he was beginning to think he did—he needed this win.

"No," Salvio said, eyeing him with a measure of suspicion that made Seth wonder if he'd been made. "You don't seem the type at all."

Late that night, Lauren reached into the economy-size box of tampons in her bathroom and fished out the last surviving rock sample from the crate that had been destroyed.

She couldn't bring herself to look at it yesterday or the day before. She'd been afraid of what she'd find. Of what it meant, given all she'd seen and heard, given everything that had happened.

She was still afraid, but she had to know.

Caribou Island 1 was a dry hole. Shale and limestone, a few interesting fossils, nothing more. She'd taken only a quick glance at the strange sample that first day when she found the unlabeled crate in front of her trailer.

It was time to take more than a glance. It was time to find out the truth.

Selecting the largest chunk of rock from the plastic bag, Lauren wiped the gray drilling mud from it with absorbent cotton, then placed it on the stage of her microscope. It was a fine-grained sandstone, crumbly to the touch, a rich chestnut that reminded her of the color of Seth's eyes.

Absently, a smile edged her lips.

She studied the sample a long time, far longer than she

had done with any sample in recent memory. Finally, plucking the chunk of rock from the stage, she touched it to her nose and closed her eyes.

A deep breath later she was sure.

Chapter 10

He couldn't sleep.

Seth rolled onto his back in the narrow bunk in the room he shared with three other guys. The damp, twisted sheet rolled with him. He swore, ripped it away from his sweat-soaked body, and swiveled out of bed.

Two of his "roommates" were on shift. The other one snored loudly in the bunk across from his, oblivious to Seth's insomnia. It was hot as hell in the room.

He checked the luminous dial on his watch. Three o'clock. In the afternoon, he reminded himself. He'd only slept a couple of hours. Pulling the blackout drape away from the window, he blinked against the harsh yard lights reflecting off the blowing snow of the blizzard still raging outside.

He'd never seen a whiteout last this long. Six days. Bledsoe was probably fit to be tied. Seth hadn't been able to contact him since the day Lauren arrived on the island and the weather turned bad—and since one of Jack Salvio's cronies had made sure the sat-link was only operational when Salvio wanted to send a transmission or make a call.

That's exactly what was happening. Salvio was faxing in his morning reports, and Lauren's, too, as if nothing out of the ordinary was happening out here. Seth wondered how Salvio had fixed it so Lauren didn't have to make contact with any of her superiors by phone.

From what Lauren had told him about Bill Walters, Seth got the impression they were used to daily phone contact on an operation like this one. Maybe Walters was in on the scam with Salvio. It was possible.

Before his talk with Lauren the other night, Seth was leaning toward pegging Walters for the business end of this corporate piracy deal. As exploration manager for Tiger's Alaskan holdings, Walters was definitely in a position to make the kinds of contacts required to pull something like this off. The fact that Tiger's CEO was thinking about promoting Lauren over Walters, provided a motive. Revenge. Not to mention the money involved. But after he'd heard Lauren's take on the family man's character and goals, it didn't make sense that Walters was the ringleader.

Seth grabbed some clean clothes out of the duffel bag stowed under his bunk and dressed in the dark. On his way out to Lauren's trailer he asked himself for the hundredth time that week what the hell he was doing.

She's getting married, you idiot.

He was a fool to even want her. He'd learned enough about her to know she wasn't the kind of hard-edged woman he'd first made her out to be. And she was nothing at all like his ex. Their high-society backgrounds were similar, sure, but Lauren hadn't been raised that way from birth like Kitty had. It wasn't in her blood.

Listening to her talk about Alaska, hearing the nostalgia in her voice when she'd told him about the time she spent with her father in the Arctic growing up, made him think the kind of life she'd been living—the diamond ring, the

Porsche, Holt's money and her own career plans—maybe it wasn't the life she really wanted.

You're delusional, Adams.

What kind of woman wouldn't want it?

He shook his head and wished Danny, one of his officers from the borough police department, was here to knock some sense into him. He wondered, idly, how things were going back at the village. Probably fine, aside from the minor problems this kind of weather brought with it. A roof blown off an old building, a sled dog missing in the storm. Stuff like that. Not much happened in Kachelik. It was quiet.

Small town and small time. There were no Porsches and only one jewelry store—and they didn't even sell diamonds. For something like that you had to go to Anchorage. Better yet, San Francisco. Lauren had mentioned it, in fact.

He knew from the case file that Crocker Holt kept a condo there—a million-dollar crib with a view of the Golden Gate Bridge. Seth thought about his two-bedroom house with the metal roof. He had a view, too—of the tundra.

Was that why he was contemplating Bledsoe's bargain? Because somewhere in the back of his mind he thought he'd be more interesting to a woman like Lauren if he was a federal agent working big cases in a big city, instead of the chief of police of a two-bit town?

That was part of it. There was another reason, too, but he didn't want to think about that now. He dropped the guide rope leading from the camp to Lauren's trailer and raised a gloved hand to shield his eyes so he could see.

"What the—?"

The door to her trailer was wide open. Wind howled past him, blowing dry snow into the lab.

"Lauren?" He started up the steps and stopped dead. What the hell had happened? The inside of the trailer was a wreck. Every cabinet door in the lab was open, equipment and supplies scattered across the white linoleum. "Lauren?"

Panic rose in his throat. Sloughing a glove, he stepped

cautiously inside, his hand slipping instinctively under his jacket to where his shoulder holster would be if he was wearing a weapon. Which, of course, he wasn't.

He swore.

"Lauren, answer me!"

The overhead lights were on in the lab and in the bedroom in the back. His gaze swept the room, all his training, his instinct sharpening every move. Moving slowly, he stepped over open boxes of all sizes and their contents littering the floor. Glass from a box of microscope slides crunched under his boot.

All of the supplies in the overhead cabinets had been pulled down and were strewn across the steel counters underneath. Lauren's microscope lay on its side in pieces. Her notebook, which was usually right next to it on her workstation, was missing altogether, along with her laptop computer.

There was no evidence of a skirmish. No blood, no footprints, nothing. Thank God. No, this mess wasn't the result of an altercation. Someone had searched the place, looking for something.

The questions in Seth's mind were *who?* and *what?*

He had a pretty good idea of the "who"—either Salvio himself, or one of his cronies. Pinkie and Bulldog. Oh, yeah. This was right up their alley.

Seth moved quickly toward the bedroom, but already sensed no one was there. The room was a wreck, the single mattress pulled off the box spring and ripped apart. Stuffing was everywhere. Lauren's clothes lay scattered across the floor. The bathroom was the same, the contents of the medicine chest in a pile in the sink.

"Oh, my God!"

He spun a one-eighty at the sound of her voice.

Lauren stood framed in the open doorway of the lab, wind whipping at her hair, her mouth gaping as her gaze swept the room, colliding with his in a shock.

"What did you do?" She took a step toward him, then stopped, fear streaking across her face.

"Lauren." He put his hands up. "It wasn't me. I swear it." He snaked toward her, sidestepping the debris littering the floor, holding her shattered gaze.

She shook her head and stepped back. "Lauren, no!" Not heeding his warning, she grabbed the door frame a fraction of a second before tumbling backward down the trailer stairs.

A moment later he reached her.

"D-don't touch me!"

He grabbed her by the shoulders and pulled her inside. She started to fight him, but he held her fast. "Listen to me, Lauren. Look at me!"

She obeyed, her face white, her body trembling beneath his hands. Her astonishment was natural, explainable, but her fear wasn't. She should have been angry, more than angry. She should have been pissed as hell to discover that someone had broken into her trailer and done this.

But she wasn't angry. She was scared to death. And that made Seth instantly suspicious. What had happened that he didn't know about to make fear, and not anger, her first reaction?

"It wasn't me," he said again, and looked steadily into her eyes. "I came out here to see you and found it like this."

He watched her take in air and work to calm herself.

"Are you okay?"

She nodded. "I was just…" Her gaze focused past him on the bedroom. When she saw the mess in there, her eyes widened. "Oh, no."

"What is it?"

She jerked out of his grasp and stepped shakily over the boxes and scattered debris blocking her path to the bedroom.

"Lauren—"

"I'll be right back." She shot him a glance over her shoulder. "Stay here. Please!"

What the hell was going on?

He started to follow her, then stopped when he heard the bathroom door slam shut. She was in there for only a minute; it seemed like forever. Seth was just about to go after her, when he heard the toilet flush.

"Are you okay?" he asked her again when she returned to where he was standing.

"Yes." She nodded, but not convincingly. Her face twisted in frustration. "No. I don't know."

Her gaze darted around the room, her brown eyes like a frightened doe's. The tough, cool facade she'd put on a few hours ago in Salvio's office for Seth's benefit was gone.

"Come here," he said, not waiting for her to respond. He simply put his arms around her and pulled her to him. She buried her head in his chest and tightened her arms around him like a frightened child.

"Sweetheart," he wanted to whisper into her hair, against the soft skin of her neck—but he didn't. "Things have happened that you haven't told me about. Am I right?"

She nodded, her face pressed into the loft of his down survival jacket.

"Look at me, Lauren." He shed his other glove and tilted her chin up. "Has anyone threatened you, or hurt you? Salvio? Any of the others?"

Her brown eyes glassed, and he swore.

"It's all right," she said. "I'm…fine. Everything's fine."

"You're lying."

"No, I'm not. It's just that—"

He couldn't help himself. He kissed her, and not gently. His head began to throb with the weight of a hundred unanswered questions—most of them about her, what she wanted, what she felt.

The case—Salvio, Walters, Bledsoe and the hell Seth would catch if the section chief found out he'd fallen head over heels like an idiot for one of their suspects—all of it fled his mind as he let himself drown in the kiss.

Lauren tried to break away, but he wouldn't let her. "Seth, I…can't do this. I don't want to—" he kissed her again "—make things harder." He could have made a joke, but he didn't. When he kissed her again, she finally gave up the fight and kissed him back.

God, he wanted her. He wanted to pull her down on top of him right here on the linoleum. Unzip her jacket and—

"Well, well, well."

Both of them startled at the sound of Salvio's voice. Lauren unwrapped herself from Seth's embrace and jumped back as if he was a pariah.

Salvio stood in the open doorway and took in the scene. His gaze leveled on Lauren. "Don't expect your *boyfriend's* gonna like this."

Lauren flinched at the way Salvio drew out the word. "What are you talking about?"

Seth started to speak, but she flashed her eyes at him in warning.

"A woman like you. A lowlife like him." Salvio nodded at him. "News like that travels fast."

Seth advanced on him, fully intending for his fist to connect with Salvio's face.

Lauren caught his arm. "Please leave. I can handle this myself."

"Place is a wreck, Fotheringay." Salvio shook his head as he looked around. "Not much of a housekeeper, are ya?"

Seth was ready to kill him. He forced himself to calm down and act like the cop he was supposed to be, instead of a man going medieval at the thought of someone threatening the woman he cared about. He sucked in a breath and reminded himself that as far as Lauren or Salvio were concerned, he was supposed to be a roughneck from Kachelik. That's all.

"I'll, uh, help you clean this mess up."

Lauren cast him a collected look. "That's all right. I can do it myself."

"No, really. I'd like to."

"Please. Just go." She stood there, rigid. Her jacket and gloves were still on, but her hard hat had fallen to the floor when he'd kissed her. The wind blowing in through the open door ruffled the fur of her hood against her cheek.

"Sure?" he said.

She nodded, her gaze riveted to Salvio. The company man turned to leave, and Seth followed him out. Lauren grabbed the door to close it behind them.

Seth shot her a look that said *later,* but her eyes had gone cold again, just as they had earlier that day in Salvio's office. He knew what had set it off this time. Salvio's mention of her boyfriend. The very wealthy, highly respected Crocker Holt. The man she was going to marry.

A woman like you. A lowlife like him.

Lauren closed the door. Seth listened for the click of the lock, but couldn't hear it over the wind.

Jack Salvio leaned back in his desk chair and snorted. Driver's license, VISA, a North Slope Borough library card and a couple of twenties. "That it?"

"Nope." Pinkie grinned. Christ, what an ugly sight. "I saved the best for last." He gathered up the items on Salvio's desk, stuffed them back into the wallet and pocketed it.

Salvio eyed the roustabout with amusement as Pinkie closed the door to the office, walked to the window and pulled the drape. Salvio knew Pinkie'd done time. Petty theft, arson, assault with intent. Perfect for the kinds of capers they'd been pulling off for over a year now.

"Check this out. You're gonna croak when you see it."

Salvio nearly did. Pinkie's eyes lit up like birthday candles.

"Son of a bitch!" He snatched the weapon from Pinkie's

grasp and weighed it in his hand. "You found this in his stuff?"

"Took some lookin', but yeah. Found it duct-taped up under his bunk. It's a Glock, ain't it?"

"Nine millimeter." Salvio checked the ten-round clip. It was flush. "But what the hell's he doing with it, and how'd he get it past security?"

Every bag coming and going from Caribou Island was searched by Tiger rent-a-cops. No guns, no cameras, no booze… The list of contraband was as long as your arm.

"Beats me." Pinkie dropped onto the sofa and swung his feet onto the battered cushion.

"Gimme that wallet again."

Pinkie tossed it to him. Salvio put the Glock down on his desk and jerked the driver's license from its plastic protector.

"Thirty-two years old, six-two, a couple a hundred pounds plus change." Hair—black. Eyes—brown. An organ donor. Salvio laughed at that one. This son of a bitch was no Boy Scout. He stared hard at the Glock, his mind sifting through every encounter he'd had with this jerk over the past week.

He'd been sniffing around Fotheringay from the beginning, and had a bad habit of showing up where he wasn't supposed to be. Snooping around the office, questioning the crew, by the reserve pit with O'Connor's body, in Fotheringay's trailer at night. Oh, yeah. Jack Salvio's mama didn't raise no dummies. Old Nanook was banging her. Jeez, what he wouldn't give to see Holt's face when he found out.

Salvio's gaze zeroed in on the bad driver's license photo of Seth Adams. "Roughneck, my ass."

Chapter 11

She was determined to do this herself.

Lauren cruised casually past Salvio's darkened office and checked her watch. 11:30 p.m. He'd be up on the rig now to supervise the shift change at midnight. She could hear men's voices and occasional laughter drift down the hall from the kitchen.

Seth was probably there now, eating before it was time for him to work. At least a dozen times since that afternoon, she'd alternately decided on and then dismissed the idea of confiding in him. Someone had ransacked her trailer looking for that sample. Thank God they hadn't found it. It remained undiscovered in the box of tampons in her bathroom. Her woman's intuition about where to hide it had been right.

She ignored her intuition now. The little voice inside her head warning her that if she was right about her suspicions, what she was about to do was more than just stupid. It was dangerous.

Nevertheless, she was going to do it, and without Seth's

help. She'd leaned on him far too much already. She didn't want them to get any more involved than they already were.

Are we? Are we involved?

She remembered the smoldering look in his eyes when he'd asked her that.

Her hand paused on the door to Jack Salvio's room, which was tucked into a blind alcove at the far end of the camp's hundred-foot-long hallway, adjacent to the emergency exit she and Seth had used the day they'd broken into the sat-comm shack.

The door was locked, as she'd expected it to be. But the camp belonged to Altex, not Tiger, and Lauren had lifted a set of master keys from the desk in the tiny office across from Salvio's that had belonged to Paddy O'Connor.

If Salvio was doing something illegal on Caribou Island—other than the typical high jinks that often went on in these oil field camps, like smuggling in booze or women—she was going to find out what it was and blow the whistle on him.

She put her ear to the door and heard nothing except the low-level hum of the camp's generators and the shrieking wind outside, which had been blowing for so long now the sound of it had become a part of the background.

She tried four different keys before finding the right one. The knob turned easily under her hand. She was in. The room was dark, and she didn't want to chance turning the overhead light on. Switching on her penlight, she scanned the small bedroom. It reeked of cigarettes and dirty clothes.

A desk was wedged into a corner next to the unmade bed. It was as good a place as any to start. A minute's search uncovered nothing out of the ordinary. Blank paper, pens, a couple of men's adventure novels, and some letters from someone named Charisse in envelopes prominently displaying the logo of The Great Alaskan Bush Company—a popular strip club in town. Lauren sat down on the bed and started to read one. She stopped when she realized it had nothing to do with what she was looking for.

What *was* she looking for?

She wasn't sure. Just *something* that proved there was more than a simple drilling operation going on out here.

She searched through the clothes scattered on the bed. Paper crunched inside a pair of mud-spattered jeans that looked as if they hadn't been washed in weeks. She smoothed the paper out on the mattress and shone the penlight on the scrawled writing.

It was a phone number. It seemed familiar to her. She knew it from somewhere, but where? Recently, Tiger had upgraded its phone system both in Anchorage and San Francisco. She hadn't gotten a new number, but lots of people had, including her boss Bill Walters and some of the other Tiger execs. In her mind she ran through the common exchanges, then some of the extensions she knew by heart. No, she couldn't place it. She pocketed the slip of paper, then arranged the clothes on the bed as she'd found them.

The built-in wardrobe at the foot of the bed was next. She didn't bother with the hanging garments, but went right to the cubbyholes on top. She held the penlight in her mouth as she sorted through folded piles of white underwear and socks. A flash of color caught her eye. She gasped. The penlight thudded onto the thinly carpeted floor and rolled under the bed.

"Damn!"

A moment later she dove for the light, jerking a whole pile of Salvio's underwear from the cubbyhole in the process. She felt it whoosh by her on its way to the floor. Good going, Lauren. She found the penlight and sat up amidst a disarray of jockey shorts and wool socks.

The glow-in-the-dark hands of her watch told her she'd been in the room only a couple of minutes, but already she heard men's voices in the hallway outside. The second shift was suiting up to go to work.

Now, if she could just gather up all this stuff and put it back where—

The narrow beam from the penlight froze on the object that had caused her to lose it to begin with. She snatched the blue felt garment from under a pair of briefs on the floor.

It was a liner. A felt hard-hat liner like the kind the crew used in winter. She used a down one, herself, but these were popular with the men because they could be washed.

This one was dirty. It had mud on it and—

"Oh, my God."

She held the penlight close and traced a finger along the brownish-black crust that glued the liner to itself, making it hard for her to smooth out the fabric.

It was blood.

The men's voices in the hallway outside grew louder, along with footfalls. They should be moving away from the end of the hall, not toward it. Lauren froze. She switched off the penlight, pulled her knees up close and sat there in the dark holding her breath.

A heartbeat later the door opened. The overhead light came on, shocking her like a jolt of electricity. Momentarily blinded by the harsh fluorescents, she didn't see his first reaction.

"Humph." Jack Salvio stood in the doorway, looking down at her. "Shoulda hired you instead of Pinkie."

"Wh-what?"

She scrambled to her feet, the bloody liner in her hand, and backed away from him as far as was possible in the small room, until she felt the edge of the desk press into her back.

Her heart beat wildly in her chest as Salvio's gaze washed coolly over her, the room, the open wardrobe and the hard-hat liner she held in her hand.

Then he did something she wasn't prepared for. He smiled. In all the years she'd known him, she didn't remember him ever smiling. It was…crooked. Higher on one side of his face than the other.

"I was just, uh…"

"Got some good news, Fotheringay."

"Good…news?"

He moved toward her, that crooked smile arching higher. If it was possible for a twenty-nine-year-old woman in excellent health to have a heart attack, Lauren fully expected hers to begin now.

A foot from her Salvio stopped, and gently relieved her of the blood-crusted liner she knew belonged in Paddy O'Connor's hard hat. His gaze never left hers. It was almost as if the whole incident was an aside, not in the least important to him.

"We found another crate in the warehouse."

Crate? What was he talking about?

"Those samples you were so hot on—the ones that kid destroyed."

Her mind worked to process his words, but her heart was still racing, her hands shaking. Salvio had caught her searching his room, he'd been here thirty seconds now and hadn't even mentioned it.

"We found more of them."

"More?" His words finally sunk in. She snapped from fear-induced paralysis to attention. "Where? Where are they?"

"Like I said, out in the warehouse. Pinkie's recrating 'em now. Go ahead." He stepped aside to let her pass, nodding at the open doorway behind him. "He's waiting for you. I told him you'd wanna see 'em before they shipped to town."

Her gaze darted briefly to the bloody hard-hat liner crushed in Salvio's hand. His smile faded.

"Okay." She sidestepped past him, her heart in her throat, and had to force herself not to run down the hall toward the mudroom. Not because she was so anxious to see that crate of samples, but because Jack Salvio was scaring the living hell out of her.

Halfway to the warehouse, the wind at her back, propelling her along, icing exposed sections of skin on contact, Lauren changed her mind.

She was alone in this, and it was clear to her now that what had happened to Paddy O'Connor might very well happen to her if she got too close to the truth of whatever it was that was going on out here.

Seth would be on shift now, more than likely up on the rig. Maybe she'd go there first, try to see him, ask his help after all. He'd said the satellite uplink was broken. Maybe he could fix it. It was worth a try. She had to call in. Get help. The situation was too much to handle on her own now, and she was smart enough to admit it.

Grasping her hood with both hands, she turned into the wind. "Oh!"

Bulldog stood not three feet from her, his feet firmly planted on the ice. "Makin' sure ya get there okay," he yelled over the wind. He pointed in the direction of the warehouse, but she couldn't see it for the blowing snow. "Come on, I'll help ya."

Her body went cold inside her survival suit as the roustabout tucked her arm under his and pulled her toward the warehouse.

When they were safely inside and out of the wind, her first impression was that there were even more wooden pallets and empty crates stacked here than there had been when she was here a couple of days ago. The air inside was warm, and she caught the faintest whiff of diesel.

Aisles were nonexistent. Bulldog led her on a circuitous path that reminded her of one of those English hedge mazes you saw in old movies, only this one was made of stacked crates instead of greenery.

"Where are we going?"

Bulldog grinned. "He's waitin' for ya. Right over here."

Lauren didn't like it. Something was very wrong. Even if Salvio had found another box of those mystery samples, he surely wouldn't have told her about it if he was behind some kind of covert operation.

No, she didn't like this one bit. She had that feeling again—one of impending doom, as stupid as it sounded—and this time she wasn't going to ignore it.

"Bulldog, wait. I—"

The roustabout pulled her around a corner, and the first thing she saw, the only thing that registered, was Seth's stunned expression.

"Lauren, what are you doing here?"

She glanced at the open crate of samples at his feet and knew at once, from her initials on each bag, that she'd already analyzed them. They weren't the mystery samples at all. They were from yesterday's regular batch.

Salvio had lied to her. She felt suddenly claustrophobic wedged between Bulldog and Seth and all the crates. She met Seth's gaze and read a hard-edged coolness there she'd never seen before.

"What are *you* doing here?"

The situation went from bad to worse.

Seth had known from the moment he'd discovered his gun missing, that he'd been made. He'd suspected it that afternoon in Salvio's office. He was ready for what was coming next, but he hadn't figured on these bastards involving Lauren in their plan.

"Crating samples," he said evenly, in answer to her question.

It was obvious that Salvio wanted both of them out here for a reason. The warehouse was isolated, far enough away from the camp that even if the wind wasn't deafening outside, no one would be able to hear them if something happened. And something was about to. For the second time in thirty seconds Bulldog checked his watch.

"But I thought that Pinkie…"

Lauren's voice trailed off, her gaze darting to the stacks of crates surrounding them. She wrapped her arms around herself as if she was cold, but Seth knew that wasn't it. She was afraid. More than that, she was afraid of him.

The thought of it made him sick. She took a step back, but Bulldog was right there, making sure she didn't leave. Seth would deal with him later. Right now he had to get the message across to Lauren that he was on her side.

"Salvio asked me to come out here and help." He willed her gaze back to his. "I didn't know you'd be here."

"You didn't?"

"No. Do you understand?"

Bulldog stood behind her, still preoccupied with checking his watch. Seth glanced at the shadows marking each snaking turn of the piled crates defining what used to be an aisle. Pinkie was here somewhere. He'd bet his life on it.

"Come here," he said, and waved Lauren over to where he was standing. When whatever was about to happen happened, he wanted her next to him where he could protect her.

He squatted beside the crate on the floor and made a show of digging through the plastic bags of rock samples. He could see it in her eyes, in the way she bit her lip, that she wanted to trust him.

That's when he saw it.

An egg timer. The digital kind like they had in the camp's kitchen, only it was wedged on the floor between two towering stacks of crates, not ten feet from him. He wouldn't have noticed it if he was standing, or if it hadn't had those big red flashing numbers.

Counting down.

A minute and twenty-one seconds, a minute twenty, nineteen…

Oh, God.

The device wasn't fancy. A timer wired to a detonator—

what amounted to a big firecracker, an M80—jammed inside a drum of gasoline. Amateur arsonists used setups like this all the time. Any kid with Internet access and half a brain could learn how to build one using stuff from around the house.

"Seth?" Lauren squatted beside him, her back to Bulldog, and placed her gloved hand on top of his.

"Uh...hey," was all he could manage to say as he tried to focus on her face.

"What is it?"

A minute fifteen, fourteen... Mentally he kept the time. When he'd first entered the warehouse, the wooden crates and pallets towering halfway to the ceiling had looked like nothing more than a lousy stacking job to him. Someone had been in a hurry, and completely haphazard.

But now, when he looked up, he realized that what he was really seeing was *fuel load,* and that there was nothing haphazard about it. He also realized he'd never be able to reach the device to disarm it, without first moving thousands of pounds of full sample crates. There wasn't time.

Ignoring Lauren's question, he said, "Here, check these out before I seal the crate." He grabbed a couple of the sample bags and thrust them into her hands.

"But I've already—"

Grabbing her wrist, he shot her a look that said their very lives depended on her doing exactly what he told her to do, without question.

A minute three, a minute two...

"Seth," she whispered, "we need to talk."

"Later."

"But—"

"How's it goin'?" Pinkie appeared behind Bulldog, seemingly out of nowhere. Seth wasn't at all surprised to see him. Salvio wouldn't have trusted Bulldog on his own as far as he could throw him.

"Fine," he said, forcing a relaxed look. "This crate'll be

done in a minute.'' Only they didn't have a minute. Fifty-nine, fifty-eight...

"Salvio wants us up on the rig.'' Pinkie nudged Bulldog, who was oblivious to everything except the second hand on his watch.

Even Lauren was suspicious of these two, and she didn't know half of what Seth knew about them. He read the worry lines in her face and revised his assumption. Maybe she did know.

"Uh, yeah. We gotta go.'' Bulldog edged around a couple of crates and started for the door.

"What's going on?'' Lauren whispered between clenched teeth.

"Let's get this lid on.'' Seth grabbed the crate's lid and pretended to search the floor for the hammer. Pinkie was still watching them, and Seth didn't dare steal a glance at the timer.

Fifty, forty-nine, forty-eight...

"There's six more crates over yonder need reboxing.'' Pinkie trained his eyes on Lauren. "That's where those samples are. The ones you wanted to see?''

"They are?'' Her brows arched in surprise.

"What samples?'' Seth asked.

Neither of them answered him. Lauren started for the aisle Pinkie had pointed to, deeper into the maze of pallets and crates.

Seth grabbed her wrist. "Wait a sec. I need your help with this.'' He gestured to the lid of the crate he was working on.

Pinkie turned, satisfied they had no idea what was going to happen in—Seth checked the timer—forty-two seconds, then followed Bulldog toward the front of the building.

As soon as he was out of sight, Lauren said, "Tell me what's going on!''

"We're outta here. That's what's going on.'' He dropped the hammer, grabbed her arm and started in the direction of the emergency exit door he knew was somewhere behind these crates.

"Let me go! What are you—"

"I'll explain later. Come on!"

He slid his grip to her gloved hand and pulled her along behind him as he dodged pallets and crates and piles of small equipment, snaking his way toward the back of the warehouse.

Thirty-six, thirty-five, thirty—

"Where are we going?"

"Out."

She jerked hard, pulling him to a stop. "It's that way." She pointed to the next aisle over.

He swore. "Come on, we're out of time."

Twenty-seven, twenty-six... At last the emergency exit door was in sight. Simultaneously he hit the bar with his hand and the door full on with his shoulder. The pain reverberated through muscle and bone. The door didn't budge.

"Son of a bitch!"

Lauren crashed into him. "What's wrong?"

"It's blocked from the outside." He hit the door again with the same result. His shoulder screamed.

"We can go out the front, like Pinkie and Bulldog."

Twenty-three, twenty-two...

"There's no time!" He cursed again, and didn't stop until his gaze lit on what he was looking for.

A ventilation plate built into the side of the prefab metal building. Tumbling crates out of the way, he offered up a silent prayer to anyone up there who was listening. A second later he kicked the plate free.

"You first."

Lauren looked at the small, rectangular hole through which frigid wind was now howling, blowing snow into the warehouse, dancing around them like a dervish. "It's too small. We'll never get out that way. What's this all about?"

He pushed her to her knees. "Do it!"

Fifteen, fourteen, thirteen...

She looked at him with a mixture of disbelief, anger and fear. Then she scrambled through the hole to the outside. Seth was right behind her.

"Okay, so we're out," she yelled over the wind. "Why did we have to—?"

He grabbed her arm and took off, scrambling for purchase on the ice. Lauren pulled back, and when he turned to look at her he saw that anger had finally overcome whatever else she was feeling.

Ten, nine...

There was no time to explain. He picked her up in a fireman's hold and bolted. He'd apologize for his less than suave tactics later. All he cared about right now was getting them the hell out of there.

Six, five...

The warehouse exploded.

Chapter 12

"Are you okay?"

Lauren lay spread-eagled in a snowdrift, wedged between a storage building and a row of empty fifty-five-gallon drums weighted down with sandbags. Seth was on top of her.

"I...think so."

They'd landed hard. Her body felt as if it had been hit by a train. She worked to catch her breath, which frosted on contact with the air.

"You sure?" Seth pushed the hair away from her face and looked at her. The lights from the yard reflected in his dark eyes. His jaw was tight, his expression a fusion of both fear and relief.

"What...happened?" She tried to push him off her so she could see, but he wouldn't let her up.

"The warehouse. It's history."

Over the wind she heard the sounds of men racing past them. The blowing snow made it difficult to see.

"We could have been..." It suddenly dawned on her why

Seth had acted so strangely in the warehouse, and why the second Pinkie and Bulldog had left them alone he'd taken her hand and raced for the exit.

"Killed. Yeah. I think that was the general idea."

"Oh, God."

She didn't want to, but she couldn't help it. She clutched at him, and his arms went instantly around her. He was in shirtsleeves, no jacket or gloves, and she realized he must be freezing.

"You're okay now. Safe."

"Salvio," she breathed.

"That's my guess, too."

"You knew! You knew it was going to happen. That he— How? How did you know?"

Two men ran past them with fire extinguishers. Seth pushed her back down into the snow, flattening his body over hers. Miraculously the men didn't see them.

"Tell you later." He got to his feet and pulled her with him. "I've got to do something, and I want you to stay right here. Understand?" He led her farther back between the building and the drums, then pointed to a space barely big enough for her to sit. "In there."

"No! I've got to get help. Call someone. Don't you understand? If that explosion wasn't an accident, then—"

"Then it means Salvio is a killer, and if he finds out you're still alive…" He pulled her to him and looked into her eyes. "I'm not taking that chance."

All at once she knew she was in over her head. With the goings on at Caribou Island, yes, but more than that. She was in over her head with him. A roughneck from Kachelik she'd met barely a week ago.

She was vaguely aware that he was shivering. The temperature was somewhere around forty below. "You're freezing, Seth. Here." She started to unzip her jacket, but he stopped her.

"Get in there." He pointed her toward the cubbyhole

between the metal drums. "Wait for me. I'll be ten minutes, no more."

"But—"

"Don't argue." He waited until she was settled, wedged cross-legged between the drums where no one could see her, then he slipped around the side of the building and was gone.

It took Seth longer than he expected to make his way back to camp without being seen. Men streamed from the rig, the shop, the camp, from everywhere, some of them hauling fire extinguishers that Seth knew wouldn't do any good.

The amber glow of the warehouse on fire was visible through the blowing snow. He could smell burning fuel, and all that wood. By the time he slipped past the Dumpsters and in through the kitchen, he couldn't feel his hands or his face anymore. The warm air burned his skin as nerve endings roused to life.

Pots boiled unattended on the industrial-size range. Cabinet doors were open. Half-eaten plates of food and cups of still-steaming coffee sat on cafeteria tables that looked as if they'd been vacated in a hurry.

Everyone was outside watching the fire. As he jogged down the corridor toward his room, the only sounds he heard were the camp's generators humming in the background, the buzz of overhead fluorescent lights, and the wind.

The bloodied rock hammer was still there, where he'd hidden it in its paper bag, behind a removable panel in the wall that housed electrical circuits. He grabbed it, stuffed it into his duffel, stole a pair of gloves and a jacket from one of his roommate's gear bags, and was out of there.

He had one more stop to make, and tried not to think about Lauren out there alone, as he continued down the hallway toward Jack Salvio's office.

The lights were on, but Salvio wasn't there. Seth hadn't expected him to be. He'd be out at the fire, making sure it burned that warehouse to the ground.

It only took him fifteen seconds to pick the lock on Salvio's desk drawer. And there it was, right where he'd thought it would be. He grabbed his Glock and stuffed it into his jeans at the small of his back. Just in case. Though he didn't plan on meeting up with anyone on his way back out to the storage building where he'd left Lauren.

The Altex crew manifest caught his eye on the bulletin board above Salvio's desk. He pocketed it, then spent a few seconds looking for a particular set of keys he thought for sure would be in the drawer. They weren't. Silently he cursed.

Okay, fine. He didn't need them. He checked his watch—it had been ten minutes already. Lauren wasn't the kind of woman who sat back and did nothing while all hell was breaking loose around her. He admired that about her, but he worried, too, that she'd do something stupid, like not wait for him. That she'd confront Salvio on her own.

As he made his way back around the storage building and between the metal drums, he prayed to God she was still there.

"Seth!" Lauren was on her feet before he got to her.

"Come on. Let's go." He took her hand and led her around to the front of the building.

"Where?"

They'd have to cross over a hundred feet of open space to get to the rig. The visibility was poor and, even if anyone saw them, they wouldn't be recognized. Everyone wore the same company-issued survival jackets. Navy-blue canvas with metallic stripes on the arms. The hoods were generous and trimmed in fur; their faces would be covered.

"Around back." He pointed past the rig. "Let's go."

He dropped her hand as they crossed the yard, so that if

anyone did see the two of them pointed into the wind, high-tailing it toward the rig, they wouldn't be suspicious.

She followed him into the narrow slot between the pipe shed and the rig, which led to the back of the site. He didn't stop, or give her any other opportunity to question him.

He'd made the decision when they were lying in the snowbank, his heart racing out of control, their breath frosting the air. She'd clutched at his shirt, looked up at him with doelike eyes, and what he read in them left him no choice but this one.

They came out on the other side of the rig, and she grabbed his arm to stop him. "Seth, where are we going?"

"Here. Right here." He dropped the duffel bag and nodded toward the tanklike vehicle sitting at the edge of the ice pad, where the island flowed seamlessly into the frozen Beaufort Sea.

"That's the Rolligon."

It was the only way now. The ice road leading back to Deadhorse hadn't been maintained, and Seth suspected that was by design. They wouldn't make it a mile in one of the SUVs Tiger kept on site. The Rolligon had huge, low-pressure tires that were meant to drive across uneven terrain like tundra, frozen or otherwise. This was their ticket out.

He dropped the duffel bag, climbed onto the steps leading up to the small cab, and jerked open the door. "Give me your hand."

"What are you doing?" He could barely hear her over the wind, but he recognized that rigid stance, her gloved fists balled at her sides.

"We're leaving the island. You and me. Now."

"What are you talking about? I can't leave. That fire was set on purpose. We've got to—"

He grabbed her arm and pulled her forcibly up beside him. Her feet scrambled for traction on the metal steps. "You don't get it, do you?"

"Get what?" She glanced at her arm, his iron grip. "You're...hurting me."

"Get in."

"No!"

"Get in the cab, Lauren." He didn't wait for her reply. Hooking one arm around the handhold on the outside of the cab, and another around her waist, he hoisted her up and onto the bench seat.

"You're out of your—"

"Slide over." He retrieved the duffel bag, swung in beside her and slammed the door. For a few seconds both of them just sat there, breathing hard, reveling in the simple fact that they were at least out of the wind.

She threw back her hood and gave him one of those "Well?" looks.

"That explosion was meant to kill. The second Salvio finds out it didn't, that you're still alive..." He didn't think he had to spell it out for her.

He could tell by the expression on her face that she hadn't thought that far ahead. He had. And he knew that Salvio wouldn't stop until they were both dead.

Salvio had found Seth's department-issue weapon and knew by now he wasn't just a roughneck from Kachelik. It made sense that Salvio wanted him out of the picture. But why Lauren? He'd find out, but now was not the time.

"We'll go to Deadhorse for help," she said.

"It's too far. Kachelik's only fifty miles, give or take."

"Your village."

"Yeah." He climbed over her into the driver's seat and studied the instrument panel and controls.

"You can drive this?"

"Probably."

He knew from the look on her face she was scared. "These things only go about ten miles an hour don't they?"

"Yeah."

She spotted the CB radio tucked under the dash and reached for the receiver.

"Don't even think about it. We're out of range of everything except the camp at Caribou Island, and once Salvio realizes there aren't two dead bodies in the rubble of that warehouse, and that his Rolligon is missing, he'll be scanning every channel."

"You're right."

"Don't worry. We'll be okay." He smiled at her, but she didn't smile back. "As long as I can get this thing started."

Her eyes widened. "You mean you don't have the key?"

"No." He shucked his gloves and the borrowed jacket, and slapped his Glock onto the dash.

"Oh, my God. That's a gun."

"Yeah." He slid under the steering wheel, ripped off the cover housing fuses and starter wires, and went to work.

"Is it…loaded?"

"Yes, it is."

She said nothing to that, only watched him as he cut and stripped wires with a penknife and twisted them together.

"You can hot-wire this?"

A few seconds later the diesel engine sputtered to life. They didn't have to worry about anyone hearing it. The sound would be masked by the wind and the huge generators rumbling on the rig and in camp.

"Okay," he said as he readjusted himself on the seat. "We're outta here."

She looked at the gun, her eyes as wide as he'd ever seen them, then met his gaze. "You've got something to do with all this, haven't you?"

"All what?" He cranked up the heat full blast, and shook off a chill that ran bone deep.

"You knew the warehouse was going to blow up, that Salvio and those roustabouts were up to something. That—"

He threw the vehicle into reverse and it lurched backward.

"Wait a minute!"

"What?"

"I can't leave without—" She tossed his duffel bag to the floor and slid toward the passenger side door. "I'm going back to my trailer."

"The hell you are." He grabbed her arm.

"You don't understand. I left something there. Something important. I've got to get it!" Her gaze darted to his hand clamped around her arm, to his gun sitting on the dash, then turned on him. "Who are you? And how do you know so much?" She nodded toward the nest of wires he'd rerouted to start the vehicle.

He'd have to tell her sometime, but not now. He shrugged. "Every teenage boy in the world can hot-wire a car."

That seemed to satisfy her, but she still looked edgy, her hand gripping the door handle. "I'll say it again. There's something in my trailer I need to get. It will only take a minute."

He pulled her toward him across the seat, and maintained his grip on her as he maneuvered the Rolligon to the edge of the ice pad. "No way. You're not going back there."

She stared at the gun and ground her teeth behind thinned lips. More than anything, he wanted to take her in his arms and kiss her, hold her, tell her that everything was going to be all right. But he didn't.

"Was it you?" she said, still staring at the gun. "Did you kill Paddy?"

He hit the brakes as the vehicle slid over the side of the ice pad and down onto the frozen sea. "No." He slipped his hand into hers. "Look at me, Lauren." She did. "I didn't kill Paddy, and I'm not involved in whatever the hell is going on out here with Salvio and the others."

They sat there idling for a moment and just looked at each other. "I believe you," she said at last. "It's just that..." Again she looked at the gun.

"It's going to be okay. I promise."

She stared out the window in the direction of her trailer, as he flipped on a navigational device and steered the Rolligon east toward Kachelik.

Blowing snow pummeled the windshield. He couldn't see a dozen feet in front of them, and didn't dare turn on the vehicle's headlights until they were well away from the site.

They'd be lucky if they made the village sometime tomorrow. Lucky if they made it at all, he corrected himself when he saw that they had barely half a tank of fuel. It would have to be enough.

At last Lauren settled back on the bench seat, resigned to his plan, and removed her jacket and gloves. He exhaled in relief. At least they were getting out of here. At least she'd be safe. He owed her that much, after having thought for the better part of a week that she was a killer and an embezzler.

But if not her, then who? He'd asked himself that question a hundred times in the past few days. Salvio, sure. But who at Tiger was the mastermind? Who made the deals and handled the money.

Money.

As they disappeared into the night, swallowed up by an endless expanse of frozen sea and blowing snow, she interrupted his thoughts to ask him one more thing.

"You wouldn't lie to me about any of this, would you Seth?"

Chapter 13

She looked like an angel.

Lauren sighed in her sleep, curled up next to him on the bench seat of the Rolligon. His jacket, which she'd been using as a blanket, slid to the floor of the cab. Seth tucked it back around her and brushed her hair back from her face. He wanted to watch her expression as she dreamed. Like an idiot, he wondered if she was dreaming about him.

Yeah, right.

They'd talked last night until four in the morning, when exhaustion had finally caught up with her, and the motion of the all-terrain vehicle lulled her into sleep. He checked his watch. 9:00 a.m. He could barely keep his eyes open. He hadn't had a wink since yesterday afternoon, and the environmental conditions did nothing to improve his alertness.

The Rolligon crawled across the tundra toward Kachelik at a snail's pace. From the mileage, and the short rise they'd climbed about an hour ago, Seth figured they were on land now, though you couldn't really tell in winter, given the flat, snow-swept expanse of the arctic plain.

Visibility had improved, but he could still only see about twenty feet ahead of the vehicle. The rumble of the diesel engine sounded more and more like a lullaby to him. He was in desperate need of sleep. He kept himself awake by looking at Lauren, her face illuminated by the soft amber lights of the instruments on the dash.

It was his fault they were out here. If Salvio hadn't found his gun...

He'd known it was a risk to carry it on this kind of undercover assignment, where he lived and worked in close contact with so many others. But he hadn't known what to expect, and wanted to be ready in case there was trouble.

Besides, he hadn't forgotten how Doyle Bledsoe had hung him and his partner out to dry on that last case they'd worked together. No way was he ever going to let Bledsoe, or anyone, do that to him again.

Lauren sighed again and snuggled closer. Her head rested on his thigh. He had to force himself to keep both hands on the wheel.

You wouldn't lie to me about any of this, would you Seth?

He'd avoided answering her question last night, but he wouldn't be able to avoid it much longer. He had to tell her who he was and why he was out here with her. But not yet.

He'd finally gotten her to trust him, and he discovered that earning that trust was more important to him than he'd realized it would be—and not because of the case.

Christ, it was impossible.

He reminded himself that, no matter what she said, no matter what he thought about her, they led lives that were worlds apart on every level. He also reminded himself that she was with him only because there was no one else. She was alone, vulnerable, and her life was on the line. She had to trust him. Besides, he hadn't really given her a choice.

Which one of them would she choose, he wondered, if

she wasn't stuck out here alone with him with no one else to turn to? In the light of day, under normal circumstances when her life wasn't turned upside down, would she choose him or Crocker Holt?

He watched her as she drew a deep, restful breath, as her eyes opened and focused on his.

"Hi," she whispered in a sleepy, sexy voice.

"Hey."

She lay there, looking up at him, and smiled. "Where are we?"

"Don't know exactly. Somewhere between Caribou Island and Kachelik." He glanced at their mileage and the fuel gauge on the panel. "We haven't come as far as I'd hoped."

She sat up and squinted against the headlight glare reflecting off the blowing snow and ice.

"Hell, we could have walked it faster, but at least in here we're warm."

She noticed his jacket around her and gently pushed it to the side. "Thanks," she said, smoothing the fur of the hood.

"Feel better?"

"Rested, but not better, if you know what I mean."

"Yeah." Only he didn't even feel rested.

"I still can't believe what happened."

"Believe it. Salvio wanted you dead, Lauren." He watched her expression cloud as the truth of things sank in. "Why?"

She didn't answer right away, just stared out the window, thinking. At last she shook her head. "I'm not sure. Something's going on that he doesn't want me to know about."

If she only knew. "Like what?"

His Glock was still on the dash where he'd put it. She stared at it for a moment, then said, "Why do you have that?"

He was overly conscious about lying to her now, and didn't like the sick feeling he had in his gut when he thought about how big a hole he'd dug for himself with her. But it wasn't the time or the place to give up the truth. Not yet.

He still had a job to do, and somewhere in the back of his mind he held on to the hope that if he did it, and did it well, the reward would justify the means.

He searched for a plausible answer. "You've been around. You know why. You work in the Arctic, you carry a gun."

"For the bears, you mean."

"Yeah." He knew from the look on her face that she didn't believe him.

"Why were you out there, in the warehouse with those crates?"

He shrugged. "When my shift started, Salvio told me to get my butt out there and help Pinkie and Bulldog."

"He wanted you dead, too, then. Why you?"

He looked at her, remembering the feel of her legs wrapped around his hips that night in the lab, how she tasted, the smell of her. "He saw us together more than once. Maybe that was enough of a reason."

She looked away, and he knew she was thinking about it, too. "I don't want to talk about it anymore." She reached for his duffel bag sitting on the floor of the cab. "Do you have anything to eat in here?"

He hit the brakes, and thrust his arm out to keep her from lurching forward. "I'll get it." The last thing he wanted her to see was the rock hammer buried inside. He rummaged around in his bag and produced a couple of energy bars. "Peanut butter or chocolate."

She smiled. "Peanut butter."

He stowed the duffel bag in the small space behind the bench seat, and they went to work on their breakfast.

"I would have pegged you for chocolate," he said after they'd finished. "Expensive chocolate."

"No way. Peanut butter's my favorite."

He would have never thought that about her. "What else is your favorite?"

She gave him a funny look, then smiled. "All right. I'll play."

"Play what?"

"Favorite things. My dad and I played it all the time when I was a kid."

"Favorite things?"

Her eyes lit up. Her smile bloomed like a summer wildflower across her face. In the pit of his stomach he felt something else now. Something that scared the hell out of him.

"Sure. I'll start." She swiveled toward him on the seat and pulled her legs up under her. "Favorite color."

"Mine?"

She nodded.

"Blue. But not regular blue. Midnight blue—like the night sky when the stars first come out."

"Mine's green."

"Dark green, like the forest."

"How did you know?"

He shrugged. "Just a feeling."

She smiled again. This time he smiled back.

"Favorite place," she said.

"That's easy. Alaska."

"Me, too."

If she would have told him that a week ago, he'd have never believed her. But now, looking at her sitting there in her father's old sweater, her hair mussed from sleep, her face lit with adrenaline, he knew it was true.

"Favorite animal. Cat or dog?" he said.

"I don't really know. Dog, I guess. But Mother wouldn't allow me to have one growing up. And now, well...Crocker doesn't like pets. Too messy, he says. Too much trouble."

Yeah, I'll bet. Wouldn't want dog hair in his Mercedes.

"What about you?"

He focused on the tundra outside and thought about how much to tell her. "I have a dog."

"You do?"

"Yeah. He's a half-breed like me. Husky and shepherd. Name's Amaguq."

"Wolf," she said, stunning him with her knowledge of his native tongue. "Will I get to meet him when we get there?"

When we get there. Christ. What the hell was he going to do with her when they did get there?

"Sure," he said. "He stays with my mother when I'm working, but he'll be around."

"All-time worst date."

He shot her a surprised look. "That's not a favorite thing."

"I know. But I'm curious."

So was he. "All right. It was with my ex-wife."

"You were married?"

"Surprised?" He could see from her face that she was, but she quickly recovered herself.

"No, not at all. I just…"

"What?"

"I guess I hadn't considered that you might be."

"I'm not. It's been a few years since the divorce. Five years to be exact."

"Oh. What was she—"

"Favorite book," he said abruptly, determined now to change the subject.

She took the hint. "You're going to laugh."

"Go on. Tell me."

"Okay, but don't laugh. *Swiss Family Robinson.*"

He did laugh. "You're kidding?"

"No. I love that book." She shot him an exasperated look. "I told you, you would laugh."

"Why do you like it so much?"

"I don't know." She shrugged. "I guess because it's

about a family—a father and mother and kids. Together, on an adventure, just them against the world.''

The more she talked about herself, the more amazed he was at how wrong he'd been about her. And how right she seemed to him now.

"Favorite movie." She edged closer to him on the seat.

"Mine? Now you're gonna laugh."

"Try me."

"*Notorious.* Cary Grant and Ingrid Bergman. Nineteen forty-six."

It was her turn to be surprised. He could read it in her face. He read other things, too, and he got that funny feeling again.

"I love that movie," she said. "Hitchcock, right?"

"Yeah."

"He's a government agent, a regular guy. And she's a wealthy socialite."

Ouch. He didn't realize when he'd answered, that the movie's characters hit so close to home.

"Her boyfriend—later they get married, of course, and he's her husband. Anyway, he's selling government secrets to a foreign power, and Cary Grant, the government agent, needs to catch him. So he enlists her help."

Brilliant, Adams. "Yeah, that's the one."

"It's not really a spy story, though. It's a romance," she said.

He gripped the steering wheel tighter and pushed the gas pedal to the floor. Their speed increased to a whopping six miles an hour.

"All through the movie Ingrid Bergman and Cary Grant love each other, but they never say it. They're too—"

Their gazes locked, and Seth swallowed hard. Absently, she twisted the frayed hem of her sweater in her hands. He stopped breathing, waiting for her to finish.

"Afraid," she said, her voice a whisper.

They looked at each other for a moment longer, acutely

aware of the fact that there was less than a foot of warm air separating them.

"Yeah, well…" he said, shrugging it off. "It's an old movie. Stuff like that doesn't happen anymore." The hole he was digging just got deeper.

She recovered her composure, and swiveled back to face the front of the cab, her gaze fixed on the storm raging outside.

Desperate to change the subject, he said the first thing that blasted across his mind. "You're not anything like what the papers say about you."

Her expression darkened.

"I read the society columns now and then. For fun."

"So…you must have known about Crocker, then."

"Yeah."

"Before you…before we…?"

He nodded, realizing that he hadn't changed the subject at all.

"Crocker's a very successful man," she said in a cool voice. She sat up straight, her spine rigid against the vinyl seat-back.

"Yeah, the guy's got everything, doesn't he? Money, power, connections, and a boatload of nice stuff, I suspect."

"You're right. He does."

He felt himself sliding into dangerous territory, but couldn't stop himself. "Is that what you want, too?"

That's what his ex had wanted, what his father had, and had wanted for him. But it wasn't his thing. It never had been. He'd worked his butt off at the Bureau, hoping, somehow, that it would be enough. That Kitty, and his father, too, would respect him for a job well done. They had, marginally. And then he'd gotten the ax. The rest was history.

Lauren stared out the window, brown eyes hard, her lips pressed into a thin line. "I don't know, Seth. I don't know. My father always said I could be whatever I wanted, and that whatever I did, I should strive to be the best."

"He sounds like a good man. A good father."

"He was. After he died, Mother pushed and pushed for me to succeed—but at the things she wanted for me, not what I wanted for myself. I rebelled when I got old enough. Finished my master's in geology and—"

"Went to work for Tiger."

"That was Mother's doing. My stepfather had connections. I wanted to work for the state, like my dad had. But the next thing I knew Tiger had offered me a job. It seemed stupid to turn it down."

"And then?"

"And then I met Crocker... He pushed me, too. Pushes me. But in a different sort of way. He's all business. All success. He says he wants us to be successful together. That he wants..." She drew a breath and exhaled, as if she was sick of the whole topic. Suddenly she turned to him. "What about you, Seth? Money, power—that's not the kind of thing you care about, is it?"

He rubbed his burning eyes, stifling a yawn. "Right now all I care about is getting to where we're going and getting some sleep."

"Oh, my God, I didn't think about that. I've been so selfish." She grabbed his arm and half rose from the bench seat. "Here, switch places."

"What?"

"I'll drive for a while. You can get some sleep."

He shot her an incredulous look. "No way. You don't know how to drive this thing."

"Come on, switch places. I've been watching you—it's easy. Just put your foot on the gas and steer."

God, what he wouldn't give for even an hour of shut-eye.

"It's not as if we're barreling across the tundra at breakneck speed. Besides, I've trusted you this far, haven't I?"

"You have."

"Well, then? Isn't it about time you trusted me?"

He couldn't argue with that. He didn't want to argue. "Okay, but—"

She started to climb over him. He twisted sideways, trying not to touch her, but his foot slipped off the gas and the Rolligon lurched to a halt.

"Oh!" Lauren lost her balance.

Instinctively he grabbed her around the waist and pulled her toward him. She ended up straddling him, her arms on his shoulders, her mouth a dangerous inch from his. Their gazes met and he slid his hands downward to her hips. She was hot between her legs where his groin pressed up against her.

"I, uh…" Before he could kiss her, she scrambled off him and perched awkwardly on the seat. "Sorry."

"It's okay." He smiled and slid sideways so she could position herself in the driver's seat.

God, he was exhausted. He balled up his jacket to use as a pillow, watching her take over the controls of the slow-moving, but enormous vehicle. "See the navigational read-out?" He pointed to the directional heading displayed on one of the small screens on the instrument panel. "Just keep it pointed east-southeast, and we'll be fine."

"Got it." She played with the seat adjustment until her legs comfortably reached the pedals.

"Wake me if you see anything at all out there." He glanced one more time at the storm outside and the flat, white plain of the tundra beneath them. "Understood?"

"Understood."

He tried to stretch out on the bench seat without touching her, but he was too tall, and couldn't get comfortable.

"Here," she said, and patted her jean-clad thigh. "Put your head here. It'll be more comfortable."

"You sure?"

"I'm sure." She gave him a small smile, and he sucked in a breath.

He lay on his back, his knees pulled up, his head practically in her lap, and watched her until his tired eyes couldn't stay open a second longer. ''Wake me if anything happens.''

''Like if we run out of gas?''

He'd hoped she wouldn't notice the fuel gauge, which was almost on empty. It was hard to tell in this kind of vehicle how much diesel was really left. ''Yeah, like if we run out of gas,'' he said, and proceeded to let his mind drift.

''Sweet dreams,'' he thought he heard her say after a while, but maybe he was dreaming. Her fingers stroked his hair and the day-old stubble on his cheek. That was probably a dream, too, but he didn't want to open his eyes and find out for sure. He felt too damned good.

Lauren stared ahead into the storm, one hand on the steering wheel, the other resting lightly on Seth's shoulder. She thought it ironic that she and Seth had *slept* together, but they hadn't had sex. With Crocker it was usually just the opposite. They had sex, but rarely slept together.

Crocker liked to sleep alone in a separate bed, preferably in a separate room. He needed absolute quiet, he said. And space. No one hanging on to him in the night, disturbing his rest. During the week he got up early to check the markets when they opened in New York. He always said he couldn't afford to oversleep. Everything was always about money.

Lauren put her driving on autopilot, and for the next couple of hours thought hard about what her marriage to Crocker would be like. More than once she caught herself wondering what it would be like to be married to a roughneck, to live a million miles from nowhere and raise a bunch of kids.

Just like the Swiss Family Robinson.

She smiled, and for the next little bit allowed the fantasy to run wild in her mind. Just as she got to the part where she arrived home to find Seth bouncing their baby daughter on his knee, the Rolligon ran out of gas.

Chapter 14

"Lauren?" Seth flew off the seat, scrambling for his gun on the dash. "What is it? What happened?"

"It's all right." She placed a steadying hand on his shoulder, and watched him as he came fully awake, quickly scanning their surroundings and realizing they were in no imminent danger. "No," she said. "I take that back. It's not all right."

"Why did you stop?"

"We're out of gas. At least I think we are." She pointed to the fuel gauge. The red needle glowed well below empty. "The engine just...stopped."

She could tell by the tight look on his face that her fears were justified. He checked their position on the navigational screen, then his watch, then the mileage reading on the instrument panel. She knew he was doing the same calculations in his head that she'd already done.

"How close are we?" she asked.

"Not close enough."

Peering into the darkness and the blizzard outside, she watched him as he considered their predicament.

"We're not going to be the next Donner Party, are we?" She laughed at her own joke, but knew it wasn't funny.

"No. We're gonna be fine." He searched behind the bench seat in the cab, and then under it, until he found what he was looking for. "Put your jacket on, and your gloves, too."

"But—"

"Just do it." He ripped open the plastic bag marked Emergency Supplies and did a quick tour of its contents. "Here, put this on, too." He handed her a wool hat, and she did as he asked.

"This cab's going to be freezing inside of an hour, isn't it?"

"Yeah."

She switched off the Rolligon's headlights to save battery power.

"Good idea," he said, and grabbed the handset of the CB radio.

"I thought you said we shouldn't use it."

"I know. But we're far enough away from the rig, and the weather's so lousy, I don't think Salvio could pick up our transmission if he wanted to."

"And we're close enough to Kachelik that…"

"Exactly."

He tried for thirty minutes, without success, to raise someone, anyone, on the radio. Lauren's hopes faded.

They sat there in silence, their breath frosting the air, staring into the darkness outside. Wind howled past them at God knows how many knots. The temperature gauge inside the cab read fourteen degrees and dropping. As for outside…she didn't want to know.

"Okay, that's it," Seth said, and grabbed his gun.

Her heart did a flip-flop inside her chest. "What? You're going to put us out of our misery?"

He shot her a wry look. "No such luck." Then he reached across her and switched on the vehicle's headlights.

"What are you doing?"

"What I should have done in the first place." He grabbed his gun off the dash, stuffed it into his jacket pocket, and swiveled toward her on the seat.

"You're not going out there?"

"Yeah, I am. I need to find out where we are."

"But what if—?"

"If I'm not back in ten minutes…"

"What?"

He didn't answer. For a moment, they both just looked at each other in the dark. "Hell, I don't know. Don't worry. I'll be back."

Fifteen minutes later she was in a panic.

Okay, Lauren, get a grip. You've been in worse situations. Actually, she hadn't. She'd been on dozens of field surveys in the Arctic—in the summer. She'd never been in a situation quite like this.

A dozen horrible thoughts crossed her mind. What if he got turned around and couldn't find his way back? What if a polar bear got him? What if—

A figure appeared in the weakened beam of the Rolligon's headlights, and she knew right away it was Seth. "Thank God." She didn't wait for him to reach the vehicle. The wind hit her like a brick wall when she jumped from the cab and fought her way toward him on uneven ground.

"Wait here," he yelled into her ear when he reached her. He jogged to the Rolligon, pulled his duffel bag from the cab, switched off the vehicle's headlights, and rejoined her on the tundra. "Come on! It's just ahead."

What was just ahead?

He took her hand and she followed him, blindly. Ice shards beat against her jacket, winnowing inside her hood, stinging her face. She wasn't wearing down pants over her jeans, and in less than a couple of minutes her legs burned cold like nothing she'd ever felt before. Where on earth were they going? And how could he possibly see? Between the blowing snow and the darkness...

"Here it is!"

Shielding her eyes with a gloved hand, she peered ahead into the storm and saw the outline of a building. At first she thought her eyes were playing tricks on her, but they weren't. A few minutes later they were inside.

"Thank God," she breathed, and slumped into the first chair she stumbled past in the dark.

Seth lit a couple of emergency candles he found in a drawer, and the room was bathed in soft light.

"What is this place?"

"It's a lodge," he said, and walked the perimeter of the oblong space, taking inventory. "For hunting and fishing. It's owned by the village. Families use it in the summer."

It was little more than a Quanset hut, and nothing like the last "lodge" she'd weekended in. Crocker had commandeered one of Tiger's corporate jets and had flown them to an exclusive Canadian resort. The kind of place whose guest list included businessmen like Bill Gates and celebrities like Madonna.

Lauren unzipped her jacket and surveyed their spartan surroundings. Kitchen counters were bare. Metal-framed twin beds stood upright, stacked in a corner, their mattresses wrapped in plastic and rolled tight. The walls were decorated with last year's calendar, opened to the month of July, and photographs of smiling children holding up strings of fresh-caught fish.

She nodded at one of the pictures. "Arctic char?"

"Yeah." Seth stopped what he was doing and held a candle up to the photo. "How'd you know?"

She smiled at him, just so damned happy they were safe, out of the weather, and alive. "I know a lot of things. You'd be surprised."

He smiled back at her, remembering, she knew, his similar comment of a few days ago. "See if you can find us something to eat. I'm going outside to start the generator."

She shivered, and noticed their warm breath frosted the air no less than it had outside. "Sounds good to me."

"Back in five."

A few minutes of rummaging around in cupboards was rewarded with a half-dozen bags of English breakfast tea, some cling peaches and two cans of what was described as "man-pleasing" beef stew. Perfect.

Seth blew in with the wind, locked the door behind him and tossed his gloves onto the small kitchen table. "There's no fuel. Besides, it's too cold. Generator won't start."

"So...?" She didn't want to state the obvious. If there was no power, and it was nearly as cold inside as out...

"So we'll have to make do with the candles. At least we'll be warm." He shrugged out of his jacket and knelt beside what looked to her like a big metal box. She frowned at the fat pipe connecting it to the roof, then realized what it was.

"A propane heater!" she said.

"It'll be eighty in here in no time."

And it was.

A half hour later Seth carried their empty stew dishes to the sink. "That was great."

"Wait till breakfast," she said, moving to one of the twin beds they'd positioned next to the heater. "I fry up a mean can of Spam."

He laughed, and for the first time in days, she felt good. Safe. Relaxed. She curled her feet up under her on the bed and watched Seth's shadow move toward her across the room in the candlelight.

He handed her a cup of tea and sat beside her on the bed. "You okay?"

She nodded, breathing in the honeyed steam. "Now I am. Thank you for what you did. On the island, I mean. Thank you for getting me out."

"No problem." He smiled, then sipped at the hot tea. She was conscious of how big his hands were wrapped around the cup. She remembered those hands on her body, capable and strong.

As was he.

There was so much about him she didn't know, but deep inside herself where random thoughts and feelings, fears and desires spun in confusion, she knew enough.

His hair, usually tied back in a short ponytail, had come loose, and spilled in disarray across his shoulders. His skin glowed bronze in the candlelight and his eyes danced, dark and mysterious, sharpening her awareness of his Inuit bloodlines.

On impulse, she reached up and brushed a stray hank of jet hair from off his face. He sat motionless while she did it, his gaze pinned on hers. The moment stretched on, the silence between them ripe with awkward feelings, questions both unasked and unanswered.

"Lauren," he said, taking their cups and setting them on the floor beside the bed. "There's something I need to tell you."

He was close enough to her that she could smell him. Warm. Male. Both foreign and familiar. All she had to do was lean forward. That's all it would take. One small move on her part and their mouths would be joined, their tongues entwined, their hands groping each other's bodies in a frenzy, as they had that night on the island in the lab.

"Later," she said, her gaze moving to his full mouth, her hand inching across the bed toward his.

She made the move and kissed him, but what followed wasn't anything like what she'd expected. There was no frantic coupling of tongues or groping hands. He didn't even put his arms around her, and for a moment she thought she'd made a mistake.

"Are you sure?" he whispered against her lips.

The funny thing was, she *was* sure. More sure about this, about him, than she had been about anything in her life.

"Yes," she said, and pulled him gently down on top of her on the bed.

Candlelight reflected in his eyes. He snaked an arm around her waist and looked at her for a long moment. "Me, too," he said, and kissed her.

The room was warm, and they took their time undressing each other. He began with her sweater, one button at a time, and paused to look at her body in the knit turtleneck she wore underneath, before sliding his hand under the fabric to cup her breast.

"Oh, Seth."

"Mmm."

He kissed her again, more fervently this time, his fingers slipping into the cup of her bra, toying with her hardened nipple. She couldn't help her own sounds of pleasure and surprise, nor could she stop herself from wrapping her legs around his hips as he deepened their kiss and pressed his already hard body between her legs.

He pushed her top up, and with one hand managed the front clasp of her bra. Her breasts were bared to the warm air and his scrutiny, her nipples growing harder and tighter the longer he looked at them.

"You're beautiful," he said, and took one into his mouth.

She nearly came off the bed.

"Easy." He smiled up at her. "We've got all night."

All night.

In the Arctic in winter, the sun set each year on an evening in late December and didn't rise again for fifty-four days. Fifty-four days of night. She wondered what it would be like to spend a whole winter with Seth. A whole lifetime.

Her fingers tangled in his hair as he gently suckled her breasts, pausing frequently to look at her face. Not to gauge her clinical response, as Crocker did each time they had sex, but to connect with her, to share their pleasure by acknowledging it in each other's eyes, in his smile, or in the way he reached blindly for her hand and squeezed it.

She was stunned by how different he was from Crocker, who never wasted energy or time on things that didn't immediately propel her toward climax. Crocker prided himself on being able to bring her to completion in a matter of minutes. He was both expedient and skilled.

But that's all he was, she realized, as Seth paused to stroke her hair and trap her lips with his. There was no true passion, no emotion in the sex she'd had with Crocker. She gazed into Seth's dark eyes and knew her world was about to change irrevocably.

"You okay?" he asked.

He still had all his clothes on, and suddenly she felt an overpowering need to feel his skin hot against hers. She clawed at his shirt, pulling it out of his jeans and halfway up the smooth, muscled expanse of his back. He obliged her by rolling onto his side and pulling it over his head.

She responded in kind by shimmying out of her T-shirt and bra. His boots came next, hitting the wooden floor with a thud, followed by hers, then jeans, socks, his shorts and her panties. And then they were naked, breathless. Together.

She drank in the sight of him, brick-hard and smooth under her exploring fingers. His skin was naturally bronze, his nipples dark, the thatch of hair at his groin blue-black in the candlelight. "You're the one who's beautiful."

He laughed at that, then she laughed, too, feeling suddenly ridiculous. He didn't allow the feeling to last long. Her smile faded, her heartbeat quickened as they both studied the startling contrast of her pale skin against his.

His gaze traveled lazily along the soft curves of her body, pausing at the triangle of hair between her legs. He hadn't, as yet, touched her there, but already she felt herself moving precariously toward the edge.

Rolling back on top of her, he kissed her hard, his dark eyes sobering, his expression tightening as he moved against her. She opened her legs to let him in. He was more than ready. She was ready, too. Closing her eyes, she held her breath, clutched his shoulders and waited.

"Look at me," he said, and kissed her softly on the mouth. She obeyed, and was wholly unprepared for the raw emotion she read in his eyes. "I love you," he whispered, then drove himself inside her.

The breath rushed from her lungs with the shock of his invasion. He held himself in check, gave her time to recover, time to allow his words to sink in.

He was close to losing himself in her, but waited, searching her eyes for the words he didn't hear in return. Perhaps he was just a diversion for her, after all. One last fling before marrying Crocker Holt.

He didn't want to think about it. Not now. Not like this, with her naked and writhing beneath him, with him inside her, consumed by her heat, his passion for her driving him nearly to the edge of his control.

She began to move, and he with her. He lost himself in her, completely and without thought. He wasn't conscious of trying to pleasure her, or she him. They just did. They simply were.

Several times that night he brought her to the edge, and each time, before pushing her over, he paused, waited, their gazes locked, their lips a breath apart.

But he never heard the words from her, and he didn't say them again.

Chapter 15

He slept like the dead.

The first thing he saw when he opened his eyes was Lauren crouched beside his duffel, examining the geologist's rock hammer he'd pulled from the Dumpster on Caribou Island.

Her rock hammer.

Oh, Christ. He hadn't wanted her to find out like this. He'd wanted to prepare her, to preface the truth with some kind of explanation.

She rose stiffly, the weapon in hand, and turned toward him as he sat up in the narrow bed. "There was something you were going to tell me." Her voice was thin, shaky, her face pale.

"Yeah."

She glanced at his Glock on the floor next to the bed, then ran her hand over the dried blood on the hammer. "But it's not what I think, right?"

Her question was really a plea, the stunned look in her eyes begging him to deliver the answer she wanted to hear.

He felt like a jerk to have put her through all this, to have lied to her—to have kept lying, even last night.

It was time to come clean.

"That's right." He nodded and slowly swiveled his legs to the floor.

She stepped back, toward the door, unconsciously raising the hammer in a posture of protection. She looked so small standing there, swimming in his thermal shirt. She must have put it on when she got up. The arms were too long for her, and she pushed nervously at the sleeves.

"Listen to me, Lauren. I found your hammer in the Dumpster behind the kitchen. And you're right, that's probably Paddy's blood."

She took another step back, her eyes locked on his.

"It's evidence, in fact, and you shouldn't be handling it." He nodded toward the paper sack on the floor. "Put it back in the bag."

"It's…why you thought I did it. You thought that I killed Paddy."

"At first, maybe, but not now." Very, very slowly he rose from the bed. Lauren froze in place. "Why don't we put it away," he said, and offered her his open palm.

"It's not you." Her voice was a whisper now. She shook her head, and kept shaking it, as if trying to convince herself. "After last night, after everything…" She took another step back and bumped up against the table with a start.

"It's not me," he said with conviction, willing her to hold his gaze while he moved toward her. "You know it's not."

The candlelight was bright enough so that he could see the change wash over her features. Visibly she exhaled and set the hammer on the table behind her. A second later she was in his arms.

"Seth." She clutched at his shoulders, burying her face in his chest. "I looked in your bag for something clean to put on. When I found the hammer, I—" he kissed her, reveling in the feel of her warm body against his "—I didn't know what to think."

"Come back to bed. It's cold." He led her back to the narrow bed, and they slid between the army-surplus blankets. He held her for a minute, stroking her hair, breathing in the scent of their lovemaking, still warm on her skin and his, wanting to make love to her again, knowing it wasn't possible. Not now. Maybe not ever.

He had to tell her, but didn't know how to begin. Last night had been incredible. She was incredible. When he'd told her he loved her, he'd meant it.

"So Paddy was murdered, after all." She gave him the opening he needed.

"Looks that way."

"Salvio did it."

He still wasn't sure if it was Salvio or Tweedle Dee and Tweedle Dum, as he'd come to think of the two roustabouts Pinkie and Bulldog. "Why do you think it was Salvio?"

"I found the liner of Paddy's hard hat in his room."

"What?" He turned awkwardly in the small bed so he could see her face. "You were in his room?"

She nodded. "I remembered that the liner wasn't in Paddy's hard hat when you returned it that day in Salvio's office." She was right. It was missing, and he'd thought it damned suspicious at the time. "I found it in Salvio's closet. When he caught me in his room he—"

"He caught you? Christ, Lauren! What happened? What did he do?" If that son of a bitch had so much as touched her...

"That's when he sent me out to the warehouse. To where you were."

His arms slid around her and he pulled her tight against him. A dozen odd events over the past couple of days—a look here, a comment there—all of it began to make sense to him.

"He did want me dead," she continued. "I've been

thinking about what happened out there, and you were right."

"We're out, now. You're safe."

"I was confused at first, because after Paddy's murder Salvio wanted to shut the whole operation down ASAP."

He knew where she was going with this. "If he was the killer, he wouldn't have wanted to draw attention to the murder. If he had shut the whole thing down, the island would've been crawling with cops in no time, if the weather had obliged."

"Exactly." She turned in his arms. "But don't you see? Salvio knew I'd never consent to the shutdown. He played me, Seth. He made *me* out to be the bad guy, the one who wanted to keep drilling after Paddy was dead."

She was right. He could see it now, though one thing still didn't fit. Why, if he didn't want to cause a stink, did Salvio send Paddy's body back to town on that chopper? "Yeah," he said, distracted by the paradox. "I think that's exactly what he did."

"He knew how dedicated I was to the job. That I wouldn't let anything get in the way of Tiger's success. My success." Her voice was laced with bitterness and self-censure. "Salvio knew me better than I knew myself."

She threw back the blankets and sat up, rubbing her temples, cradling her head in her hands.

"It's over now. Lie down." He coaxed her back under the covers.

"*Why* was Paddy murdered? Why, Seth?"

"He knew too much. Maybe he was ready to blow the whistle."

"Blow the whistle on *what?*"

He couldn't see keeping it from her any longer. He looked at her, burning into his mind the memory of last night, the passion in her eyes, the tenderness and trust he saw there now. In a moment it would be gone. Vanished. As if what they'd shared had never happened.

Get it over with, Adams.

"What, Seth? Tell me."

"The FBI suspects that someone at Tiger, someone high in the organization, is secretly selling Tiger's proprietary geologic data to a foreign interest."

"What?" She sat up in bed, and he moved with her.

He told her the name of the foreign oil company, and she knew it. She was familiar with the lucrative oil tracts the company had won in Alaska in last year's federal land lease. Tiger had bid on adjacent tracts. Both companies had scored big time, and now held billions of dollars in oil reserves.

"That still wouldn't explain the samples."

"What samples?"

"Of course! That's what all this is about. When I first arrived on the island, there was a crate of unmarked rock samples outside my trailer. All they had on them was the date—a week ago Tuesday, before the crew change. When Salvio found out I had them, he went crazy. He confiscated them. Later they were inadvertently destroyed."

"So...?" Seth didn't get it.

"Don't you see? Those samples weren't from Caribou Island. They were from somewhere else. But where?"

"Are you sure?"

"Yes. Positive. I hid one of them in my trailer before Salvio took the crate. I didn't think he realized I had it, but—" she shrugged "—I guess he figured it out."

"Which is why he had your trailer ransacked." So many things he hadn't understood before made sense to him now.

"Yes. He was looking for it."

"Lauren, why didn't you tell me?"

"He didn't find it. It's still there, right where I hid it, in a box of tampons in the bathroom."

He remembered the afternoon they discovered the trailer had been searched, how she ran to the bathroom in a panic. He'd thought... Hell, how much more hadn't she told him?

"That's what you wanted to get before we left the island. That sample."

She nodded. "Yes."

"So maybe Caribou Island has nothing to do with all this. Maybe it's the other samples that are important, that were going to be sold."

She looked at him, but didn't see him. She continued to nod, her eyes unfocused, as if she was looking right through him. "Yes, I think you're right."

He told her the rest of what he knew about the case, leaving out his own role in the undercover operation. The funny thing was, she didn't seem all that surprised. As he talked, she stared blankly into near space, her mind working, a manicured fingernail tapping rhythmically on the edge of the metal bed frame.

"Salvio's the kingpin here in the field—I'm sure of that, now—both on last year's operation and this one." Though it wasn't clear now what this year's operation actually was.

If Lauren was right, and those other samples were the contraband goods in question, and if they hadn't come from Caribou Island, then...

"Pinkie and Bulldog are in on it with him, aren't they?"

"Yeah," he said absently, still trying to figure it out. There were too many pieces still missing. "They worked for Altex, but Salvio owned them."

"And Paddy's involvement?"

"He was probably pressured into it, into whatever scam they're running out here. Altex isn't exactly a picture of financial health. It would have been dead easy to coerce him."

"Oh, God." Her expression mirrored a sudden realization.

"What?"

She turned to him and grasped his hands, gripped them tightly in hers as she spoke. "When I first arrived on the island, Paddy was desperate to see me alone. I've never seen him so agitated. He was probably going to warn me.''

"Did he know, beforehand, that you were the geologist assigned to the well?''

"No. No one knew. It was a last-minute substitution.''

"Maybe he was willing to go along with things until he found out you would be involved and be in danger.''

She nodded. "That makes sense. Paddy's known me since I was a child. He would have been protective.'' Her eyes filmed. "It's my fault he's dead.''

Seth slipped an arm around her, pulling her close. "Don't think like that. It's not your fault. If anything it's...''

As his voice trailed off, she looked up at him, swiping a hand across her eyes. Her brow furrowed. "How do you know all this, Seth?''

It was time to tell her. He met her gaze and sucked in a breath. "My father was the one who tipped the Feds to the shenanigans with that foreign oil company last year.''

"Your father?'' She looked more confused than ever.

"Yeah. He's a big shot in the industry. Corporate wheeling and dealing, stock swaps, negotiating deals between oil companies and government agencies—that kind of thing.''

Her eyes widened. "You mean *Jeremy* Adams? Your father is *that* Adams?'' Her mouth gaped in astonishment.

"Yeah.''

He didn't have to say another word. Everyone in the business knew who Jeremy Adams was. Hell, for all he knew, Lauren might even know him personally. For sure Holt knew him. Money Man ran in exactly the kinds of circles that...

"It's Holt,'' he said suddenly.

"What?''

All of Tiger's VPs were on the Bureau's short list of suspects, but Seth had discounted Crocker Holt from the beginning because he, out of all of them, seemed to have no motive. He was already rich as Midas, and held prestigious positions in banking, the oil business and, socially, the upper crusts of society Lauren was raised in.

"Crocker Holt. He's the one selling out Tiger."

"That's crazy! I thought you said Salvio was the ring-leader."

Seth's head was spinning, trying to piece together the details, everything he knew about Holt. "He is. Here in the field. Collecting the data and samples to be sold. But Jack Salvio doesn't have the connections or resources to broker secret deals with foreign interests."

He still hadn't figured out how Salvio, a guy with no geologic training, would know which data was important and which was useless. But he would, and soon. Maybe they used an outside lab to analyze the rock samples. It would be risky, but it could be done.

"No, you're right, Jack doesn't have those kinds of con-tacts. But Crocker?" She shot to her feet. "He would never do anything like that. Never. You don't know him. He's the most honest, upstanding—"

"You sure?" Most white-collar crooks were already big shots, he reminded himself. It wouldn't be out of character at all for a guy like Holt.

Then again, maybe he just wanted to believe it was her fiancé. That would be damned convenient, wouldn't it? It would wipe Holt right out of the picture. The picture being Lauren and him.

"Crocker would never lie to me. If he was involved in something like this and didn't tell me, it would be just like lying." Nervously, she twisted the diamond engagement ring on her finger. Candlelight shattered in fiery brilliance against the stone. "If you love someone, if you're going to marry them, you don't lie to them, Seth."

Years ago at the Academy, he was kicked in the gut by an instructor as part of his self-defense training. Her words had exactly the same effect on him.

"Lauren, there's something else I need to tell you." He reached for her hand, but she wasn't listening.

She paced the floor, barefoot, chewing at her bottom lip. He watched her mind working. She was thinking about the possibility. About Holt. What it would mean if he was the one the Feds were after.

Suddenly he felt strange.

Something was different. Not right. He'd been so focused on Lauren from the moment he woke up, he hadn't even noticed. "The wind," he said, and shot to his feet.

Lauren froze in place. "Oh, my God."

Metal shutters covered the few windows in the lodge from the view outside. They couldn't see, but they could hear.

Nothing. Not a breath of wind.

Seth reached for his shorts.

Lauren moved toward the door, but before she could yank it open, he grabbed her arm.

"Wait! Listen." He'd thought he heard something, far off in the distance, but maybe it was just his imagin—

A buzzing sound cut the silence.

"I hear it," she said.

"Snowmobile." He moved quickly to the bed and retrieved his Glock from the floor.

Lauren followed. "What do we do?"

"Stay behind me. Understand?"

She nodded, her face tight with fear.

"It'll be all right. Trust me." He brushed a kiss lightly across her lips.

Her gaze locked on his. "I do trust you." She forced a smile.

He wanted to tell her everything, right then and there. But mostly, he wanted to tell her again that he loved her. As crazy as it sounded, he did, he was sure of it—and he wanted her to believe it. To love him back. To forget Crocker Holt, whether he was a criminal or not.

But there wasn't time.

The high-pitched buzzing of the snowmobile's engine grew louder, closer. Seth moved quickly toward the door, pulling Lauren with him. Abruptly the engine cut off. Footfalls crunched in the dry snow outside.

Seth looked at her hard, put a finger to his lips, gesturing for her to be quiet. Lauren nodded compliance. He moved her behind him, behind the door, his eyes riveted to the dead bolt lock, his gun leveled chest-high.

The knock startled them both. Three dull raps with a gloved fist. He heard Lauren suck in a breath behind him. He went statue-still, his trigger finger poised, ready for whatever came next.

What did, surprised the hell out of him.

It was the sound of a key fitting snugly into the lock. Seth backed up, crushing Lauren to the wall behind them, shielding her body with his. "Don't move," he breathed.

He felt her hands trembling against his back, the weight of her breasts as she gulped in air. The dead bolt turned with a crisp click, and Lauren gasped.

Cold air hit him like a wall as the door swung inward. A hooded figure stepped into the room, his breath frosting the air. Seth pressed his gun against the man's temple before his mind processed the familiar emblem on the standard-issue jacket he wore. "What the—?"

Lauren let out a strangled cry.

The man turned.

Seth exhaled in relief, lowering his gun as he recognized the crooked smile and those dark, boyish features.

"Hey, Chief." The crooked smile broadened as he took in the situation: the twin bed, slept in, their clothes in a pile on the floor, Seth standing there in his shorts, and Lauren peeking out from behind him, naked except for his shirt.

"Christ, Danny, I almost shot you."

"Nah, you wouldn't do that." He tipped his hood back, his gaze washing over Lauren as she moved from behind the shelter of Seth's body. "Danny Chilit, ma'am. Pleased to meet you."

Turning his attention back to Seth, he said, "Heard somebody on the radio last night. Thought it might be you. Buzzed up here to check it out."

"Chief?" Lauren said, her gaze zeroing in on the North Slope Borough law enforcement emblem on the officer's jacket.

Seth didn't want her to find out like this. He'd wanted to tell her himself. She looked up at him, silent, her mouth open, her brows arched not in question—because she already knew the answer—but in dazed realization of who and what he was.

Danny cocked that crooked smile at her again. "That's right." He jutted his chin at Seth. "Chief of Police Adams, Kachelik Outpost, North Slope Borough. He's the man."

"Yes," she said, nodding slowly, her eyes glazed hard as the two-carat stone on her finger.

Seth felt that gut-busting kick again, and wished to God he could relive the past half hour.

"I'm beginning to think he's a lot of things."

Chapter 16

"You used me."

Lauren marched toward the snowmobile idling in front of the lodge. Behind her she heard the snow crunch under Seth's boots as he jogged after her.

"Lauren."

"Save it," she said, and stopped in front of the vehicle, breathing hard, not from exertion, but raw anger, which she hadn't been able to contain the past half hour since discovering Seth's little masquerade.

Danny Chilit, *Officer* Chilit, was busy inside the lodge, securing it for the duration of the winter. The decal on the snowmobile he'd arrived on matched the patch sewn onto the sleeve of his law-enforcement-issue survival jacket—North Slope Borough Police Department.

Her anger burned so hot, she was certain if she stood in one place long enough, the ice beneath her boots would simply melt.

"I tried to tell you." Seth grasped her shoulders and spun her toward him.

"Let go of me!"

"I wanted to tell you, days ago, but I couldn't. How could I, Lauren? It was an undercover job."

"For the FBI." She wrestled out of his grasp. "So you've said."

"Lauren, it's my job. I'm a cop."

She snorted. It was unladylike, but she didn't care. "It *was* a stretch believing Jeremy Adams's son was just a roughneck. I should have known, right then and there, that you were lying."

"I wasn't lying. I was…"

"No?" She glared at him. "What would you call it, then?"

He exhaled loudly, his breath crystallizing on the air. The sky was dark all around them, and the wind was picking up again. They had to get out of there fast before conditions deteriorated. She glanced at the snowmobile, wondering how the three of them were going to manage the six-mile trip in to Kachelik.

"It was just another case, an assignment. That's all." He gestured for her to get on.

"Oh, I see. An *assignment*. Is that what I was, too? Is that what last night was?" She stepped onto the running board, threw a leg over the seat, and promptly lost her footing.

Seth was there in an instant, his arms circling her. Before she could stop him, he lifted her off her feet.

"Put me down!"

"No." He pulled her tight against him, and angled her chin upward with a gloved hand. "Listen to me."

"I'm done listening. Unless, of course, you've got some other choice lies to add to last night's pièce de résistance."

The startled look in his eyes told her he knew exactly what she meant. "What I said to you last night…"

She struggled against him, but he wouldn't let her go.

"I meant it, Lauren."

For a millisecond she allowed herself to remember his face when he'd said it, the feel of him inside her, the joy and confusion, the visceral ache when she'd heard his words.

I love you.

For a split second their gazes locked, and she knew he was remembering, too. And then the moment passed.

"Oh, right. And if I buy that, next you'll want to sell me some land in Florida."

"Stop it." He dumped her onto the seat of the snowmobile and ran a gloved hand through his hair.

It had to be at least thirty below. Both of them were breathing hard now, their breath frosting the air. His cheeks were ruddy from cold, and probably frustration, but that wasn't her problem.

"All set," Danny said, and jogged over to join them. One look at their faces, and his expression sobered. "Uh, you two need a minute?"

"No. We don't." Lauren scooted to the back of the narrow snowmobile's seat and waited. "Let's get this over with. I have people to call, places to be. And one of them isn't here."

"Yes, ma'am." Danny positioned himself in front of her, gloved hands on the controls, and nodded at Seth. "Chief?"

Chief.

There it was again. That subtle reminder that everything he'd made himself out to be, all that he'd said to her, her trust in him, what they'd shared...all of it was lies.

"Move up," Seth said, and gestured for her to slide to the middle of the seat.

"No way." Hell could freeze first before she'd allow herself to be sandwiched in between the two of them.

Seth didn't give her a choice. He simply got behind her and forcibly slid her forward on the seat.

She swore.

Danny laughed, and she was tempted to slap him. It

would have been difficult given that they were all in survival gear, hoods cinched tight and gloved hands about as dexterous as elephant's feet.

Seth slid up behind her on the seat, jamming her in so tightly she couldn't move. "Let's do it," he said.

Danny engaged the transmission.

It was the most uncomfortable half hour of her life.

They bumped along the tundra, and Lauren held on to the officer for dear life. Seth pressed closer, shielding her from wind so frigid it cut like a razor on contact with her skin. His thighs cradled hers, and she could feel his heat behind her.

Every moment of their lovemaking replayed in her mind on that six-mile trip. When she closed her eyes she saw him naked, his body bathed in soft light, dark eyes trained on hers. His smile, his touch, the smell of him lingering on her skin. She could still taste him—salty, hot, smooth and hard against her tongue.

They bounced over a hard-packed snowdrift onto a trail, and she was jolted back to the present.

Don't do this, Lauren. Don't talk yourself into believing last night was something it wasn't.

She didn't want to think about it. She couldn't. What a fool she'd been. For a week they'd danced around the mad attraction that had been there from the beginning, and last night she'd finally succumbed. She'd allowed him to get close to her, to know things about her no one else knew.

But it wasn't about her, she reminded herself.

It was about the case. His *assignment*.

And to think she'd questioned her upcoming marriage, her career at Tiger, her goals in life—all because she'd been lied to by a borough cop masquerading as a roughneck. A law enforcement officer who'd come to Caribou Island for just one purpose—to know her, seduce her if that's what it took to get her to trust him—solely to get the information he needed to crack the FBI's case.

"Hey," Danny yelled over his shoulder.

"Oh, sorry." She realized she'd been gripping the arms of the officer's jacket so tightly, she was dragging him backward.

"Almost there," Seth shouted over the buzzing of the snowmobile's engine.

The twinkling lights of the tiny village of Kachelik were exactly as she remembered them. A bittersweet pain clutched at her heart as she recalled the first time her father had brought her here. So long ago.

It seemed like yesterday.

Though it was nearly noon, hardly any natural light bled from the southern horizon through the ice fog and lightly blowing snow. Large sodium lights attached to poles, like the ones on Caribou Island, lit their approach.

After a moment, a small airstrip came into view on their right. It was nothing much to speak of: a couple of Quanset huts, an old North Slope Borough chopper, and a handful of privately owned ski planes.

The officer slowed the snowmobile into a turn, and ahead Lauren made out a green Jeep Cherokee sporting a police department emblem parked in front of one of the buildings. They pulled up alongside it, and the deputy cut the engine.

"Thank God."

"Thank Officer Chilit," Seth said, as he slid off the seat and offered her a hand.

She ignored it, and turned to Danny. "I really appreciate you coming to get us. I'll see to it that Tiger Petroleum pays you for your time, and for the gas."

"The borough pays me for that. Besides, it's my job to keep this guy out of trouble." The officer's smile cracked into a mischievous grin as he tossed Seth a set of car keys. "Looks like this time I was too late."

Seth shot him one of those stony I'll-talk-to-you-later looks. Lauren was embarrassed.

"Head on in to the station, why don'tcha?" Danny said,

ignoring their reactions. "Coffee's hot, and there's a stack of paperwork a mile high needs signing on your desk."

"You're not coming?"

"I'll catch up. I wanna do a once-over on the chopper before the weather goes to hell again." He nodded at the ancient borough helicopter tied down on the ice by one of the hangars. "That wreck a couple of days ago spooked me."

"What wreck?"

"Some chopper outta Deadhorse. Went down in the storm twenty miles off Caribou Island."

Lauren snapped to attention.

"Anybody hurt?" Seth asked.

"One guy dead, fried to a crisp in the wreckage. Must have been some crash. Surprised you didn't hear about it."

"Communications were down on the island. We've been in the dark for more than a week."

"Yeah, but he was one of yours. From 13-E, I mean. They found his wallet in the wreckage. Driver's license still intact."

Lauren knew what was coming, even before the officer said his name. Her stomach did a slow roll.

"Name's Paddy O'Connor. That old guy who owned Altex Drilling. Wonder what'll happen to the company now that he's dead?"

"Oh, my God." Lauren put a gloved hand over her mouth to stop the scream welling up inside her.

"And the pilot?" Seth said evenly.

"That's the funny thing. Wasn't a sign of him in the wreckage. He just...vanished."

Lauren's gaze cut to Seth.

"Yeah," he said, nodding. "Funny is right."

She closed her eyes and swallowed hard, felt herself sway on her feet. For days she'd wondered why Salvio was hell-bent on sending Paddy's body back to town if he was the one responsible for the murder. It hadn't made sense. She

knew, now, that Salvio had never intended for the body—
or her—to arrive safely. She blinked her eyes, unable to
focus.

If she'd gotten on that chopper she'd be...

"Come on." Seth grabbed her arm to steady her, guiding
her toward the Jeep. "Let's get you inside, and get you
something hot to drink."

A hot brandy. A big one, she thought, as he tucked her
into the vehicle and closed the door.

A second after Seth had ushered her into his office—a
functional space in a prefab metal building housing the police department, the single-engine fire department, and a
small jail—Lauren reached for the phone.

Seth's hand closed over hers. "Not so fast."

"I need to call in to Tiger."

"I can't let you do that, Lauren."

"Are the phones out here, too?"

The weather wasn't nearly as bad here as it had been on
the island. Besides, she would have thought a borough fa-
cility like this one would have a telecommunications system
able to handle almost any conditions.

"No. I suspect they're working fine. I just can't let you
call in."

"You're kidding, right?"

His expression was as hard as she'd ever seen it. "No,
I'm not."

She made a derisive sound in the back of her throat, and
snatched her hand from under his. "What, am I under ar-
rest?"

"No. But I want to think about this first."

"Think about what? I need to call my boss. I need to call
Crocker. Tell them what's happened."

"No way."

"Why not?" Again she reached for the phone. "Even
prisoners get one phone call. Is that what I am, *Chief?* A

prisoner?'' She tipped her chin at him and steeled herself for his response.

"You're not a prisoner, or a suspect. But any move you make now could compromise the Bureau's investigation."

"Oh, right. The investigation. Your job."

"That's right."

He didn't try to stop her this time when she jerked the receiver from its cradle. At least not physically. As she punched in the numbers to Bill Walters's office in Anchorage, Seth slid a hip onto the edge of the cluttered desk and leaned toward her.

"That sat-comm system on the island was operational all the time," he said.

"What are you talking about?"

The call connected and her boss's phone in Anchorage a thousand miles away started to ring.

"It was rigged to work when Salvio needed it to work, like every morning when he faxed in his reports—and yours."

"What?"

A recorded message came on informing her that Bill Walters's number was out of service. Absently, she placed the receiver back on the hook.

"What do you mean he faxed them in?"

"I saw the reports in his desk drawer. Each one had a confirmation report stapled to it. I'm guessing that back at Tiger Petroleum they thought everything on Caribou Island was business as usual."

She thought about it for a minute, and wondered if he could be right. "But how could they think that? The chopper crash, Paddy's body. Surely they'd know—"

"Nothing about what really happened. Not yet, anyway. Salvio's made sure of that."

She nodded. "I get it. The only people who suspect Paddy's death was anything other than an accident—and now they think it's a chopper accident—are you and me."

"And we're supposed to be dead."

She'd forgotten about that. "Salvio will know by now that we're not."

"And he'll be doing everything possible to cover his tracks. See why I don't want you calling in?"

"Because Salvio would have already called in—to his partner at Tiger. Whoever that is." She refused to believe it was Crocker. It couldn't be. It just couldn't.

"Yeah. And filled him in on you and me, and how much we know about what's really going on."

An idea formed in her mind. "That means anyone who's innocent, who thinks things *are* business as usual on Caribou Island, wouldn't think anything of me calling in. See where I'm going?"

"Yeah." She watched him think it through.

"Wait a minute. Why did I get a recording when I called my boss's number?"

"You got a recording?"

"Of course! Last week all the executives got new phone exchanges. Bill's number, Crocker's, too, would have been changed."

She fished the forgotten scrap of paper out of her cardigan pocket. Thank God she still had it. "I found this in the pocket of Salvio's jeans when I searched his room." She handed him the paper with the unfamiliar phone number scrawled across it in blue ink.

Seth reached for the phone.

"No, wait!"

He paused, his hand on the receiver.

"Let me. Please."

If it *was* Crocker who was the ringleader of this whole ugly caper, she needed to find out for herself. To hear his voice. To make the leap, which, right now, seemed so impossible.

"Okay, but don't say anything. As soon as you recognize the voice, we hang up."

She nodded, her hand shaking as she took the scrap of paper from him. She punched in the numbers and held her breath. Seth leaned in close to listen. She felt his heat against her shoulder, his arm brush against hers.

The call connected. There was a lot of static, and both of them glanced outside at the blowing snow. The sound of the wind provided an eerie backdrop to the shrill ringing on the other end of the line.

"Walters," the gravelly voice said.

"Oh, God," Lauren breathed. Seth tried to grab the receiver from her, but she held on tight.

"Lauren? Is that you? Where are you?"

Seth depressed the hook and the connection was lost.

"I can't believe it. He's such a nice man. Bill Walters is the last person on earth, besides Crocker, I would have thought…" She slumped into the chair behind Seth's desk, and stared blindly out the window. "What do we do now?"

"Nothing—yet. I've got to be sure it's him. If Walters isn't involved, he wouldn't have been so surprised to hear your voice. He wouldn't have asked—"

"Where I was." She nodded. "He knew I wasn't on the island. He knew because Jack Salvio told him."

"Come on. Let's get out of here and get something to eat, some rest."

"Don't you need to—" she nodded at the phone "—call someone? The FBI?"

He shook his head. "No. I want to think it through first. Make sure I'm right."

"I'm calling Crocker."

"No." He grabbed the phone and set it out of her reach. "You've got to promise me you won't call him, or anyone. Not yet. Promise me, Lauren."

She met his gaze and tried to fathom what was reflected back at her in his dark eyes. She couldn't. "All right. I promise."

"Good. Let's go."

"Where?"

"My place. It's just a few blocks."

She drew a breath and stood up, her head throbbing from the events of the past two days, the past two hours, last night. "No." She had to distance herself from him, get a grip. Put her life back in perspective. "Isn't there a hotel somewhere I could check into?"

"The closest one's in Deadhorse, a hundred and fifty miles from here." It might as well have been a thousand. "It's my place or nothing."

His place was a complete surprise.

As she stood in his living room and he built a fire in the fireplace, she studied the sturdy, high-quality furniture: comfortable sofa, hand-carved table, a big, squashy chair with matching ottoman. Deep impressions in the seat cushion, along with a stack of books and mismatched, half-full coffee cups on the floor next to the chair, told her he spent a lot of time in this room, reading and listening to music.

Solitary time.

She glanced at the eclectic mix of CDs scattered across the coffee table, then smiled as her gaze lit on a couple of ragged chew toys wedged between the cushions of the sofa.

"Where's Amaguq?" she asked, remembering the animation in his voice when he'd told her about his dog.

"At my mom's. I'll pick him up when all this is over."

On a side table she spied a copy of *Business Week,* open to a full-page article on oil financier Jeremy Adams, Seth's father. He caught her glancing at it, frowned, then tossed the magazine onto the crackling fire along with a handful of kindling.

"Tell me about him," she said.

"Who?"

"Your father."

His face hardened. "There's nothing to tell. We don't see each other."

She wondered why that was, but knew better than to probe deeper. Besides, she didn't want to know any more about him than she already did. She didn't even know if what he'd already told her about himself was true. She didn't know and she didn't care. And that's the way she meant to keep it.

She focused on the objects in the room. Padding across the thick, handmade carpet covering old hardwood floorboards, she marveled at the workmanship that had gone into the traditional Inuit design.

"Danny's grandmother made that rug for me."

She glanced up at him, surprised. "It's beautiful."

The room was decidedly warm, and not simply because he'd built a fire. Buttery-colored walls were graced with native artifacts and limited-edition prints, mostly Alaskan landscapes and wildlife. Rows of books—lots of them college texts—flanked the old-fashioned double doors leading into the small dining room where a desk and late-model computer fought for space with a rough-hewn dining room table and sturdy chairs.

It was a man's domain, but not like any man she'd ever known. There was no trace of cold steel, glass or black leather that seemed to be the unifying force in every room of Crocker's San Francisco condo.

Crocker.

She vacillated between wanting desperately to call him, to reconnect with him and reground herself, and wanting to push him from her mind altogether.

Pictures of Seth's family and friends, packed onto the cluttered surface of a sideboard against the wall, drew her attention, and all thoughts of Crocker vanished.

She recognized the smile of a much younger Seth in one of the photos. He and a couple of other guys—one white, one native—stood grinning, on what looked like a frozen pond. They were in hockey uniforms emblazoned with the name of the village. Mirth danced in his eyes. She smiled unconsciously, then caught herself.

"Hungry?"

She realized with a start that he was standing right behind her.

"Not really. Just tired."

He tried to take her hand, but she wouldn't let him and turned away. "Don't."

"We need to talk about last night."

"I told you. I don't want to discuss it. I just want to forget it."

She felt him move up behind her. She closed her eyes and tried not to be affected by his familiar scent, his warm breath ruffling her hair.

"I'll never forget it," he whispered. "And I don't think you will, either. Even if you are still planning to marry that guy."

She turned on him. "What are you talking about? Of course I'm still planning to marry him. Why wouldn't I be?"

"I just thought…maybe…"

"Maybe what? That once I calmed down, I would change my mind. Not likely." She put distance between them. "I told you, I have a life, a career. It's all planned out, and it's nothing like—"

Her gaze darted across the objects in the room, the cozy fire, the photos, the books—all the things that told her she was in his world now, not hers, and completely out of her element.

Or was she?

"Like this place?" He picked up the coffee cups from the floor, juggling them awkwardly. Cold coffee splashed from one of them onto the rug.

"That's right."

"I like it here, and I like the village," he said, anger

flashing in his eyes. "I grew up here. I liked it then, I like it now."

"So do I."

He made a sarcastic sound.

"I mean, I did like it, when I was here with my father."

"That was a long time ago. You were a different person then. A kid."

She was a grown woman now, living in a world completely unlike the one he lived in. But was she so different? Was she really?

The phone rang, interrupting her thoughts and their conversation. She relieved him of the coffee cups so he could answer it, and bussed them into the kitchen to give him some privacy for the call.

A minute later he joined her. "Look, we're both tired. Why don't we just get some sleep?"

"Fine. Got a guest room?"

"Down the hall." He cocked his head toward the darkened hallway. "First door on the right. There's only one bathroom. On the left."

"Thanks," she said, and moved past him. "I'm dying for a shower."

He reached out and grasped her hand.

Her breath caught, and she stopped. Rigid. Waiting.

For a long moment he didn't say anything. They stood there silently, the ticking of the old-fashioned kitchen wall clock and the howling of the wind outside the only sounds.

"Last night had nothing to do with the FBI's case, or my job."

She stiffened in his grasp.

"Whatever happens, Lauren, I just want you to know that."

Chapter 17

When she woke up the next morning Seth was gone.

Lauren showered and dressed in the same jeans she'd been wearing for the past three days. Last night, she'd rinsed out her bra and panties in Seth's bathroom sink, and had hung them to dry over the tub.

This morning she'd discovered them folded neatly on top of her jeans, along with a clean flannel shirt and pair of socks. His, she realized, when she put them on and found herself swimming in them.

His doing something as simple as putting a pot of coffee on before he'd left the house, or making sure she had something clean to wear, caused a stab of regret to pierce the emotional armor she'd donned to keep him out of her heart.

She poured herself a cup of the coffee and read the note he'd left for her on the kitchen table.

Be back around ten. Wait for me. Seth.

Maybe she'd overreacted yesterday when she found out who he really was. Maybe she'd owed him the benefit of the doubt when he'd said last night that what had happened between them had nothing to do with his assignment or the FBI's case.

Maybe. Maybe not.

She stared at the yellow phone on the wall next to the refrigerator, and thought about what she would say to Crocker if she called him now. She'd promised Seth she wouldn't.

Her hand was on the receiver. Her heartbeat accelerated. She was just about to dial his pager, when the kitchen door opened behind her.

"Hello?"

Lauren slapped the receiver onto the hook and turned toward the unfamiliar voice. An Inuit woman wearing a fur-trimmed parka and carrying something bulky, wrapped in a dish towel, blew through the open doorway on a blast of icy air and blowing snow.

The woman fought the door closed behind her with a grunt, then smiled. "You're Lauren."

"Uh, yes." How on earth did the woman know her name? "Um, that door wasn't locked?"

"Nobody bothers. Not in the village."

"Oh." In her whole life Lauren had never lived anywhere where it was safe to leave your front door unlocked.

She and the woman looked at each other for a few seconds, the woman not missing the fact that Lauren was dressed in what was obviously Seth's shirt.

"And you are…?" Lauren prompted.

"Violet. Violet Adams. Seth's—"

"Mother." Lauren realized that this was the same woman she'd seen in some of the pictures scattered on the sideboard in Seth's living room.

"That's right." The woman smiled. "How did you know?"

She was about to mention the pictures, but what came out of her mouth instead was an observation. "He looks a lot like you."

Her smiled broadened, highlighting laugh lines that made her round face look unusually beautiful. She must have been in her mid-fifties at least, but she didn't look it.

"He has my eyes."

"He does," she said, marveling at how dark they were, exactly like Seth's.

The older woman shrugged off her parka and pushed a strand of salt-and-pepper hair out of her face. "I smell coffee," she said, unwrapping the dish towel, which she'd set on the table.

"Seth made it, before he left this morning. But…how did you know my name?"

"He stopped at my house this morning on his way to the school. He told me all about you."

"Did he?"

"Well, not everything." Her dark eyes washed over the long tail of Seth's flannel shirt. Lauren realized she was twisting it nervously in her hands. "But some things a mother knows."

Lauren felt her face grow hot. She turned to the coffee pot, embarrassed, and searched for another cup. "It's not what you think. I mean, we're not…"

"Nice ring," Violet said.

Lauren went statue-still, her left hand poised on a cup on the top shelf of the cabinet. Her diamond shone dully under the overheard kitchen light. "Uh, thanks."

"I brought sweet rolls—homemade. Sit down, have one."

Feeling incredibly awkward, Lauren poured Seth's mother a cup of coffee and joined her at the table. The sweet rolls were still warm, and smelled delicious.

"You made these yourself?"

"Sure." Violet handed her one on a napkin.

Lauren tried to remember the last time her own mother had made her something to eat. She couldn't. All the meals at the Fotheringay house were prepared by a cook. Even before her father died, her mother hadn't cooked much. She'd said cooking was for people who couldn't afford to eat out.

When Lauren was a child and was asked to join in school bake sales or potlucks, her mother had always provided something store-bought. Later, after her mother remarried, there hadn't been any more bake sales, and potlucks were out of the question. The private schools Lauren attended simply didn't have them.

"This is delicious," she said as she wiped a bit of frosting from her cheek. "God, it's the best thing I've eaten in…" She laughed. "I don't know. A long time."

"Good." Violet nodded, pleased by her enthusiasm.

"You said Seth went to the school. The village school?"

"Yes. He said the principal called him last night, wanted him to speak to the kids about the weather and safety—what to do if they got into trouble in the storm."

Lauren recalled with a shudder their own experience on the open tundra the past thirty-six hours. "Well, he's the right man to talk to them, that's for sure. I wouldn't be here, if it wasn't for him. I'd be…"

She stopped and caught her breath, remembering what had happened in the warehouse, and on the ice when they'd run out of fuel.

Violet sensed her distress. She reached across the table and patted her hand. "But you're here now, with my son. Things are good." She smiled.

"Are they?" Lauren said, not realizing she spoke aloud.

"Come on." Violet cleared up the mess they'd made at the table, and beckoned her into Seth's living room. "I want to show you something."

Lauren followed her to the sofa, where they both sat down. Violet lifted a heavy-looking book, a scrapbook, Lauren realized, from a stack of magazines and books jammed in neat stacks under the coffee table.

"My son is a hard man to understand sometimes."

"You've got that right."

Violet shot her a pithy glance. "Here. Have a look." She handed Lauren the open scrapbook. It was filled with photos and mementos of Seth's childhood and youth, from infancy to high school graduation.

Lauren spent time studying each page, asking questions, trying to understand the man from the memories his mother had of the boy. What she learned was that Violet Adams loved her son with both a fierceness and a freedom that awed her.

Although one thing struck her as strange. There were hardly any pictures of Seth's father in the scrapbook. Family get-togethers, youth sports, fishing trips with other kids and their dads... Jeremy Adams's face was conspicuously absent from the photographic record of these events.

"Seth told me he doesn't see his father. Do you mind my asking why not?"

"No, I don't mind," Violet said. "Jeremy and I were young, and times were different then. He married me because he had to."

Lauren tried to conceal her surprise. "Oh."

"The novelty of the situation wore off after a while, and Jeremy wasn't the kind of man who'd let an Inuit wife and half-breed son stand in the way of his ambition."

"I see."

"All Seth wanted was for his father to be proud of him, like other fathers were of their sons." Violet grazed a finger across a photo of Seth in a baseball cap, holding a trophy over his head.

To love him, Lauren read between the lines. But Jeremy Adams hadn't loved his son. That was clear from the bittersweet look in Violet's eyes.

"Poor boy. He spent a lifetime trying to get his father to notice him." Violet shook her head. "He's still trying."

"What do you mean, still trying?"

Violet closed the scrapbook and placed it back under the

table between the stack of magazines and books. "This FBI thing. You'll understand when you know him better."

"You know about that? About his...case?"

The older woman shook her head. "Not the details. Just that if he does a good job, the Bureau will take him back."

"Take him back? You mean he actually worked for the FBI? As an agent?"

"Oh, yes. In Washington, D.C." Violet said the city's name as if it were some kind of panacea. "And that did make his father proud—for a while."

"I didn't know that." She remembered when he told her he'd been to D.C. She'd had no idea at the time that he'd lived there, worked there. Perhaps that's where he'd been married, too.

"I think he thinks if he wins the job back, his father will be proud of him again."

She looked into the woman's eyes. "But you don't think so."

"No."

Lauren slowly nodded. "That explains a lot."

"Good. Then I was right to come here."

After thanking her for the sweet rolls, Lauren walked Violet Adams to the kitchen door and waved from the window as she pulled away in an old Bronco.

A dozen odd references Seth had made over the past ten days made sense to her now. She understood him, his motives, and why the Caribou Island assignment was so important to him.

I want to think it through first. Make sure I'm right.

If he brought down the bad guys, he'd win his job back at the Bureau, and possibly another shot at his father's love. Though his mother didn't think so, and, from all she'd seen and heard today, neither did Lauren.

But Seth thought so, and that's what mattered.

She stared, unfocused, into the blowing snow outside, and

realized Seth would do anything for that chance, anything to crack the case. Lie, seduce a suspect, even tell her he loves her to gain her trust.

The walk to the village school was mercifully short. Along the way Lauren passed a general store, the post office, town hall, and a tiny white church right out of a Norman Rockwell painting. In the distance she spied a hockey pond, and recalled the photo of a young Seth and his smiling friends.

On that short walk she thought hard about what Violet Adams had told her about Seth's father.

She thought about Seth.

She'd decided to keep her promise to him and not call Crocker, though her reasons had nothing to do with the FBI's investigation. She simply wasn't ready to talk to him yet. She had things to sort out first in her own mind.

Just minor stuff like her upcoming marriage, her career at Tiger, the uncontrollable feelings she had for a borough cop she'd only met ten days ago, and what she wanted to do with the rest of her life.

"You're a mess," she said to herself as she cinched the hood of her jacket tighter and jogged the last block.

In the past, whenever she was unsure about something, Crocker would always step in and persuade her to make what he liked to call "the smart decision."

Crocker could be very persuasive. As could her mother. Both of them, she realized, had had an enormous influence on her life, especially recently. She'd been so busy with her career, a career she wasn't even sure she wanted.

Oh, hell. What *did* she want?

She burst through the door into the school and stopped dead. A smile curled, unbidden, on her lips as her gaze danced along hallway walls papered with children's artwork.

She had the strangest feeling she'd been here before. It was certainly possible. The summer before her father died she'd accompanied him on a field survey along the arctic plain. It had been Hatch Parker's last.

They'd stopped here in Kachelik for supplies. She distinctly remembered the village, and now, standing here surrounded by bright Crayola drawings of seals and polar bears, breathing in the familiar scents of construction paper and paste, she remembered the school.

The hallway was empty, but as she drifted down the corridor, not really sure where she was going, or why, she heard the sounds of children laughing, chalk tapping on blackboards, a teacher reading aloud from a book.

After Violet left the house, Lauren had thrown on her jacket and boots and had rushed out without thinking, making a beeline for the school. What, exactly, was she going to say to Seth when she found him? What couldn't wait until he returned?

She didn't know. All she knew was that she needed to see him, talk to him, get things straight in her own mind. Find out if his feelings for her were real, or if…

His voice, clear and confident, drifted down the hallway from the last classroom on her right, causing her breath to catch and her feet to feel like lead weights, pinning her in place to the well-worn linoleum.

She must be out of her mind.

A brightly colored flyer tacked to the bulletin board on the wall next to her caught her attention for the barest second, as she worked to get a grip. It was a job posting—teaching assistant, science and math.

"Okay, let's see how well you've been listening. What do we do in a whiteout?"

Almost against her will, she was drawn forward by Seth's voice. Just a few more steps. Edging up to the classroom door, she peeked through the window.

"Bobby," Seth said, nodding to a little boy, seven or eight years old, with his hand raised.

She didn't hear the child's answer, so focused was she

on the man perched casually on the edge of the teacher's desk. He looked incredibly relaxed. The children gazed up at him, hanging on every word.

"That's right," Seth said. "We stay inside." He smiled at the boy who'd answered, and her heart melted.

She watched him through the glass as he continued to test them. Something about seeing him there at the teacher's desk, interacting so easily, so naturally with the children, made her feel... It was almost as if...

The hairs on her nape prickled.

Of course!

That's why the school seemed so familiar to her. She *had* been here before, perhaps in this very classroom. She'd watched and listened, her attention every bit as focused on the man who'd spoken that day as was the children's attention now, only their eyes were fixed on Seth.

The man had been her father.

The year was 1984, and Lauren was eleven.

Hatch Parker had been invited to the school that day to give the children an impromptu talk on the local geology. He'd started out on that topic, she remembered, but that wasn't where he'd finished.

He'd gone on to tell them about his own career, how he'd grown up poor but had worked his way through college to become a geologist.

He'd told them that they had the potential to be anything they wanted, that each and every one of them owed it to themselves to find out what it was they did want, and to go after it.

Go after it.

Lauren had never forgotten those words, she realized. They'd burned inside her after he died, even after her mother had moved them from Alaska to New York, remarried and changed Lauren's life so drastically she hardly recognized herself.

Getting her degree in geology had been her one bout of

rebellion, but after that she'd been swept along on a tide—not of her own making, but her mother's, her stepfather's, Tiger's and now Crocker's. She shook her head, realizing that somewhere along the way, she'd lost herself. What *she* was. What she wanted.

It had always been there, just below the surface, vague yet insistent, an intangible feeling of discomfort that had gripped her each time she was pushed further away from herself by those who would shape her into something she was not.

Briefly, she closed her eyes and felt the sting of tears. She swallowed hard against the emotions boiling up inside her. When she opened them again, the first thing she saw—the only thing she saw—was Seth, staring back at her.

Go after it, she heard her father say.

Seth was on his feet, moving toward her, his smile warm, light dancing in his eyes.

Lauren turned and ran.

He found her two hours later at the village museum.

Lauren was sprawled on the floor of an upstairs storage room in the sixties vintage building, surrounded by old rocks and rolled maps with time-yellowed edges.

In the corner Seth saw an open display case covered in dust, which she'd apparently rifled. She was holding one of the rocks up close to her face, looking at it through a geologist's hand lens—a tool much like a jeweler's loupe, but more powerful—that she kept in the pocket of her cardigan.

"Lauren!" he said, and jogged toward her.

She looked up, startled. She'd been so focused on what she was doing, she hadn't heard him come in. "Oh, thank God it's you! I was just about to come find you. You won't believe this."

"I've been looking for you for hours. When I saw you at the school, and you ran, I didn't know what to think, I didn't know where you'd gone. Don't you know how worried I've been?''

She grabbed his hand when he reached her. ''Sit down. I've got something to tell you.''

He'd never seen her so excited. Well, he had, but in a different way. For an instant he recalled their lovemaking two nights ago. God, he wanted to hold her. He wanted to scoop her up in his arms and just hold her.

When he saw her standing there outside the classroom door at the school, staring into space, tears glassing her eyes, he hadn't known what to think. He'd made as hasty an exit as he could without alarming the kids, but by the time he got outside, she was gone.

''Sit down.'' Insistent, she pulled him down beside her. ''Look.''

He took the hand lens she offered him and the rock that she'd been studying. He remembered from his college geology class how to use the low-magnification lens.

''You're not going to believe it. I still don't believe it.''

He angled his head back so the light from the bare overhead bulb reflected off the rock. ''Sandstone, right?'' he said, after he'd looked at it. ''So what?''

''So what?'' On the floor she smoothed one of the yellowed maps she'd unfurled, and held it in place with a couple more rocks from the display case.

''This is exactly the same kind of rock as the sample I took from the crate that Salvio snatched from me on the island. *Exactly*,'' she said with emphasis.

He looked at the rock, but to him it was just a rock. He didn't get it. ''So…?''

''Remember I told you that rocks like this don't exist at Caribou Island?''

''Yeah, I remember. You said the crate of rocks Salvio was hell-bent on keeping secret had to be from somewhere else.''

She nodded. ''Guess where they're from?''

He didn't have to. Already she was poring over the map, her finger tracing lines of topography across what he recognized as the arctic coastline near the Caribou Island site.

The map was old, hand drawn in India ink with a calligrapher's pen. His gaze cut to the legend in the right hand corner. "How old is this?"

"Nineteen forty-seven," she said absently, still tracing the topography with her finger. "Postwar there were a lot of government-sponsored field surveys in the area. Most of the records are buried somewhere in old files. They weren't thought to be that important, because at the time no one was looking for oil in Alaska."

"And now?"

"And now—" her finger stopped in the middle of the map, just east of Caribou Island "—no one's looking for oil *here.*"

He stared at the map.

"Because it's illegal." She tapped her finger impatiently on the spot.

The realization hit him like a slap in the face. "The wildlife refuge!"

"Bingo," she said, and snatched the rock from his hand. "Due east of Caribou Island. That's where this rock is from. And that's where that box of rocks Salvio confiscated was from, too."

"But those were drilling samples, right? From below the surface, from a well."

"From the Caribou Island well," Lauren said, and studied the rock again. "Only no one knows it. No one except Salvio and Walters and that foreign company."

His mind worked to process the information, but she didn't give him time to think it through.

"That's why the operation was so far behind schedule. That's why there was so much sophisticated equipment out there. Equipment that shouldn't have been there. Oh, God!"

"What?"

"*Directional* equipment! The kind you need to drill a well at an angle. I saw Pinkie and Bulldog moving some of it off the rig one night. At the time, I didn't recognize it for what it was, but now I know. Now I'm sure of it."

Seth had spent his first few days at Caribou Island, before Lauren arrived, getting a feel for the operation and the players. Nothing about the drilling of the well had seemed unusual. But then, Salvio had gone to a lot of trouble to make sure it appeared that way.

"By the time you arrived, by the time I arrived, everything was normal. Paddy and Jack were drilling the well Tiger had commissioned. A vertical hole, ten thousand feet down, easy as pie."

"But before we got there..."

"Exactly. They'd already drilled another well from the site. A secret well, at an angle from the island, into the wildlife refuge."

"A secret *illegal* well, you mean." The Feds were going to have a fit when they heard about this. The whole industry would be in an uproar.

"I can't believe I didn't piece it together before now. It all makes sense. The samples, impossibly deep depth measurements flashing on Salvio's computer—it was all from the other well."

Seth made the next logical leap. "It's the data from *that* well, the secret well, that's supposed to be sold."

"Exactly. I'd guess rock samples, engineering data, anything Salvio could get his hands on without raising suspicion or leaving a paper trail. Seth, that crate of samples would have been worth a fortune. More money than you can imagine."

"But the wildlife refuge isn't open to oil exploration or drilling. What possible good could—"

"It's not open to drilling *yet*," she said. "But it could be. Look at gas prices. Americans are in an uproar."

She was right. He knew there was legislation pending that

could open wildlife sanctuaries like the one near Caribou Island to oil exploration. If that happened, anyone who knew ahead of time whether or not oil existed below the surface, and where, would have a huge advantage when the government leased the land for drilling. An advantage potentially worth billions of dollars.

It was a whole new ball game as far as Seth was concerned. In his mind he reopened his original list of suspects.

Lauren pocketed the rock and gathered up the map as she scrambled to her feet. "I have to go back. I have to get that sample."

Jolted from his musings, he said, "What are you talking about?"

"Caribou Island. I'm going back."

"The hell you are." He followed her out the door and down the stairs into the museum.

"Everything all right?" the volunteer docent asked as Lauren sidestepped her, making a beeline for the exit.

"Fine. Thanks, Dottie." Seth shot the elderly woman a quick smile, slipped out the door behind Lauren and caught her in the icy parking lot.

She turned, the look on her face telling him she was ready to go to the mattresses on this one. "What?"

"You're not serious." He clamped down on her arm and guided her toward his Jeep.

"I'm dead serious. And don't push me around."

He loosened his grip, but didn't let go. Once they were in the vehicle, she said, "That sample may be the only evidence left of what's happened out there. I've got to get it."

"Come on, Lauren. If a secret well was drilled from Caribou Island into that wildlife refuge, there's got to be a paper trail a mile long that will show it. You, better than anyone, know what it takes to drill a well like that—truckloads of drill pipe, wellhead equipment, steel casing, hundreds of pallets of cement and hundreds more of supplies and equipment. You can't hide the movement or sale of all that stuff."

She arched a brow at him as he turned into Kachelik's main street and headed for his house. "You can if you're Jack Salvio and Paddy O'Connor, and if you have enough cash backing you."

"Even so, the hole they drilled is probably still there, intact. If it's there, the Feds will find it. The sample's not important."

She shot him a look of astonishment. "You don't get it, do you? No one, not even the FBI, will be allowed back in that hole. There'd be lawsuits, injunctions. You can't imagine the legal ramifications of something like this. The sample is *everything*."

Before he could stop her, even before he had the damned ignition switched off in his driveway, she leaped out of the Jeep and dashed around the back of the house toward the kitchen.

Seth was right behind her, swearing. He slammed the door behind him and she jumped, nearly dropping the receiver of the yellow wall phone next to the fridge.

"Hang up," he said. She ignored him and dialed 411. Directory assistance. "You're not going back there, Lauren. I won't let you."

"Why not?" She twisted around to look at him while the call connected.

"It's too dangerous." He snatched the receiver from her hand and slammed it down on the hook.

"But I've got to."

He kissed her. Hard.

"Seth, please."

He kissed her again, backing her out of the kitchen into the hallway. He couldn't stop himself.

"Where are we going?"

"The bedroom," he whispered against her lips.

This time she kissed *him*.

Chapter 18

Animal lust.

That's what it was. But not all it was, she told herself, as Seth scooped her into his arms and carried her down the shadowed hallway into his bedroom.

Their emotions had been ratcheted into high gear, and the thrill of at last unraveling the Caribou Island mystery fueled their ardor. Not that it needed fueling. Their desire for each other had crouched between them from the first day like a predator waiting to strike.

She didn't care any more. She simply gave in to it, allowed herself to be consumed.

Light bled from the kitchen, just enough so they could see each other as he stripped off his jacket, then hers, then picked her up again, this time cupping her bottom. He lifted her off her feet and kissed her with a voracity that shocked her.

She reciprocated. Her legs wound tightly around his hips, trapping him, as he pressed her into him and backed her toward the bed.

She told herself not to get carried away by her emotions this time, to simply enjoy the sex. Forget Caribou Island, her career, her confused feelings about Crocker.

Forget everything except him. His hard body grinding against hers, hands tearing at her clothes, the weight of him as he toppled her onto the bed, his tongue like hot glass searing hers.

His anger at her, his obvious frustration, a maelstrom of muddled emotions tangled with raw lust—all of it was unleashed on her at once. She reveled in it, kissing him wildly, clawing at his buttocks and back.

Together they broke the speed record for undressing.

Boots hit the floor. His belt, her jeans. She barely got her sweater off without losing all the buttons. He was hard as rock. She was challenged to unzip his jeans and get them off him.

Her bra gave him trouble. He all but ripped it off her. Panties and boxer shorts fared no better. Once they were naked they came together in a tangle of limbs, shallow breaths, and unchecked groans voiced between violent kisses.

She drowned herself in sensation—the taste of his skin, his smell, the stubble of beard raking the soft skin of her breasts as he moved his mouth across her body.

"Seth," she breathed, begging him to take her, using words she'd never uttered with any man in her life.

She spread her legs and he thrust inside her, his fingers slipping between their bodies to stoke her heat. She climaxed almost at once. Then again, along with him.

Later, as they lay there entwined, silent, stroking each other, she remembered what she'd felt at the school when her gaze had collided with his.

She'd felt the same on those nights in the lab when they'd talked until late, again in the Rolligon, and when they'd made love in the hunting lodge and he'd said the words she feared believing.

Maybe she *could* have a new life, the life she'd always wanted. A new man to share it with.

A man like Seth.

Stretching, Seth rolled over, feeling the empty expanse of sheets. The bed was still warm where Lauren had slept, curled in his embrace, after they'd made love.

He didn't know what had come over him. He'd acted like a wild animal. So had she, he recalled, allowing a smile to break across his lips.

He sat up in bed and checked the clock on the nightstand. Five o'clock. In the morning? No way. It had to be afternoon. Wednesday afternoon. He tilted the blinds on the window and peered out into darkness. A lot of good that did.

His watch kept military time. Switching on the bedside lamp he squinted against the light and fixed on the time. Seventeen hundred. Good. He hadn't slept around the clock, as he'd feared.

But where was Lauren?

Swiveling out of bed, he stepped into his shorts and surveyed the clothes scattered across the room. All of them were his.

"Lauren?"

Her voice, low and urgent, drifted toward him as he padded down the hallway toward the light shining from the kitchen.

"Fine. Seven o'clock tonight then." She turned as he came into the room. She was dressed, her jacket looped over a chair by the door, ready to go.

He saw the tiny Kachelik phone directory open on the table to Air Charter Services. His stomach clenched.

"At the airport. I'll be there." She started to hang the phone up, but he snatched it from her hand.

"Who's this?" he said into the receiver.

Lauren protested, but he ignored her.

"Al. Yeah, hi. Seth Adams here." After some small talk, he said, "About that charter. Forget it. It was a mistake."

"It's not a mistake! I told you, I—"

He turned away and finished his conversation with the bush pilot, assuring him that Lauren's call had been an error, and that she didn't need his services after all. When he hung up the phone and faced her, she launched at him.

"We've been through this, Seth."

"That's right, we have. You're not going back there."

"I am. I have to."

"Why?"

She spun toward the counter, gripped it, emitting a strangled sound of frustration. He wasn't backing down. Not on this. No matter what.

"You know why. That sample could prove oil exists in the wildlife refuge."

"You've already looked at it. Does it?"

She didn't answer.

"Well, does it?"

"I have looked at it, yes. But it's just one sample. I... can't be sure."

She was lying. He could tell by the way her shoulders bunched up, the way she drummed her nails on the tiled countertop.

"So *that's* it."

"What?" She turned to face him.

He shook his head and softly laughed. "And all this time, after everything, after what happened at the lodge and in there—" he jerked his head toward the bedroom "—it's still about Tiger, about your career. Isn't it? You're obsessed."

"No. Yes." She exhaled in what he recognized as frustration, for he felt the same damned way right now. "I don't know what it's about. All I know is, it's my obligation to get that sample. For Tiger."

"For Tiger or for you?"

"What do you mean?"

She knew exactly what he meant. Or maybe she didn't, he thought, as he searched her face.

"Think about it, Lauren. What if you were to prove the existence of a new Alaskan oil field with that sample. Think what that would do for your career. You'd be the most sought-after geologist in the industry."

The truth of it dawned on her. He saw the change in her expression as she thought it through.

"I didn't really consider that. I was just thinking about what was the right thing to do."

"The right thing for Tiger? The right thing for you? The right thing for the wildlife refuge and this village?"

Her brow furrowed. "What has any of this got to do with the village?"

"Come on, get real. If that wildlife refuge has got oil under it, this whole place'll turn into a circus. You know it will. You also know that nobody in Kachelik will get a red cent from the oil royalties coming off that refuge—if there *is* oil."

She shot him a quick glance, but her face was unreadable.

"The refuge is owned by the government. They'll make a bundle. So will the oil companies. But this place will never be the same again."

"Speaking of obsessed, what about you? What about this—" she waved her arms in the air "—this FBI stuff? The case against Salvio and Walters?"

"I'm not so sure it is Walters."

"I thought we'd decided that it was."

"I haven't decided anything. That's why I haven't called in the Bureau. In fact, the more I think about it, the more I think that piece of paper with his number on it means squat."

"But Walters knew when I called him that I wasn't on the island. If he wasn't involved, how would he have known?"

"Caller ID." Seth shrugged. "You said it yourself. There's a new phone system at Tiger. They probably have all kinds of new stuff."

She went stock-still on him. "So, what are you saying?"

"I'm saying I'm rethinking the Bureau's short list of suspects. And right now your fiancé's name is coming out on top."

Her eyes widened. She stood there, fists clenched at her sides, staring at him, that sexy mouth of hers stretched in a tight line.

A handful of hours ago he'd had the best sex of his life with her, and now she was standing an arm's length away, glaring at him with a mixture of contempt and disbelief.

"You said it before, yourself. Walters isn't the type. He's not cut out for it, doesn't have that killer instinct you need in order to pull off something as big as this Caribou Island thing."

"Crocker is innocent. I'm telling you. Besides, you're just changing the subject again."

"From what?"

"From the point I was getting to. That *you're* the one obsessed, not me. I'm just doing my job."

"So am I."

She shook her head. "It's more than that with you, Seth. I know, your mother told me."

"What the hell does my mother have to do with—?"

"She was here, this morning. We talked."

He let out a breath, stunned. "About what?" Christ, he could just imagine.

"Things. Your life, your father, your…I don't know… *quest* to prove you're worthy of his love."

He felt blood rush to his head. "What the hell are you talking about?"

"This FBI thing. The case. If you catch the bad guys you get your job back, right?"

"Who told you that?" He didn't have to ask, and she

didn't answer. Unable to control himself, he swore. His mother, God love her, and he were going to have a serious talk about his privacy.

"Maybe you're doing it to win your father's love. Maybe mine, too, I don't know."

He covered the short distance between them and grabbed her. She had him so wound up he couldn't speak. He just stood there, looking down at her, breathing hard, his heart beating out of control in his chest.

"All those things you said about Crocker, about his money and what a big wheel he is in the oil business, how he probably even knows your father—which, by the way, he does—"

He started to tell her to shut up, but she interrupted.

"The whole time you were comparing yourself to him, weren't you? I know you were. I could hear it in your voice, in the offhand way you mentioned the sports car he bought me or my engagement ring." She glanced at the rock on her finger. "Once you even compared his salary to that of a borough cop's. I remember it now. I didn't think anything about it at the time. It was in the lab one night when—"

He kissed her with enough unleashed emotion to power every oil rig in Alaska from now until the earth was sucked dry.

"Stop it," he whispered against her lips when he, at last, had the presence of mind to let her draw breath. "Just stop it."

"I'm right, aren't I?" She looked up at him, and what he read in her whiskey-brown eyes made his gut clench. "Do you think I care about that? About Crocker's money?"

"Don't you?"

She extracted herself, carefully, from his grasp and crossed to the other side of the room, putting the kitchen table between them.

"No. But I do care about other things. My commitment

to him, for one. And my responsibilities to Tiger. Right now all I know is I need to get that sample."

"So we're back to that."

"Yes, we're back to that."

He ran a hand over the beard stubble on his face, considering the options.

"I could be in and out in—"

"No!" he said emphatically.

"You can't stop me, Seth."

"The hell I can't." They stood there for a moment, breathing hard, staring at each other across the table. Then he said, "I'll go get it, if it's so goddamned important to you."

"It is."

"Fine." He started down the hallway, meaning to get dressed, but she called him back.

"Where's the FBI in all this? Why aren't they here? Why haven't you called them?" As soon as the words left her lips, a change washed over her expression. "Oh, I get it."

He met her gaze and knew that she did.

If he called Bledsoe now and told him what had happened, that he'd blown his cover on Caribou Island, and that he still wasn't sure who the Tiger crook was who'd set up the deal with the foreign company and who'd bought Salvio and O'Connor...

"Tell me something, Seth? What's wrong with just being you? The town's chief of police? A nice guy who makes sure people are safe and that schoolkids know what to do in a storm?"

He honestly didn't know what to say to that. For the first time in his life he felt disoriented, unsure. He was used to knowing what he wanted without questioning why he wanted it. But now...

"I...have to go to the station for a few minutes. An hour at most." He needed to defuse the situation, to get a grip on his emotions. His first instinct was to put physical space between them. Maybe then he could think straight.

"Okay," she said, her voice soft, the animation of the past few minutes suddenly gone.

"Will you be all right here?" What he really wanted to ask her was if could he trust her to stay put.

She must have read it in his expression. "Don't worry. I won't go anywhere."

"Good."

Her expression brightened, but in a forced sort of way, as if to abruptly distance them from the heated topics of a minute ago. "Are you hungry? I'm hungry."

"Sure," he said, distracted. "Food sounds good." He grabbed his jacket and moved toward the door. "There's stuff in the freezer, or I can bring something back."

"I'll cook something." She glanced at the freezer, then nodded toward his police department Jeep in the driveway. "Go ahead."

"See you, then."

She didn't respond, just turned her back on him and opened the freezer door.

He ground his teeth as he slid into the icy driver's seat of the Jeep, and let fly a pack of swear words as he barreled down the street toward the station.

Two hours later Seth returned home to the smell of stew simmering on the stove. The clock on the wall read seven. Lauren wasn't in the kitchen. He checked the living room, but she wasn't there, either. He didn't think she'd deliberately sneak away, not after she'd said she wouldn't, but then again...

He pushed the door open to the guest room and breathed with relief when soft light from the hallway illuminated her sleeping form. Curled into a ball, she'd drawn a quilt—one that his mother had made him—over herself. Her boots looked so small lined up carefully next to the bed where she could easily step into them when she woke.

He smiled. In some ways they were exactly alike.

She was exhausted. She had to be. When they'd argued in the kitchen he'd noticed how pale her skin was, and had seen the dark circles under her eyes. Both of them had been pushed to the limit. And it wasn't over yet.

He closed the guest-room door, deciding it was better if she just slept. For a while, anyway. Once he did what he was about to do, and the hours of questioning began, she wouldn't have much of a chance to sleep.

Neither would he, but that didn't matter.

"Bledsoe," the drawling voice said on the other end of the line after Seth's call connected.

"It's me. Adams." He dragged a kitchen chair over to the phone and slumped onto it. "I've got news."

The faraway whomp of chopper blades woke her. At first Lauren thought she was dreaming, then realized she wasn't when she squinted against the hallway light framing Seth's silhouette in the guest-room doorway.

He didn't come in and sit on the bed, brush the hair off her face and lean down to kiss her. What did she expect? She'd gone too far with him this time. She wished that she'd never brought up the situation with his father.

A handful of hours ago she and Seth had made love, but now he simply stood there in the doorway as if they were total strangers, and in a low and serious voice said, "Wake up, Lauren. They're here."

"Who's they?" she said in a voice thick with sleep.

Ten minutes later she found out.

"Doyle Bledsoe, FBI," the gum-chewing man in the dark suit drawled as he shook her hand and gave her a once-over she found irritating.

She was wearing the flannel shirt Seth had loaned her,

and that fact wasn't lost on Bledsoe. She was practically swimming in it, given its size and her petite frame.

Three more suits crowded into Seth's small kitchen behind the stocky, blue-eyed man who explained to her that he was Seth's superior at the Bureau, and in charge of the Caribou Island investigation. Given his smug expression, it was apparent Bledsoe thought he was Seth's superior outside the Bureau, as well.

Seth propped himself casually in the doorway leading from the kitchen into the hall, his fingers looped into the waistband of his jeans. But Lauren could tell from his tight expression and hard eyes that the situation was anything but casual.

Seth's gaze was riveted to Bledsoe. It was clear to her there was no love lost between these two. An underlying current of tension and mutual distaste crackled between the two men like electricity.

Bledsoe smirked at him, still chewing. "So, you *effed* up again, eh, Adams?" He glanced at Lauren and apologized for his language.

She didn't offer him a response, not even a shrug. She took a step toward Seth, but something in his body language and the way he flashed cool eyes at her stopped her. From the moment he'd awakened her in the guest room, she'd felt his emotional distance.

Perhaps it was better this way.

She tried to clear her head of all that had happened between them, and focus on the situation. "How much have you told them?"

Seth didn't spare her a glance. "Pretty much everything."

"About Paddy's murder? The explosion? Salvio and Walters and—?"

"Holt," he said, shifting his gaze to hers.

"Yeah," Bledsoe drawled, working the chewing gum between meaty jowls. "Crocker Elliot Holt, the boyfriend."

"Fiancé," she snapped, returning Seth's glare with one of her own. "I told you that's not possible."

"Maybe it's not," Bledsoe said as he yanked out a kitchen chair and wedged himself into it. "Then again, maybe it is." He shot Seth an amused glance. "Too bad you didn't stick around the island long enough to find out."

Seth drew himself up in the doorway, throwing off the nonchalant guise that Lauren knew wasn't working anyway. His eyes flashed anger. "I told you. It wasn't safe for Lauren to be there. I had to get her out."

"So it's Lauren, now. What happened to Miss Fotheringay?" Bledsoe's gaze washed over her again, and this time he didn't attempt to disguise his overtly sexual appraisal. He grinned.

Seth took a step toward him, and for a heartbeat Lauren thought he might hit him.

"All right, all right." Bledsoe held his hands up in mock surrender. "Don't go off half-cocked. I can see why you did what you did." Bledsoe flashed his eyes at her again. "I mighta done the same thing, myself."

"Let's get to the point," Seth said.

Lauren was anxious, too. She had no idea what the FBI would do next, or what she was supposed to do while they did it. She had to get that sample back. She had to call Crocker and—

And what? Tell him she was in love with another man? A man who thought he was a criminal and that she was obsessed with some twisted idea of success? A thousand thoughts raced through her mind. It was useless trying to process them. Maybe she just didn't want to.

She closed her eyes for a moment and rubbed them. She'd slept nearly five hours, but was still tired. Why hadn't Seth wakened her sooner? The kitchen wall clock read eleven. She glanced at her watch. Twenty-three hundred.

"The point is, by now Salvio knows you're alive—" Bledsoe looked pointedly at Lauren "—and that's a liability for him. A bigger liability for whoever the hell is running this little operation.''

''That's why I got her out of there,'' Seth said.

Bledsoe grinned. ''Yeah. And that's exactly why I'm sending her back.''

''You're not doing this, do you hear me?'' Seth trapped Lauren as she came out of the bathroom in the drafty Quanset hut that served as the terminal for Kachelik's tiny airport.

''I have to do it. The FBI wants me to.''

''To hell with the FBI. *I* don't want you to.''

It took all her resolve not to respond to the unspoken meaning behind his words. She pushed past him, zipping her survival jacket as she marched toward the open double doors leading outside to two unmarked choppers sitting on the pad.

The night was clear and cold, the first clear night they'd had in ten days. The storm was over—at least where the weather was concerned. Stars twinkled overhead.

''It's too dangerous.'' Seth stopped her again at the open doors.

''I'll be fine. Bledsoe's arranged for six agents to go in with me.''

Their eyes met, and she read a bitter fusion of anger and helplessness in his. Bledsoe had refused to let Seth go with her. In fact, he'd given him his walking papers, had taken him off the case.

Seth had spent nearly an hour arguing with him at the house while arrangements had been made to fly her back to Caribou Island. At first he'd flown into a rage that Bledsoe would even consider the idea of sending her back there. But Doyle Bledsoe was immovable as stone. He wanted the ringleader, and he wanted him now.

Lauren was the bait.

From Bledsoe's perspective, Seth had failed in his mission. All he'd managed to do, according to the section chief, was to tip the bad guys to the Bureau's investigation. He'd blown his cover and nearly the whole case, which was the exact reason for Seth's dismissal from the FBI five years ago.

She'd gleaned that much from Bledsoe's cutting comments during the past hour. He was good at twisting the knife. She'd seen Seth's face when Bledsoe mentioned Jeremy Adams had called him—tonight, in fact—to find out how his son was doing on the case. It was clear Bledsoe had delighted in telling the powerful oil man that his son had blown it—again.

"I don't trust that bastard as far as I can throw him," Seth said. "He says he's sending in backup, but—"

"I'll be fine."

She hoped to God she would. It had chilled her to the bone when she realized Bledsoe placed literally no importance on the fact that Seth had saved her life in that warehouse.

"It's the sample, isn't it? That's why you're going."

She wanted so badly to touch him, to graze a finger along his chiseled jawline, brush a kiss across his lips, but she held herself in check.

"That's part of it," she said softly.

"That's all of it." He stormed toward the first chopper, whose rotors were beginning to turn in wind-whipping revolutions.

That wasn't all of it, but she didn't want to share with him her other reason. She needed to deal with it on her own, to think clearly without her feelings for him clouding the issues.

Seth ripped opened the chopper door for her. Bledsoe was already inside, along with the pilot and, as promised, six agents in full combat dress, weapons hanging off them like Christmas ornaments.

"Take this," Seth said, and handed her his Glock. "Know how to use it?"

She did. Her father had taught her to shoot when she was a kid. "Yes, but what about you?"

He laughed bitterly. "Yeah, like I'll really need it here, in the middle of the night, in this bustling metropolis." He nodded at the twinkling lights of the village.

She took the gun from him and stuffed it into the pocket of her survival jacket.

"You didn't tell him, did you?" She flashed a look at Bledsoe, who sat in the copilot's seat, jawing his wad of gum as if his life depended on it.

"Tell him what?"

"About the sample."

Their gazes locked. "No. I told him about the second well, but not about the sample."

"Why not?"

He looked at her hard. "I figured I'd leave that to you."

They both knew that once the government confirmed the presence of the second well—the illegal well drilled into the wildlife refuge—it would immediately be plugged and abandoned. Tiger would never be allowed to go back in and collect more rock samples or run more tests to confirm or refute the existence of oil.

That one sample was everything.

"Thanks," she said simply, and climbed into the waiting chopper.

Seth grabbed the door before one of the agents could slide it closed. "Lauren, wait!"

She turned and looked down at him. The harsh sodium lights illuminating the tiny airstrip reflected back at her in his eyes. His breath frosted the air, and she could tell he was breathing hard.

"You were right," he said.

"About what?"

"My father. Everything."

He grasped her gloved hand in his and held it—seconds, a minute, an hour, she didn't know how long. The raw emo-

tion in his eyes undid her. At last, she let him go so the
agent could slide the door shut.

As the chopper lifted off she tried to remember the exact
moment she knew that she loved him.

Chapter 19

"He's a little out of his league, don'tcha think?"

"What?" Lauren hadn't been paying attention. The rhythmic vibration of the chopper's engine had lulled her into a calming trance. They'd been in the air about twenty minutes now.

She twisted around in the rear-facing jump seat so she could see Doyle Bledsoe. It was dark, and she could just make out his squishy features in the dim glow of the chopper's flight instruments.

He had to shout over the near-deafening din. "Adams. With you, I mean."

She ignored the comment. She'd met the FBI section chief only a handful of hours ago, and had known in the first minute she didn't like him.

Bledsoe nudged the pilot and laughed, which was mercifully drowned out by the engine noise.

Lauren settled back into her seat for the remainder of the trip out to Caribou Island. They would touch down nearly a mile from the site on what remained of the ice road from

Deadhorse. She would travel the rest of the way in a dogsled that was already standing by.

The musher was an FBI agent posing as a villager from another of the tiny outposts skirting the Alaskan coastline. The story Bledsoe had leaked over local airwaves was that a Tiger geologist was found wandering and disoriented after the storm. That her companion was dead. That as soon as she was strong enough, she'd asked the people who'd rescued her to take her back to Caribou Island.

It was plausible. In fact, it was probably exactly what Lauren would do if those circumstances were true, and not a fabrication designed to make her a target the bad guys couldn't resist.

Salvio, Bulldog, Pinkie…they'd all be waiting for her. Bledsoe was betting someone else would be waiting, too. That's what this ruse was all about, bringing down the puppeteer of the whole, ugly operation.

At the airport Seth had argued with Bledsoe that he should go instead of her. That if his cover was truly blown, Salvio and the others would want him just as dead as they'd want her.

She believed Seth cared about her safety, but maybe there was something else he cared about more. She couldn't help but wonder if the heated argument he'd had with Bledsoe had simply been one last, desperate attempt to get himself back on the case, to redeem himself in his father's eyes.

She recalled his mother's revelation about the deal he'd cut with Bledsoe, winning his old job back with the FBI if he identified the Tiger ringleader and obtained enough evidence for a conviction.

That wasn't possible now.

Bledsoe hadn't bought Seth's argument that he should be the one to return to the island. They all knew that nothing short of Lauren's reappearance would draw out the key player. Even that was a long shot. What if he simply didn't come?

Bledsoe was banking on the fact that this guy was a whole lot smarter than Salvio. That he'd want to know exactly how much Lauren knew about the covert operation before he decided what to do with her. He wouldn't risk murdering a prominent Tiger geologist unless he had to.

"It can't be Crocker. It just can't," she whispered to herself.

She turned in her seat again and was about to tap Bledsoe on the shoulder, but realized he was speaking into the pilot's radio handset. The conversation lasted about a minute, then he twisted around and gave her a thumbs-up.

"Big fish took the bait." Bledsoe's grin was downright eerie in the glow of the instrument lights. "Our boy's in the air right now."

"Oh, God." Lauren's stomach clenched. "Wh-who is it?"

"Don't know. We have agents at the airports in Anchorage and Deadhorse, but this guy's smart. He didn't take the usual route, or make use of the corporate jet. All we know is that, a couple of hours ago, some guy flashing a wad of hundreds and a Tiger ID chartered a long-range chopper outta Barrow headed east."

"Then, he could reach Caribou Island before I do."

"Not likely, but you never know." Bledsoe's grin spread like a nasty disease across his face.

"Wh-whose name was on the ID?" She wasn't sure she could stomach the answer.

Bledsoe shrugged. "Nobody knows. The guy dealt directly with the pilot. He was wearing a hooded jacket, standard Tiger issue. Nobody got a look at his face. All anybody remembers is the money."

She sucked in a breath and tried to clear her head. "Where's Bill Walters tonight?"

"Home in bed. Just had it confirmed. Your boyfriend's unaccounted for, though. He's supposed to be in San Francisco at some charity thing."

Oh, God.

Vaguely, she remembered the function. She was supposed to have been there, too, along with her mother, but that was before the Caribou Island job had landed on her plate.

"Holt never showed."

She didn't want to believe it. She couldn't believe it.

That's why she was out here.

Not because of a rock sample worth a fortune. Not for Tiger, or to further her own career. She was returning to Caribou Island for one reason only—she had to know for sure if Crocker was the one. She had to see his face before she'd believe it.

"This is it," the pilot yelled.

The helicopter flashed its lights at something on the ice, then made a wide, slow turn before touching down.

Show time.

Lauren felt the comforting shape of Seth's Glock in the pocket of her survival jacket as she stepped from the chopper. Bledsoe alighted first and was already talking to the undercover agent who would escort her the rest of the way to the island. She crunched over to the sled and petted one of the dogs.

"Good boy," she said, and tried to keep her teeth from chattering. It was a clear night, but the temperature had dropped considerably. A dizzying array of stars peppered the ink-black sky above her.

She wondered if Seth was looking out on the same sky, if he was thinking about her, and, if so, what he was thinking. She forced herself to push him from her mind, to focus on her part in the FBI's plan to catch a criminal who might very well be the man she was supposed to marry.

Bledsoe barked some last-minute instructions at her, snapping her back to the moment. She nodded, repeating his orders back to him.

"I guess Adams wasn't so useless after all," he said.

"What?"

Bledsoe shrugged. "At least he had the sense to pack it in and call me after he bungled his cover. I wouldn't have been able to set up this little charade if he'd decided to go 'rogue warrior' on me."

"What do you mean, he called you?" Lauren grabbed his arm. "You mean you didn't just show up? He actually called you in?"

"Yeah. It was the only smart thing he did do. Good thing, too. If he hadn't, I'd have had his ass in a sling quicker than you can say Eskimo Pie."

She stood there, stunned, breathing in huge gulps of frigid air that burned her lungs on contact.

"He said you wanted back on the island, and that he didn't think he couldn't stop you, or protect you, on his own."

"He said that?"

The light of a half-moon illuminated Bledsoe's smirk. "Yeah, well, it's not like it's the first time Adams has made a fool of himself over some babe too rich for his blood." He was referring to Seth's first wife, but Lauren ignored the comment.

She was too stunned for words. She'd thought Bledsoe and his men had simply shown up in Kachelik. But they hadn't. Of course they hadn't! Why would they?

Seth had called them.

He must have done it when he was at the station earlier that evening, or while she was asleep. He must have known Bledsoe would take over the case once he told them about Salvio, Paddy's murder, the secret well. Oh, Seth. He'd given up his last chance to solve the case, to win his job back, his father's respect.

He'd done it for her.

He'd done it because she'd been hell-bent on returning to the island, because she wouldn't listen to reason. He'd done it because her safety was more important to him than his own success. More important than his pride, and a last-ditch effort at winning Jeremy Adams's love.

"Okay, let's get this show on the road," Bledsoe said, arresting her thoughts.

The six FBI field operatives who were supposed to protect her on the island stood off to the side, awaiting Bledsoe's orders. They'd go in on foot from here, accompanying the dogsled until Lauren was dropped on the island. Supposedly one of them would have her in sight every second from now on.

They looked almost unreal, dressed all in white like spies from a James Bond movie set on a Russian ski slope. The guns they were carrying...now they looked real.

"Ready?" Bledsoe asked.

As ready as she'd ever be. "Let's do it," she said, and climbed into the sled.

Seth poured another shot of black sludge into a stained ceramic mug bearing the motto, Kachelik—My Kind of Town.

"That's your fifth cup," Danny said, swinging his feet off a desk cluttered with reports, pictures of his nieces and nephews, and yellowed editions of the *Anchorage Daily News.*

"Yeah, so what?" Seth shot him a warning glance.

Danny shrugged. "Just think you oughta back off a little, Chief. You're already wound tighter than a yo-yo string."

"You'd be, too." He paced the strip of carpet in front of the officer's desk, stopping every so often to glance at his watch.

"Four o'clock in the morning," Danny said. "You just checked it."

Seth ignored him and moved to the window. The street outside the station house was dark and quiet. All of Kachelik was asleep. He'd be, too, if he was smart.

But he wasn't smart.

He was a man in love with a woman who didn't know what she wanted. And that made him crazy. Maybe she did know, and was just too afraid to act on it. The thing was, he had no idea if she was afraid to dash his hopes or make him the happiest man on earth.

Seth swore silently under his breath.

He knew what *he* wanted. He hadn't known before tonight, not entirely. But now he was sure.

"I said, I checked out that crew manifest you brought back."

Seth hadn't been listening. "Uh, yeah. Find anything?"

"You were right about one of them. Charles P. White, aka Pinkie. His sheet's as long as your arm. Did time in…geez, three different states."

That didn't surprise him.

"Assault, assault with intent, petty theft, grand theft, arson, rape—" Seth ground his teeth "—another rape, and the list goes on."

Arson. Seth mentally added the Caribou Island warehouse fire to the list of Pinkie's crimes.

Rape. If Bledsoe's men so much as blinked while Lauren was under their protection, Seth swore to God he'd—

The radio crackled to life behind Danny's desk, and both of them jumped.

"I got it," Danny said, and flipped a switch on the box.

It was Al Cheriut who ran a charter service over at the airport. The same guy Lauren had tried to hire to take her out to the island yesterday afternoon.

"Yeah, Al," Seth said into the mike, pushing Danny out of the way. "What is it?"

The pilot's voice was groggy with sleep. "Just thought you oughta know… 'Bout fifteen minutes ago, some guy rolled my kid outta bed over at the airstrip at Takluk." It was another village, about as far south of Caribou Island as Kachelik was east.

"Yeah, what about it?"

"Some chopper pilot. Needed fuel. Said he'd just dropped some big wheeler-dealer Tiger exec off on Caribou Island. Seein' as how that lady yesterday wanted me to fly her out there, I just thought you'd wanna—"

"Who was the guy?"

"The pilot?"

"No, the Tiger guy?"

"Dunno. My kid said the pilot was on his way back from the island. He'd already dropped the guy off."

Seth swore.

In the back of his mind, he'd never really thought Bledsoe's ploy would work, that the brains of the operation would take the bait. Lauren was out there alone, and while he knew, hoped, Bledsoe's men could handle Salvio and his cronies, he didn't know what to expect from this so-called mastermind.

If it *was* Holt, surely he wouldn't hurt her. The guy was supposed to marry her, for God's sake!

And if it turned out to be Walters? Walters had every reason to want Lauren dead, and not just because of what she might know about the covert operation on Caribou Island. Walters was about to be passed over for promotion— a promotion Lauren would get in his place.

Seth had the sick, gnawing feeling he'd done the wrong thing—trusting Bledsoe, letting Lauren go—but for the right reason. For her. Because that damned rock sample meant more to her than anything else in her life.

"Son of a bitch!"

Danny grabbed the mike from Seth's hand a split second before he ripped it from the box. "Uh, thanks, Al. We'll catch you later, okay?"

Seth didn't wait around to hear any more.

Danny caught up with him in the back room where they kept the department's gun safe. "What are you doing?"

"What I should have done in the first place." He spun

the cylinder of the combination lock—right, left, right—and the safe's heavy door clicked open.

"Which is?" Danny caught the shotgun Seth tossed him from the rack inside the safe, then started to shake his head. "You're not doing what I think you're doing?"

"The hell I'm not." He nodded toward the Kevlar vests hanging on the wall behind them. "Put one of those on."

"Me?"

"Yeah, you." He donned one of the vests, a shoulder holster, then slapped a Beretta into it. He reached into the safe for another of the department shotguns, annoyed as hell that only SWAT or Feds were issued assault rifles.

"You're out of your mind," Danny said, continuing to shake his head in amazement. "Bledsoe told you to stay put. You're off the case."

"I may be off the FBI's case, but I'm a North Slope Borough cop, goddamnit, and I've got my own case."

"Yeah, a redhead about five-two."

"Five-three," he said, and started for the back door.

When he found her, after he made sure she was safe, he was going to get some answers. For starters, did she love him or didn't she? A simple question, requiring a simple answer. Was she going to marry that—he let fly a choice expletive for Crocker Holt—or was she going to marry *him?*

"Just how do you think you're going to get there? All the way to Caribou Island?"

Seth shot him a look.

"That wreck? Oh, no. It's barely flyable. I put the maintenance order in weeks ago. It's still tied up in approvals."

"Screw the approvals. It'll get me there." He pushed open the back door and headed for his Jeep.

"And I suppose you want me to fly you?"

"That's right. Unless you want to give me a quick lesson and send me off on a wing and a prayer."

Danny climbed into the passenger seat of the Jeep a second before Seth threw it into gear and barreled out of the parking lot. They argued all the way to the airport.

"So tell me again, why I'm doing this?" Danny skidded across the ice after Seth, toward the rusting, thirty-year-old chopper the department had snagged only because Danny had saved it from the scrap heap.

Seth tossed him a wry look. "To nail the bad guys, save the girl."

Danny's face effected a look somewhere between thoughtful calculation and surprise. "Okay. Sounds good."

Twenty minutes later they were in the air.

Bill Walters?

Lauren's jaw dropped.

Her boss stood in the doorway of Salvio's office, blocking her only means of escape.

Where were those federal agents? They were supposed to have kept her in sight every second. Lauren fought the panic twisting her stomach into knots.

It had taken them much longer to reach the island than they'd expected. It turned out their undercover dog musher had only been on a sled once in his life, and he hadn't been driving. In the end Lauren had had to mush the dogs herself, the embarrassed agent jogging along beside her.

"I heard about what happened," Bill said, moving into the room.

Lauren took a step back.

"God, Lauren, are you okay?" He reached out to touch her shoulder, and she flinched.

"Y-you're supposed to be at home, in bed."

"Me?"

She swallowed hard, backing toward the small window overlooking the brightly lit yard. Somewhere in the background she was conscious of the roar of heavy equipment as a skeleton crew worked round the clock to disassemble the rig and shut down the Caribou Island operation.

"The...I...thought you were home, is all." This was crazy. Bledsoe had just confirmed her boss's whereabouts not an hour ago.

Walters grinned, but his eyes weren't smiling. "I ought to be home. My brother's visiting from Ohio. We're twins. He's at the house now."

"Oh, God." Lauren felt her knees go weak. Bledsoe's agents had mistaken her boss's brother for Walters himself. "When did you get here?"

"I left as soon as I got the news you'd been found and were on your way here. Didn't bother with the corporate jet or even a charter. Hitched a ride with a buddy who flies a mail route up this way."

He *was* smart. Exactly as Bledsoe had predicted. She bumped up against the window and sucked a shallow breath.

"You don't look good, Lauren. Have you seen a doctor?"

She shook her head, which was spinning like a top, over-heating with conflicting information.

"Salvio told me about the accident in the warehouse."

"Accident?" Her voice cracked as she said the word.

"Amazing you made it out alive. Too bad about that roughneck. I heard he didn't make it."

She couldn't speak. She couldn't even move.

On the sled trip in, she'd prepared herself for the inevitability that Crocker was the one. She'd figured out that he'd probably been playing her from the beginning.

Crocker was the one who'd asked her mother to introduce them two years ago, who'd infiltrated himself into the Fotheringays' social circle and into Lauren's life. When they'd started dating he'd been in banking, but soon after he'd asked her to introduce him around to Tiger's top brass. That's how he'd landed the job of VP of finance.

Their courtship, his proposal, even moving their wedding date up nearly a year...she'd concluded that all of it had been part of Crocker's plan to position himself inside Tiger

Petroleum for the purpose of selling millions of dollars of proprietary data to black market buyers.

The question was *why?*

She even recalled some unmarked rock samples Crocker had asked her to analyze last year. He'd said it was a favor for a friend. She'd done it, and the samples had, in fact, contained oil. She suspected those samples had ended up in a foreign oil company's pocket, just as the FBI suspected, and that Crocker's own pockets were lined with green.

As she stared in undisguised amazement at Bill Walters, Lauren realized her faulty conclusions had been the result of nothing more than an overactive imagination, fueled by Seth's insistence that Crocker was the one. They'd both done her fiancé a terrible injustice and, in her case, that injustice ran deeper than simply believing for the span of a few hours that he was a criminal.

"I can't believe it's you," she breathed, shaking her head, her gaze moving slowly over Walters's cool features.

"What do you mean?" He screwed up his face and cocked his head. "And about that roughneck...why'd he take you off the island?"

"Seth?" Her mouth was dry. She was still in her survival jacket, and Salvio's office was warm.

She'd seen Jack only briefly, about an hour ago when she'd first arrived. His reception was so warm, so over-wrought with concern for her safety, it was almost eerie. She'd felt as if she'd entered a bad episode of *The Twilight Zone*. He'd acted as if nothing had happened out of the ordinary before the warehouse had exploded.

He'd called it an accident, too. I guess there would never be any proof that it wasn't, since the burned-out remnants of the building were already plowed off to the side of the site.

Pinkie and Bulldog had actually smiled at her when the undercover agent—her musher, breathless from his jog along the ice road—had dropped her off and careened into the night, the sled dogs barely in check.

Nothing was as she'd expected.

And where the hell were those James Bond, dressed-all-in-white agents when you needed them? The ones with the guns. The ones that Bledsoe promised would protect her.

"Yeah," Walters said, ripping her from her thoughts. "That's his name. Seth Adams. Why'd he take you away in that Rolligon?"

"Why?" Her hands began to sweat as Walters inched closer, reaching into the pocket of his down vest. "He, I…don't know. He had some crazy idea that something was wrong here."

She held her breath as Walters drew something out of his pocket. It was a…handkerchief? She'd expected a gun. In fact, she had her own shaking hand buried deep in her jacket pocket, wrapped tightly around Seth's Glock.

"Maybe something *is* wrong here," Walters said cryptically as he calmly dabbed the sweat off her brow.

Lauren nearly fainted.

"There nothing frickin' wrong, got it?" Salvio blustered into the room and clapped a paw on Walters's shoulder. "Come on, Bill. I got a pool cue in the rec room with your name on it."

Lauren felt as if she was in a dream state. "Jack, I…want to go out to my lab now."

He hadn't let her near the trailer since she'd arrived. He'd made the excuse that Bulldog was cleaning it up for her, clearing away the mess that had been made when some "misguided person" had trashed it. Salvio hadn't said who had done it, or why, only that the crew member had been sent back to town.

He'd been spinning lies like that one since she'd arrived. The scariest part was that he knew she knew it, but it was almost as if he didn't care, as if she didn't matter.

As if she were already dead.

"Go ahead," Salvio said, steering Walters into the hall-way. "Trailer's all ready for you."

The moment she realized the two of them were going to let her go—and if not let her go, at least let her get out of Salvio's office alive—she nearly whimpered in relief.

She was out the front door of the camp in seconds, pulling in icy gulps of air as she jogged across the yard toward her trailer. The place was in an uproar, crewmen and equipment everywhere.

Where were those agents? She hadn't seen a sign of them since the musher had dropped her off. Maybe that was normal. Maybe they were just that good, hiding in the shadows where they could see her, but she couldn't see them.

They certainly hadn't been able to see her when Bill Walters had her cornered in Salvio's office. She realized that Bledsoe didn't even know Walters was here!

The trailer door was ajar, and soft light bled from the back bedroom into the lab, reflecting off the newly mopped linoleum. Perhaps Bulldog really had cleaned the place.

Everything seemed in order when she stepped inside and closed the door behind her. She considered locking it, then decided against it, in case her FBI white knights needed to get to her fast.

She hadn't considered the idea that the trailer might be booby-trapped, as the warehouse had been. She simply figured that if there was any danger, the FBI agents wouldn't have let her come in here alone.

She ran a hand along the steel countertop as she moved slowly toward the bedroom. It seemed a million years ago when she and Seth had nearly made love here.

She allowed herself to remember—his face, those penetrating eyes, the way he felt inside her, the words he'd whispered to her just days ago.

I love you.

She stepped into the narrow bedroom and gasped.

Crocker was sprawled casually across her bed. He looked up at her, ice-blue eyes glittering in the soft light, and smiled. In his pale, manicured hand he cradled the plastic bag housing the only remaining rock sample from Caribou Island's secret well.

"Can't this thing go any faster?" Seth yelled to Danny over the deafening staccato of the borough chopper's over-taxed engine.

"Pedal's to the metal. Five minutes. Almost there."

It was a clear, cold night. In the distance, the lights on Caribou Island gave off a phosphorescent glow. Seth narrowed his eyes, scanning the ice for signs of Bledsoe's team. About a mile from the island he saw the black, unmarked FBI choppers at rest on the ice. A dogsled sat nearby. The mixed-breed team went crazy as the borough chopper passed overhead.

Lauren was already on the island, Bledsoe's team in place.

Seth held his breath as Danny slowed the bird into a wide turn over the site. The rig was already partially disassembled, the yard and staging areas cluttered with outgoing pallets of equipment. The burned-out warehouse and a handful of federal agents sporting arctic camouflage lurking in the shadows, scattered across the site, were the only signs that Caribou Island wasn't just another exploration well.

"I count five," Danny yelled, as he completed the turn.

"Six," Seth said, and swore. The sum total of Bledsoe's team, the team that was supposed to keep Lauren in sight every goddamned second.

"Why are they all outside? Wouldn't she be *inside?*"

Seth checked his weapons and reached for the rattling door handle. "Land this thing, Danny! Now!"

"So this is it." Crocker said, weighing the sample bag in his hand. "Hard to believe something so small could be worth so much money. Hiding it in that box of tampons was nothing short of brilliant, Lauren. Too bad I know how you think."

"It *was* you. It was you all the time." Lauren was frozen in place, her gaze riveted to Crocker's cool blue eyes.

"Of course it was me. Who else could do something this big, this...magnificent?" He waved a hand in the air.

"I...I thought Bill..."

"Walters? That buffoon?" He made a disparaging sound in the back of his throat as he swung his legs to the floor and rose in that elegant way that was his alone.

"So, Bill's not involved?"

"Oh, he had his uses," Crocker said, skirting the bed. "But, no, Walters doesn't have a clue about what we've managed to pull off out here. He did do a fine job of making sure we had the most up-to-date technologies, I'll give him that."

She remembered that Bill had, indeed, lobbied for those things months ago. The computerized drilling system, state-of-the-art communications, the works. "But why would he do that?"

"I told him I'd support him in his big play for the job of his dreams."

"Exploration VP? You would have done that?"

Crocker laughed. "Of course not. That job's going to you. And think of what a great team we'll make once you get it."

"You're not serious."

"I'm very serious, sweetheart." He kept advancing, backing her into the darkened lab.

"But, Crocker, why? What possible motive could have driven you to *this?*"

"Money."

Her incredulity blossomed into sheer amazement. "But you're rich, even wealthier than my stepfather."

"I was. I lost it all in the stock market. Two years ago, now."

"What?"

"Sad, but true. I've borrowed a bit from some friends, but that's nearly gone."

Her bones felt as if they were made of butter. "But, my engagement ring...how did you...?"

He shrugged. "It's a fake. A very good one mind you, but the stone's not real."

"And the Porsche?"

"Leased. Again, I have some very understanding friends." He moved toward her, and she kept backing up. "My condo's mortgaged to the hilt, but I'll take care of that as soon as this baby pays off." He tossed the sample bag in the air and caught it.

What she'd deduced before, on the dogsled ride in to the island, was all true. Every last ugly detail. Her whole relationship with Crocker had been a sham, every bit as fake as the ring on her finger. As soulless as the life she'd been living for years now, a life she'd allowed others to control— first her mother, then Crocker.

It all stopped here.

She tugged the ring off her finger and threw it at him. It bounced off the expensive cloth of his custom-made, Italian suit, and skittered across the floor toward the open door of the lab.

An icy draft from the outside chilled the room, though to Lauren the ambient air felt hundreds of degrees warmer than the frigid look in Crocker's eyes.

"Don't worry. I'll buy you a new one. A *real* one."

"You seriously believe that after what's happened here—" she waved an arm into space "—after all that you've done, that I'd still want to marry you?"

He smiled, but his straight white teeth and blond good looks had no effect on her anymore.

"I'd think you'd want me more than ever now. You have to admit, we're a great team. Everyone says so. Your mother adores me."

Her mother was about to get the biggest shock of her life, but that could wait.

"Think of it. Together we can have everything we want.

This is our chance.'' He tossed the sample into the air again, but this time he missed it, and it thumped onto the floor.

"Our chance?" she shouted, moving toward him, anger seething up inside her.

Somewhere at the edge of her awareness she heard the sound of a helicopter. She ignored it, focusing all her attention on the monster standing before her.

"Yes, our chance. Yours and mine. Partners in crime, so to speak. Lovers, too. A nice married couple."

"You're insane."

"I set up the deals, Salvio gets the wells drilled, and you, my dear, analyze the rocks. It's easy."

She exploded. "And was it easy murdering Paddy O'Connor?"

"Oh, I'd forgotten about that. Nasty business, but it had to be done. He was about to talk. I liked him, I really did."

"*You* did it. You murdered him." She flew at him, but he sidestepped her.

"Calm down. I could never do anything like that. You know I couldn't. Salvio did it, and a fine job he did, too. Too bad those dimwits that work for him tossed the murder weapon out in the trash."

"My rock hammer," she said between clenched teeth.

"Precisely. I've got the two of them digging through that Dumpster right now, looking to retrieve it."

"They won't find it, because *we* have it. The FBI has it."

"Do they?" The news didn't seem to faze him. "Well the only prints they'll find on it are yours, I'm afraid. In any case—"

"You seriously believed that once I knew what was going on here, what you and Salvio have been doing, that I'd join you?"

Crocker sighed, then approached her. "Salvio doesn't think you will, but I have faith that my bride will make the right decision."

She was speechless. Her amazement was off the charts.

Crocker's gaze slid to the open zipper of her jacket, where

a man-size flannel shirt was clearly visible beneath, its tails hanging nearly to her jean-clad knees.

"Salvio did tell me that you'd been a bad girl." He inched closer, his expression hardening. "The thought of you letting that lowlife touch you—" his thin lips twisted "—makes me sick. A roughneck. A *native*."

She glared up at him, barely containing the rage roiling inside her.

"But I forgive you. Things like that happen in tense situations. God knows, I've had my share of lovers while you and I were together. I'm just glad Adams is dead. If he wasn't I'd have to kill him."

"He's not dead, and I don't want your forgiveness. You're the lowlife, not him."

The blow was sharp and unexpected, and nearly knocked her off her feet. Crocker hit her again with the back of his hand, and she caught the edge of the counter just in time to keep from careening backward. As it was, she slid to the floor, shaking.

She tasted blood, and fear exploded inside her as the man she'd planned to marry drew a gun from his inside jacket pocket and pointed it directly at her.

She scrambled for the Glock in her own jacket, but already knew she wouldn't be able to draw it in time.

"Go ahead, you son of a bitch. Give me one more reason to kill you."

"Seth!"

He was framed in the doorway, light illuminating his tight features, reflecting off eyes so dark she'd once compared them to a winter's night.

As he stepped into the room, leveling a gun at Crocker, a shadow appeared on the steps behind him.

Salvio!

"Seth, behind you!"

Seth rolled right. Crocker turned and fired. Salvio fired, too, and all of them went down.

Chapter 20

"I forgot how much that hurts," Seth said as two of Bledsoe's agents peeled the Kevlar vest from his body and recovered one of two bullets that Crocker Holt had fired.

The other bullet would have to be recovered by the medical examiner when he performed the autopsy on Jack Salvio's body, which was laid out about three feet from where Seth was sitting propped against a row of cabinets.

Federal agents were everywhere. About goddamned time, too. The sound of more incoming choppers could be heard above the cacophony of voices in the packed trailer.

He glanced at Lauren across the room, where she was being questioned—more like doted on—by four of Bledsoe's agents. Where were those jerks fifteen minutes ago? He told himself it didn't matter, that she was safe now, that it was over.

Testing the flesh just above his right pec, Seth winced. He was going to have one hell of a bruise. When he'd realized Salvio was behind him on the steps, he'd rolled right, and Salvio and Holt inadvertently fired on each other.

Salvio was killed instantly, but had only winged Holt. Seth hadn't fired his weapon up to that point because Holt had been standing dangerously close to where Lauren was sprawled on the floor. By the time Holt had turned to fire on him, Lauren had slid sideways, leaving Seth a clear shot.

They'd both discharged their weapons simultaneously. Holt was receiving medical attention now—in handcuffs. He'd live a good long time, Seth suspected, in some nice, warm, federal prison somewhere.

Seth struggled to his feet and tried to make his way to where Lauren was standing. Bledsoe was interviewing her now. There were so many people in the room, so many agents surrounding her—and him, and Salvio's body, and Holt, who was being carried out on a stretcher—he couldn't get to her.

In the resulting chaos, all they'd had were a few shared glances. Her eyes were bright, vitreous. Her hands were shaking and her skin pale. She was probably in shock. Why hadn't that damned medic seen to her yet?

He ached to hold her, to tell her everything he was feeling inside, to have her hold him, and hear the words from her he wanted to hear—that she loved him, wanted him, as much as he wanted her.

"Geez, Adams, what are ya, in a trance?"

He jerked his head around at the sound of Bledsoe's voice.

"Got a couple more friends of yours over here." Bledsoe nodded toward the trailer's open door.

Danny, grinning from ear to ear, nudged Pinkie and Bulldog up the steps with the business end of a shotgun. The two roustabouts were in cuffs, Bulldog's eyes round with fear, Pinkie's glittering with the hard-edged arrogance of a seasoned con.

"What do you want me to do with these two?" Danny said. "I found 'em in the Dumpster behind the kitchen.

They stink something awful.'' He screwed up his face in revulsion.

Seth didn't smile. ''Put them back in there until Bledsoe's ready to take them away.''

Pinkie swore. Bulldog looked as if, at any second, he'd need a change of underwear.

''Good one, Adams.'' Bledsoe nodded in what was, surprisingly, appreciation. ''You're all right, you know that.''

''Lauren!'' he called, ignoring Bledsoe, trying to get to her.

The medic was finally checking her out, sponging the dried trickle of blood from her nose where Holt had hit her. What Seth wouldn't give to get his hands on that guy for just five minutes.

When the medic was finished with her, he started toward Seth. Seth waved him off. ''I'm fine.'' He tried to push past the medic so he could get to Lauren. The people, the chatter...his head was throbbing. Where the hell was Lauren?

When the path was finally cleared, he saw her, squatting on the linoleum floor of the lab, retrieving a plastic bag that had, in the chaos, been kicked out of the way under the cabinets.

The rock sample.

She pocketed it before anyone saw it, not that it would matter. He hadn't told Bledsoe about the sample, nor had she, it seemed. As she rose from the floor their gazes locked. Lauren went stock-still. Seth forced himself not to go to her.

So they stood there like that, not ten feet apart, just looking at each other. If he had one wish, right now, at this moment, it would be to know what she was thinking. Funny thing about wishes...they only come true after you've about decided you don't want them to.

''I guess you got what you wanted,'' he said.

''What?'' She stepped toward him, her brow softly furrowed. A flood of new agents poured into the room, and what little progress she'd made toward him was arrested.

"Okay, Miss Fotheringay." One of the fresh-faced agents took her arm. Another one flanked her other side. "Time to get you out of here."

"Seth," she said, twisting her head around to look at him as they escorted her out.

He didn't respond, he didn't smile, he didn't move.

A moment later she was gone.

He stood there like a guy who, for a few fleeting days, thought he'd had in his possession a winning lotto ticket, only to find out it was all a mistake.

"About your old job at the Bureau," Bledsoe said, strutting up to him like a fat peacock. "It's yours if you want it."

"Hmm?" Seth wasn't listening. He was thinking about Lauren, about what would happen next. Maybe nothing. Maybe everything. It was up to her now.

"Your job. A *real* job. Back in D.C., away from that frozen hellhole of a town you play cop in."

"What?"

"You did all right. My boys were on top of it, but it helped that you showed when you did."

"It *helped?*"

"Yeah." Bledsoe nodded. "I didn't want my guys in too close. I wanted to see what went down. I was thinking that maybe the Fotheringay broad was really in on it all along, that once she got together with her boyfriend, it would all unravel, and we'd be there to clean up the mess."

"That's what you thought? That's why you left her unprotected?"

"Yeah. Guess I was wrong."

Seth launched at him.

"Whoa!" Bledsoe sidestepped him. "Cool down, boy. It all worked out in the end. So, about that job. What's your answer?"

Seth didn't even have to think about it. "You want my answer?"

Bledsoe stood there, grinning. "Yeah."

"Here it is."

It was the first time in his life Seth had actually broken a guy's nose when he'd hit him. It felt good. Damned good.

By the time Lauren lifted off in the FBI chopper, Caribou Island was crawling with people, vehicles and more helicopters than she'd ever seen at one time in one place. Federal agents, borough police, Tiger personnel and representatives from half a dozen state agencies swarmed the brightly lit yard.

Lauren sat back in her seat and closed her eyes, breathing in cold, calming drafts of arctic air.

The nightmare was over.

She'd spent over an hour locked in Salvio's office with her boss, Bill Walters, who'd known nothing of Crocker's illegal activities or what had happened on Caribou Island. Bill had explained that he'd started to worry after he'd heard her voice on the phone that day, and had tried countless times to reach her ever since. Each time, Salvio had put him off with some excuse. Bill had known something was wrong even before he'd gotten the news about Lauren's disappearance and subsequent return to the island.

During their conversation, Tiger's CEO had arrived on the site and had joined them in Salvio's office, along with Doyle Bledsoe who, curiously, sported a bandage on his nose. When Lauren had asked him what happened, he changed the subject.

By the time she'd finished bringing her boss and the CEO up to speed on the events of the past two weeks, on what she'd deduced about Crocker and the conversation they'd had in the trailer, Seth was already gone.

She hoped he'd be waiting for her at the airport in Kachelik when she arrived. The FBI wanted to take her back to Anchorage to make statements, fill out paperwork, submit to more questioning, but she'd insisted they fly her to Ka-chelik first.

Though the nightmare was over, the rest of her life was still up in the air. Bad pun, she thought, looking out from the low-flying helicopter over the boundless expanse of ice blanketing the arctic slope.

The rest of her life started now, she realized, but she had something to set straight before she could start it.

Back on the island, the FBI had relieved her of Seth's Glock, but there was still one thing left in her jacket pocket. She pulled off her glove, slipped her hand inside the insulated fabric and retrieved it.

The most valuable rock sample in Alaska.

She weighed it in her hand, considering its importance— what it would mean to Tiger, her career, to the wildlife refuge, even to Seth's village in a roundabout way, not to mention a million gas-guzzling SUVs that might be able to run one more day on the oil hinted at by the sample.

"Hungry?" One of Bledsoe's agents offered her half a submarine sandwich from a cooler stowed under his feet.

"Hmm?"

It was nearly noon, she realized, glancing at her watch in the growing light. Since they'd been in the air, the sky had gone from inky black to a clear midnight blue edged with an impossibly brilliant orange, indicating to her that the sun, which had slipped below the southern horizon nearly two months ago, was about to show its face.

A lone polar bear came into view on the ice ahead of the chopper. The pilot slowed to a hover so they could look at it.

"Ya know those babies can eat a seal whole, bones and all," the agent said, leaning across her to get a better look. "I hear they've got stomachs like sharks, can digest just about anything."

A mischievous smile bloomed on Lauren's face. "Let's

hope so," she said, and accepted the half sandwich he'd offered her.

When the agent turned his back to peer out the opposite window, Lauren ripped open the sandwich, along with the plastic bag housing the valuable rock sample. It was half-crushed already, practically sand. It was easy to stuff it between the thick layers of salami and cheese.

A bracing *whoosh* of frigid air iced her skin as she wrestled the chopper's window wide. As the pilot thrust forward, with no one the wiser, she tossed the sandwich to the bear. *"Bon appétit."*

Seth was standing on the ice when Lauren's chopper set down in Kachelik. The look on his face when she climbed out of the jump seat and walked calmly toward him was nothing less than astonishment.

He dropped the line he was using to help Danny secure the borough chopper to the pad. Danny smiled at her as she approached, then slipped off to deal with the federal agents, leaving her and Seth alone.

"What are you doing here?" He took a step toward her, then stopped.

She stopped, too, less than an arm's length from him. Sunlight bled over the horizon, turning his skin to bronze, his eyes a brilliant chestnut suffused with wonder and warmth.

"I, uh, came to return this." She unzipped her heavy jacket and pulled on the long front tail of the borrowed flannel shirt. "It's yours."

The light went out of his eyes. "Keep it," he said, and turned his attention back to the dilapidated chopper.

"I'd like that." She moved toward him, her gaze washing over the helicopter's rusted, patched-together frame. "I can't believe you came all the way to the island in that."

He shrugged, his back to her.

"You saved my life, you know. Crocker meant to kill me."

He stopped what he was doing and looked at her. "You saved mine. I didn't know Salvio was behind me until you called out."

"We're even, then." She risked a smile.

He didn't smile back. "Yeah. Even." Dismissing her with a cool look, he reached down to retrieve the tether he'd dropped a minute earlier. It was then he noticed it.

"Your engagement ring. It's...gone."

"That's right. The engagement's off. You were right, Seth. It was Crocker all along. I knew it in my gut on the trip back out to the island, but I had to see it for myself— see him—for my own peace of mind. I had to go. Don't you see?

He rose, towering over her, his jaw set, eyes hard but searching. "What if it hadn't been him? What if he was innocent?"

"It wouldn't have mattered. I'd have had to call off the wedding anyway."

"You would?" She watched the pulse point throb at his temple, saw his Adam's apple as he swallowed hard.

"Yes. I would have had to tell him that I was in love with someone else. Though I suspect he already knows that."

Seth took her in his arms. "Lauren."

"Wait. There's more I need you to know."

He held her away from him, and again his dark eyes shone with uncertainty. "On the island, you found what you wanted, the thing that was most important to you."

She nodded, and his features turned to stone. "Part of it. On the island I found *you,* ten days ago." She smiled up at him. "Eleven, I guess, I don't know. I've lost all track of time lately."

"Come here," he said, and pulled her close.

"The other part I found here, in Kachelik." She nodded at the menagerie of buildings in the distance, bright sunlight reflecting off metal roofs.

"The other part?"

"That's right. *Me*. I found myself, what I am, what I always was before I allowed others to change me."

He looked at her, and she knew he understood. Still, he frowned in question. "What about the rock sample? I saw you put it in your pocket."

"Oh, that."

"Yeah, that. You're a geologist, a damned good one. That sample would mean a lot to your company, to your career. And I've been a selfish idiot. Whatever you decide to do with it, I want you to know I'm behind you one hundred percent."

"I appreciate it, Seth, but I don't have a company anymore, or a career."

"What?"

She enjoyed watching his expression change to one of stunned confusion. "At least not yet. I told Walters I was quitting. I gave two weeks' notice, but as of right now I'm on vacation. I think I have about a zillion days saved up. That will give me time to interview for that teaching assistant job I saw posted at the Kachelik school. Science and math, stuff I'm pretty good at."

"What?" He pulled her closer, a slow grin spreading across his ruggedly handsome face.

She shrugged. "I figured I could take some university classes over the Internet to get my credentials to teach. Earth science, most likely. It's what I've always wanted to do. It was my father's dream, too. Did I ever tell you that?"

He kissed her, and her knees turned to jelly. She gave up her weight to his crushing embrace and reveled in the feel of his mouth on hers, his scent, the taste of him.

"Lauren," he breathed against her lips, nuzzling her neck, pulling her so tight she feared bones would break.

"So…you think it's an okay idea, then? To work here, live here?"

"As long as you don't mind living with me." His smile was dazzling in the dawn's blinding light.

She kissed him softly, tenderly, unsure of how to demonstrate the magnitude of her feelings. In the end, she realized simple words would have to do. "I love you, Seth."

"I love *you*." His eyes shone with it, her heart nearly burst from it.

She realized she had one nasty task left to do. He saw the change come over her features, and tilted her chin up so he could see her eyes. "What is it?"

She shrugged. "Mother is not going to be happy when I tell her my wedding's canceled. She ought to be overjoyed I didn't end up married to a criminal, but knowing Mother, she'll find some way to make it out a travesty."

"So why disappoint her?" he said, grinning like the cat who ate the canary. "Why not tell her the wedding's still on? But with one minor substitution—the groom."

Warmth spread inside her. He kissed her again, long and slow and hotly.

"Two substitutions," she whispered against his lips. "I want to get married here, in Kachelik." She recalled the little church near the post office.

"That can definitely be arranged. I'm the chief of police, remember?"

"I remember. But—" Her face clouded as she remembered something else. "What about the FBI, your old job. Did Bledsoe ask you back?"

"Yeah, he asked."

She couldn't read what was in his eyes, and for a panicky moment she thought she'd made an embarrassing mistake. "Your father might have more, I don't know…"

"Respect for me, if I took it?"

He'd read her mind. She nodded.

"Maybe. Maybe not." He shrugged. "It doesn't matter."

"It doesn't?"

"No. My whole life I thought I was the one who didn't measure up. You know what? I was wrong. *He* was the one who didn't measure up, as a father or a husband. I'm the one who's okay."

Her love for him spread like the sun over the ice, melting all her remaining doubts. "You're more than okay," she said, and kissed him. When they finally came up for air, she said, "So Bledsoe asked, and...your answer?"

Seth grinned. "Didn't you seen him? He's wearing my answer."

They both laughed.

"So what about the rock sample?" His eyes turned serious again.

"Oh, that." She flashed him an impish grin. "Actually, I sort of...dropped it."

"Dropped it?" There was that look of incredulity again, that she was definitely beginning to love. "Dropped it where?"

"I don't know exactly. Somewhere on the ice between here and the island?"

"You mean you dropped it out of the chopper?"

"Uh-huh."

He started firing questions at her, but she ignored them, peppering his face with delicate kisses. Finally, he relented, and let the subject drop.

"I've never seen you in the daylight before."

They turned together into the sun and let its warmth fuel their joy.

"Disappointed?" he asked, smiling.

She brushed an errant lock of blue-black hair out of his face. "No way."

He laughed, his eyes dancing. "Me, neither. Though, on second thought, I would like my shirt back." He slipped a hand into her jacket and tickled her through the flannel.

"Take me home," she said, giggling, "and I'll give it to you. And while we're at it, you can see the rest of me in the light of day, too."

"You're on," he said, and chased her all the way to the Jeep.

* * * * *

Coming in January 2003 from
Silhouette Intimate Moments, watch for

NORTHERN EXPOSURE

by Debra Lee Brown.

You won't want to miss the breathtaking
tale that's filled with passion, suspense and
heart-stopping adventure!

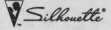

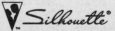

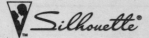

COMING NEXT MONTH

#1189 SECRETS AND LIES—Maggie Shayne
The Oklahoma All-Girl Brands

Agent Alex Stone's assignment sounded simple: impersonate a missing foreign dignitary who had a habit of hiding out with his new bride. The hard part was working with Melusine Brand, the brash beauty playing his wife. When Alex's perfect plan turned deadly, he found capturing kidnappers easy compared to fighting his feelings for Mel.

#1190 THE PRINCE'S WEDDING—Justine Davis
Romancing the Crown

Jessica Chambers had no idea the Colorado rancher she fell in love with was actually Prince Lucas Sebastiani of Montebello. For their son's sake, she agreed to marry Lucas and return to his kingdom. As she prepared for her royal wedding, Jessica searched for her former lover in the future king, but was she really willing to wed a virtual stranger?

#1191 UNDERCOVER M.D.—Marie Ferrarella
The Bachelors of Blair Memorial

A drug ring had infiltrated Blair Memorial Hospital, and it was up to DEA agent Terrance McCall to bring them down. The plan moved smoothly, with Terrance posing as a pediatrician, until he saw Dr. Alix DuCane, the woman he'd walked away from six years ago. Now he had two missions: defeat the drug lords *and* win back the only woman he'd ever loved.

#1192 ONE TOUGH COWBOY—Sara Orwig
Stallion Pass

Suffering from amnesia, Laurie Smith couldn't remember her own name, but she knew that her car crash was no accident. Someone had run her off the road—someone who was still out there. Handsome cowboy Josh Kellogg promised to protect this beautiful mystery woman from the killer on her trail, but who would protect Laurie's heart from Josh?

#1193 IN HARM'S WAY—Lyn Stone

Falling in love with a murder suspect wasn't the smartest move detective Mitch Winton had ever made. But in his heart he knew that Robin Andrews couldn't be responsible for her estranged husband's death. Once Robin became the real killer's new target, Mitch was determined to prove her innocence—and his love. But first he would have to keep them both alive....

#1194 SERVING UP TROUBLE—Jill Shalvis

After being rescued from a hostage situation, Angie Rivers was ready for a new life and hoped to start it with Sam O'Brien, the sexy detective who had saved her. Love, however, was the last thing Sam was looking for—or at least that was what he told himself. But when Angie unwittingly walked straight into danger, Sam realized life without Angie wasn't worth living.